FAMILIES
THE FRONTLINE OF PLURALISM

OTHER BOOKS OF INTEREST

Illness & Grace, Terror & Transformation
Heather Tosteson and Charles D. Brockett, Editors
Wising Up Press, 2007

Hearts as Big as Fists
Heather Tosteson
Wising Up Press, 2007

FAMILIES
THE FRONTLINE OF PLURALISM

HEATHER TOSTESON
CHARLES D. BROCKETT
Editors

Wising Up Press
Decatur, Georgia

Wising Up Press
P.O. Box 2122
Decatur, GA 30031-2122
www.universaltable.org

Catalogue-in-Publication data is on file with the Library of Congress.
LCCN: 2008928890

Wising Up ISBN-13: 978-0-9796552-3-4

TABLE OF CONTENTS

CHOICE

RIFT/REPAIR

SPIRIT OF ADOPTION

HEATHER TOSTESON

FOREWORD

I regard my family as typical if not normative. I was raised in a family layered by divorce. My older half-sister's father was Jewish, and in our episodically Episcopalian household we regularly feasted on borscht my mother made from her ex-mother-in-law's recipe. My younger half-siblings, the same age as my own son, have a mother who is both Argentine and Jewish. My favorite niece and nephew speak Spanish as their first language. Our grandchildren, with skin as fair as that of people from the land of midnight sun, call us *abuelo* and *abuelita*, unaware, as yet, of all the steps involved here. My step-daughter is bi-sexual, my husband's brother is gay. My own son's wife is South Korean. The daughters of my heart come from Iraq. But this is all foreground become background for the day. It sounds like what it is, a well-practiced story.

I can't remember exactly when the idea for this anthology came to me—were we planning to go to some family event, relaxing afterwards, engaged in our by now comfortably habitual *Sturm und Drang* about family dynamics—Yours! Yours! Or looking back at our thunderstorm with a sense of bemusement. Where did all that energy come from? Where did it *go*?

What inspired the idea is understanding what it means to have pluralism forced upon you—at very close quarters. Where all the tidy niceties of relativity don't apply. I believe it was my friend Connie Veldink who said, "There is no relativism at the breakfast table." Or was that in bed?

In any case, where it matters most. These stories and poems explore how we respond to differences where they matter most, our own intimate lives. Where we can't finesse our own needs or the needs of those around us. Where words are said, deeds are done. Harm and blessing are now, and forever will be, twinned. Where it is the truth, not the tidiness, of our own experience that will free us. And those around us. For perhaps these stories, of difference inherited or actively chosen, of deep rift and even deeper repair can help create a more resilient, stormy, and gracious norm for us, one that sees necessity not just as the mother of invention but also the mother of a scapegrace love that, in Gerard Manley Hopkins words, "lights a lovely mile."

Reading through the stories, memoirs and poems we selected, they seemed to fall naturally into four general categories: inheritance, choice, rift/repair, and the spirit of adoption.

If we have inherited pluralism, then it is both of us in some unconscious and ineradicable way and also something that needs to be consciously accepted as well. In the first section, INHERITANCE, many of the stories, memoirs, and poems hold this tension between the unwanted but inescapable and the generously accepted, with all the difficult freedom that acceptance implies.

Anna Steegmann in "Phantom Pain" writes intimately about the difficult pluralism of history—of a father in post-war Germany who sings the now prohibited Nazi Party's anthem when the pain of his phantom limb assails him. In "Provisions" she writes of a world known only by hearsay where starvation was once the great equalizer, but where the only battlefield she and her mother now know is one splattered blood red by delicious currant jelly. These are not tensions or fidelities that fit tidily into categories.

Lorena Smith, Michele Markarian, and Elinor Benedict begin to understand, at different levels, what it means to embody multiple cultural realities. Smith tries to integrate the reality of her Swedish mother's impoverished childhood with her own privileged life as a Sri Lankan with, now, her adult life in Texas. Abundance comes in many forms. Cultural fidelity too. Michele Markarian, at ten, native-born, begins to take in the seismic tremors that accompany immigration—her parents', her newly arrived distant cousin from Lebanon's, whose name, she understands, Americans will mispronounce, misunderstand, think odd. She now understands herself, as well, as inextricably involved in the same dynamic. Elizabeth Benedict seeks to understand the implications of her aunt's choice to marry a Chinese man and live most of her life in China. Her poems touch on the mystery and terror of involuntary identity—her cousin sees his own face staring back at him in the Chinese market, while she, the physical likeness of her aunt, has the same experience with her aunt's daughter.

Carl Palmer's brief poems to his parents capture the normal undertow of family life, love ungiven, misplaced, so different from the bright precision of a child's emotional accounting. This confusion is echoed in Sheryl Nelms' poem about her legacy from her grandmother: "how many times do I boil the poke/and was it the leaves or the berries".

The moving short story by Kerry Langan, "Eternal Youth", and the poems by Donna Richardson, Cherise Wyneken, and John Grey all explore racial tension and forgiveness. "Sad to say this tell is true," Donna Richardson writes in her poem Mulatto-Colored Pain. Langan's narrator, Sarah, wonders what forgiveness would smell like: "a neutral, honest scent that wouldn't be too strong or too weak." Later, she muses on her grandmother's racial intolerance, "She always had someone to blame. I didn't."

Benjamin Arda Doty and Andrei Guruianu are, in very different contexts, living into the reality of their own inheritance and what it means to them as they enter adulthood. Doty, in Georgia, begins to understand how his skin color may define him more than his ethnicity. There is something bitter in the narrator's observation, "So that's what it is, I think, like I know what I'm talking about if I opened my mouth." Something bitter and something that still holds the yearning of an open question. Andrei Guruianu's poignant memoir of finding his footing as a young man, a Romanian immigrant who needs to shoulder the burdensome blessing of his parents' self-sacrifice, is, again, a story of what it means to find our own balance within multiple cultural force fields.

In the second section, CHOICE, the stories and poems focus on making active choices to come into intimate relation with difference. Both Janice Levy and Donald Jaffe's stories deal with the undertow of cross-religious marriages, choices that are not made once and for all, but repeatedly.

Debra Gingerich's poised and thoughtful poems explore what it means to absorb the ineradicable otherness of her husband's life history. Watching a video, she muses on the fate of those like her husband, in whom the ". . .blood/of enemies mixed together in the cavities of their hearts. At least/he ended up on the right side/of my bed. . .." While Bonnie Kwong writes of what she has learned from her mother, twice migrated: "In the undertow of history/we swim parallel to shore/until the sea itself is tired."

Wendy Nakanishi's "A Life in A Day in Japan" explores how her decision to marry a Japanese farmer—and become the mother of three sons—

affects her sense of self-identity. Does she hate men? The culture she's married into? Does her love, even now, up end all her categories, all easy conclusions? Are these choices, so difficult to describe in all their intricacy to those who haven't made them, ones that weather our faces but enlarge our hearts?

Yu-Han Chao's story of a young Vietnamese mail-order bride takes place in Taiwan. Like Kwong's mother, Lei Lee too is swimming parallel to the shore. But we are impressed with her resilience, the intricacy of her response to the intrinsic oppression of the relationship. The very act of choosing, to leave her father, marry herself off to someone in another country, has its own redemption in it, a blend of fatalism and action. Choosing once means we are subject to consequence *and* free to choose again, and yet again.

In the third section, RIFT/REPAIR, the selections focus, sometimes poignantly, sometimes humorously, on how deep schisms in families go—those distinctions that are necessary, those identifications that redeem. Cheryl Hicks ponders the legacy of violence that runs through both her mother's marriages, the isolation and fragmentation it causes: "I guess you could say my brother and I grew up in a house of secrets. It was as though each member of the family lived in an iridescent bubble of potential sealed off from the rest of the household, and most decidedly from the rest of the world."

Karen Aschenbrenner and Annabelle Baptista focus on the tug and tears of relationships between siblings in adolescence and early adulthood. "*Maybe*, I thought, *a perfect body doesn't give you a perfect life*." So Karen Aschenbrenner muses as she studies her brother, whose loyalty and freedom from physical disability both astonish her—now that they both can accept the freedom he has to give, or rescind, that love. Baptista, awakened by her sister's slap to the cruelty of her own words, "felt my compacted heart wrench free from the bands that held it in place as I grasped for the first time our self-hatred."

A subject not so often talked about, the impact of class shifts within families, their powerful divisiveness, is at the heart of Precious McKenzie's memoir. She comes to see herself as living a life that partakes of the best of her mother and her grandmother's worlds—a drive to excel and a warm holding environment as well.

Daniel Martinez's poems are filled with distances—a father he runs from leaving his brother behind, an abandoned daughter with whom hopes for connection are "not as strong as any of the words/we still can't find to explain/how distant we are now." But he also finds affinities that have nothing to do with blood, but much to do with family: "He isn't my son,/but he is my boy,/and that day I became his old man."

Patti See's "Family Story", captures such a day—the reality, the yearnings and limitations, of a chosen family, and the acts that don't transform our next sixty-six years, make us into a "spit into the wind Harley babe who no longer pines for a family to accept her." In the same humorous, detached vein, Bruce Taylor's story "Her" explores what assumptions shift for a divorced man who must now assume befuddling responsibility for his relationships with his children—and receives their own category eliding assistance in return. His daughter, sounding eerily like her own mother, offers him a second chance: "You did fine with the first one. You can do this one too."

In Teresa Tumminello Brader's delicately poised story, "Age Appropriate", we experience the range of emotions, the complexity of the choices, that accompany single-parenting, remarriage, fostering grandchildren, the loss of one's own parents. We experience relationships that have no names for their affective reality, claims that have nowhere to lodge. What *are* the claims, the rights and responsibilities, of her husband's grandchild to a room in their house? Are the anger and grief, for dead fathers, insouciant mothers, entitled grandchildren, displaced—or exquisitely located so they can be transformative?

In the final section, THE SPIRIT OF ADOPTION, we experience the impact, over generations, of the decision to parent—or *not* to parent—across race, culture, sexual orientation. Phyllis Langton's brief, haunting memoir of the "Mother lady", which contrasts the ebullience and stability of her life in an orphanage with the sad devastation of reunion with her blood relation, sets the implicit context for the stories that follow. In these next memoirs, we find the clarity of individual choice, but there is also something musing, a little chastened, an awareness of being moved by forces—affections, drives—deeper than one's conscious mind and of consequences beyond prescience that one is making a blind commitment to live out, with all the rift and repair that implies. Kalia Abiade bluntly describes her relationship with her step-daughter Asha's hair: "It ain't pretty. This is probably not one of those bonding moments that she and I will recall fondly as some mother-daughter pairs do. Like many other aspects of our relationship, hair time is a struggle—often it is a complicated mess." She also describes the small but radical choices that elicit from the two of them an overwhelming Yes! and a decision to move on into a deeper, more joyful relationship.

There is an intriguing tension in John Rybicki's lyrical poems about his black foster son, the tension of inviting the ghetto into a pastoral landscape. Through the rush of words, we are stilled by images—the boy's dry shadow dissolving into rain when he rises up from the street, the gun shot holes he slips his fingers into in his own house, the foster mother's dream that he is shooting her, the death knell in her neck, which rings as well in every empty bed in their hereto childless house. In these poems, the collide of diction and image, of two incongruous realities, creates a lyrical tide that may, in time, come to lift the child, so simultaneously out of place and wanted, who "likes the fur coat of corn the best."

Elizabeth di Grazia and Diane Raptosh describe their decisions to adopt and how they affected their sense of community, both large and small. Di Grazia's story is about the expanding sense of community she and her partner experience as the adoptive parents of two Guatemalan children--not only the family they have chose to support them, but the community of their local neighborhood. They are also bound, in intricate ways, permanently with the issues of race, cultural identity. For these children, who effortlessly dissolve so many boundaries for them, find their closest sense of home in each other's similar faces, not their mothers'.

Diane Raptosh's decision to engage in single motherhood a second time, through adoption, is a meditation on the drive to motherhood and also a half-conscious commitment to "a world that doesn't quite cohere"—but a sensibility that does. Here we see the great freedom available now to women to have and support children on their own, to assume voluntary, joyous strains—so different from Phyllis Langton's silk-stocking clad "mother lady" in the 1940s.

Jess Well's memoir, "The See-Saw Family" takes us through how far-reaching and category-shuffling the experience of parenting can be—and why.

> And that, it turns out, was the crux of my becoming bi-sexual, to jumping the fence, or deserting the flock, or throwing in the towel: The sexual allure of nurturance drew me in. There's nothing sexier to me than evidence of generosity.

This new bond allows her to see men—and maleness—from a very different vantage point. She both has twice as many closets now, but also a wider range of options, new places to identify, empathize, differ. "You know fragile," she says to her husband. "No, baby, I don't know," he responds. "My friends call it shallow," she says of his freedom from self-reflection, "I call it stable." Rigidities give way to the precious but time-limited reality of family life. They are, for now, a clan—not just a partnership: "Some of the clan members move more than others, but we're a clan anyway and trying to be careful and kind."

I came away from reading these stories pondering the importance of voluntariness, even in involuntary relationships. And the importance of the mysterious gifts we receive by inheriting the complex consequences of the freedom of others. There is, in all these stories, a settling into the yearning for connection, and an awareness that any relationship, chosen or inherited as burden or blessing, always exceeds our imaginings. Thank goodness. Just so, we are always being invited into new relations with our deepest selves and the tumultuous and rewarding and so fully human world around us.

INHERITANCE

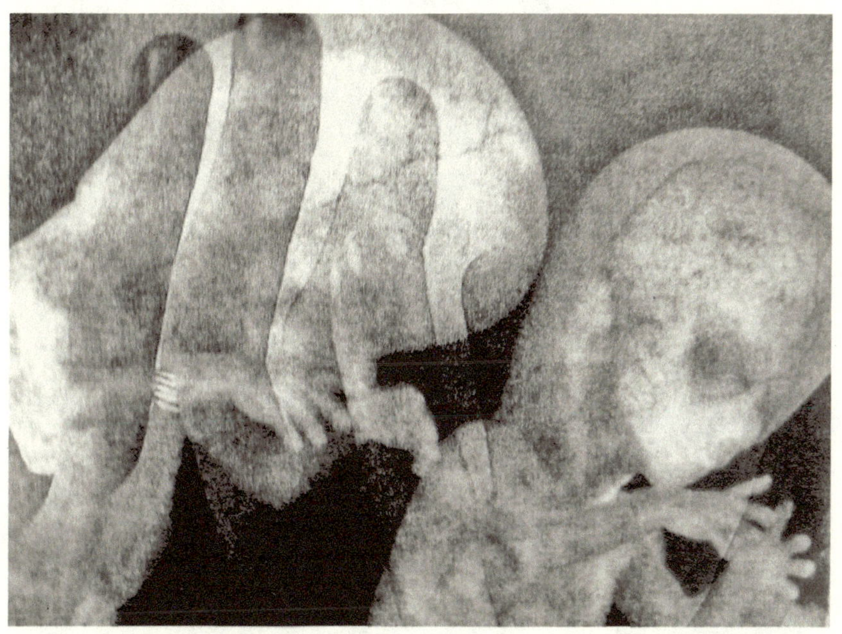

ANNA STEEGMANN

PHANTOM PAINS

On New Year's Eve, we placed votive candles on the windowsill as a tribute to our brothers and sisters in the *Ostzone*. Separated from us by a wall, barbed wire and mine fields, the East Germans were not free nor as fortunate as we West Germans were. We were never to forget their plight. The aroma of *Berliner Ballen*, special New Year's Eve doughnuts, permeated the house. Perfectly round, filled with marmalade, fried in fat and sprinkled with powdered sugar, they were my favorite pastry. On New Year's Eve each *Berliner* had a small object inside. A pig predicted a lucky year, a ring a wedding, a coin wealth. If you got the one filled with mustard, your year ahead would be full of bad luck.

My mother took the pink rollers out of her hair, coated her hair with hair spray and admired her helmet head in the mirror. Then she changed into her Sunday dress. My father stayed in his stretched out blue track suit; the empty pant leg rolled up and fastened to his trousers with a safety pin. His wooden leg rested in the corner of the living room.

We gathered around our kidney-shaped coffee table. I looked at the pickled herring, liverwurst and Gouda cheese canapés decorated with gherkins and pretzel sticks, but decided to wait for the *Berliner Ballen*. The minute hand on the grandfather clock hardly moved. The more I stared at it, the longer it seemed. My brother Heinrich and I, bouncing on the sofa, could hardly wait for midnight to storm outside into the freezing cold and watch the sky light up with fireworks.

About to jump up and do my version of a rain dance, I froze when I saw my father's contorted face. His bushy eyebrows, furrowed together, produced a deep canyon on his forehead. He let out a piercing scream. I knew what was coming. I had experienced it all too often. The stump of his amputated leg was acting up. Once unleashed, the pain might last for several hours, perhaps the entire night and turn my father, a huge strong man, into a sobbing tortured mass.

My father grabbed his cane and hobbled to the kitchen. My mother ushered us upstairs to the bedroom. Heinrich and I sat down on my bed and stared at each other. We were both trembling despite the heavy sweaters we wore to save money on the heating bill. It was only half past ten. Heinrich was pessimistic. "We're gonna miss all the fireworks." Sucking my thumb, I listened to the intensity and the ebb and flow in my father's wailing.

My father locked himself inside the kitchen every time the phantom pains attacked. No one was allowed to enter. Sitting alone in the dark, he sang for several hours with a loud, mournful voice that resonated throughout the entire house and prevented us from sleeping. I knew all my father's moods and the songs that mirrored them. I knew the words to all the melodies.

He started to sing my favorite, *In einem Polenstädtchen*. In the song, German soldiers march into a small Polish town and encounter a seductive maiden. I pictured my father among a group of soldiers, knapsacks on their backs, marching and singing in the open air. I tried to imagine the long Russian winter, the battle of Stalingrad, being hit by a grenade. My father was sad over losing the war, sad over losing his leg. I wondered why his pains always arrived on holidays in time to spoil our celebrations.

My mother balancing a plate of *Berliner Ballen* on her palm entered our bedroom. "It's a quarter to twelve. Have a *Berliner*," she said and sat down on the bed between us. "You have to understand your father. He's afraid of New Year's Eve. The fireworks sound like an artillery attack to him."

I was tired of having to tolerate my father's moods. I was ten years old. It was New Year's Eve and I wanted to have fun. Ignoring the pastries, Heinrich and I went over to the window and pressed our noses against the glass. The street was full of people. I recognized our neighbors and my best friend Frank. "Holy cow, did you see that *Kometenhagel*. Amazing," Heinrich said. Like a silver serpent, it shot up and opened into a cascade of tiny stars. There were mini explosions everywhere. "Two more minutes," Heinrich whispered. The people outside started to shout "*Zehn, neun, acht, sieben…*" As the numbers decreased they yelled louder and louder. A thunderous, deafening blast erupted when everyone set off their fireworks at the same time. There were Roman candles, pinwheels, single rockets, cherry bombs, and my favorite: *Chinaböller*. Brilliant silver, green, red and gold flashed in the sky.

Half an hour later the detonations petered out. Once in a while a

Bengali cylinder flame or *Bombette* shot up. It had been a great show. Heinrich wiped a tear from his eye. Our own New Year's Eve Family Fun Pack sat unused at the foot of the stairs. We had not fired our shells and mortars. Outside our neighbors were locking arms, clinking glasses and downing shots of liquor. With the outside noises quieting down my father's voice soared above the sporadic flare-ups of fireworks. He sounded strong and confident, almost optimistic "Breslau, Danzig, Königsberg. We'll take you back!" he shouted. Those towns once belonged to Germany. In school, we had learned that the price for losing the war was surrendering parts of our country to Poland and the Soviet Union. My history teacher didn't think we would ever get these territories back. My father demanded them back. He launched into a combat song.

We National Socialists
Want no reactionaries
We hate Jews and Marxists
*The Führer calls, follow him now**

Mama, looking like a frightened little girl, began to tremble. That song always upset her. She stood up and closed the curtains as if she didn't want our neighbors to hear my father's singing. Heinrich sank his teeth into a *Berliner.* I was ready for mine. My father sang himself into a rage.

Die Fahne hoch! Die Reihen fest geschlossen
SA marschiert mit ruhig-festem Schritt
Free the streets for the brown battalions
Free the streets, for the Storm Troopers
*The swastika, the hope of millions....***

My mother sighed. "Why does he have to sing that song all the time?"

"Why are you worried, Mama?" I asked.

"That's the Horst-Wessel Lied. It's illegal to sing that song. Your father could get into trouble."

Anticipating a delicious plum or cherry marmalade filling, I took a big bite of my *Berliner.* The strange taste made my mouth pucker up. What was the yellow stuff inside this doughnut? It couldn't be true. I had gotten the one doughnut filled with mustard. My brother didn't care. He was beaming; he had found a lucky pig in his. Disgusted, I spit pieces of the *Berliner* into my hand.

* The *Kampflied der Nationalsozialisten,* the Nazi Combat Song, was the battle song of the Nazi party.

**Horst-Wessel-Lied*, the Nazi Party's anthem, was part of Germany's national anthem from 1933 to 1945. A regulation required the right arm to be raised in a "Hitler salute" when singing the first and fourth verse. In 1945, the *Horst-Wessel-Lied* was banned. Both lyrics and tune remain illegal in Germany to this day.

PROVISIONS

When my mother ate an apple, she slowly and systematically ate the entire fruit including its core and left nothing but the stem. When we threw out a half-eaten piece of fruit, she rescued it from the garbage and finished it. When we failed to clean our plates, she took our unfinished pork chops and gnawed the bones clean. She once made the mistake of baking a crumb cake with salt instead of sugar. The taste was revolting and the family refused to eat it. But without blinking an eye, she ate the entire cake.

It was 1964 and all of Germany was on a feeding frenzy. Even our Chancellor Erhard was chubby. The war had ended and food was no longer rationed. People stuffed themselves to make up for the times they had to do without. One room in our basement was set aside as a root cellar. Apples, potatoes, preserved fruits, pickles and sauerkraut in mason jars sat next to several five-pound bags of flour and sugar. We had no sense of security. Another war might break out anytime. "The next war won't be fought with tanks and horses. It will be a nuclear war and the entire world will go to hell," my mother said with teary eyes. I wasn't worried. My hometown had air raid shelters and bunkers left over from the last war. We had food to survive for a few months.

My mother spread a slice of black bread thick with butter and put a piece of *Schwartemagen* on top. I hated *Schwartemagen*, a jellied loaf, made from the edible parts of the pig's head and stuffed into a casing of pig's intestine. It tasted as horrible as it sounded. I hated butter, but our family had had to do without butter, *the best butter,* for so long that it was a crime to refuse it. No matter how disgusting it looked or tasted, my brother and I were forced to eat everything.

"Why that face?' my mother asked. We had just gathered for *Abendbrot,* our evening meal.

"I'm not hungry," I lied, then turned to my brother and rolled my eyes. Heinrich was happily loading up on the slimy stuff. He had no problem with *Schwartemagen.*

"The poor children of India are starving, and you're not even finishing your *Butterbrot*," my mother scolded.

"Send it to India, then," I mumbled.

She slapped me across the face before I had time to duck. My mother did not put up with my lack of respect. "Ungrateful brat! You're lucky to have enough to eat. You have no idea what it's like to go hungry."

I did know; I was reminded of it every day. I had heard her story of deprivation a thousand times and could recite her litany by heart. When she was my age, her stomach had growled with hunger pangs all the time. The family lived on cabbage for months. Dinner was often *Einbrennsuppe,* a soup made with a drop of lard, flour, and water. A teaspoon of butter was a real luxury. A hardboiled egg had to be divided among four people. There was no coffee during the war, only *Muckefuck*, a grain beverage that tasted just as repulsive as it sounded.

For punishment I had to help my mother make preserves. I stared at the mountains of boysenberries, currants, sour cherries and rhubarb on the kitchen table. My mother started on the cherries and her lecture: "In the hard winter of 1942 people traded their jewelry, damask tablecloths, and even their wedding rings for food. I was sixteen, the oldest. They sent me and my aunt on day trips to the *Hunsrück,* to beg or trade our own wine for food." I thought I had heard it all before, but this opening made my ears perk up. I had been to the *Hunsrück*, a small mountain range, and tried to imagine my mother hiking from village to village.

"You mean you went from door to door like Gypsies?"

"Kind of. We knocked on many doors. Most people didn't even open their door. But when they did, I always tried to peek in."

"What did you see?" I was curious now.

"Watch that knife. You almost cut yourself."

"Don't worry, I'll be careful. Just go on."

My mother emptied a sieve full of cherries into a gigantic pot by the sink, rinsed her hands, wiped them on her apron and returned to the table. "I saw tables bursting with black bread. I saw pitchers of milk, sausages, ham and pickles. I saw all the foods we had done without. What tormented me most was the smell of bacon and *Handkäs.* "

I hated that stinky, smelly cheese, her favorite, and could not comprehend why she liked it so much.

"Look at you, your mouth all red from eating too many cherries. Work a little faster or else we'll be sitting here all night. Start on the currants now." Cleaning the currants was a struggle. The tiny berries never came off the stem easily. Having to peel off the even tiny black flower remnants was maddening.

"How did the people react? What did they say to you?" I asked.

"They kept on eating, stared at us, and then told us to go home. They weren't interested in trading a bottle of wine for a piece of bread or sausage. Maybe we would have been luckier if we had fine linens or gold."

"That's mean," I said. "What happened next?"

"I tried not to faint from hunger. I was so excited by the aromas from the kitchen."

I looked at my mother, her large breasts and wide hips. It was hard to imagine her as a skinny teenager.

"I was so mad, I prayed all the way back to Langenlonsheim 'Lord please remove my hatred for these people from my heart,'" she said.

My mother then told me about my grandfather, a day laborer, who did not earn enough to feed his wife and four children. The Flommersfeld family lived in the Nahe valley, a wine growing region near the French border. They owned a small vineyard which produced enough grapes for a few bottles of wine. They were often saved by their little garden patch where they grew leeks, cabbage, carrots and onions. From this garden by the railroad tracks, they encountered people much more desperate than they had ever been. One hot summer afternoon my mother and her younger brother were helping their father pull out the weeds and checking on their pear and plum trees, when they noticed cattle cars filled with men, women, and children. The train was still there when they returned the next day. The people inside noticed them, and stretching their arms out of the windows, pleaded in German, French, and other languages my mother had never heard before.

"What did they want?" I asked, abandoning the currants temporarily.

"They begged for water. They begged for bread. 'Have a heart,' they said."

"Who were these people? How did they end up in Langenlonsheim?" I asked.

My mother got up from the table. Her bowl of sour cherries was only half full. Standing with her back to me at the sink, her voice so low I could barely understand her, she said: "They were political prisoners, Gypsies, Jews, and Communists."

"Communists, like Herr Lehmann?" I asked.

Herr Lehmann lived above us. My father detested him because he had been on the wrong side during the war. "That Communist fool," my father would say. "Rode his motorbike all the way to Moscow!" I didn't know what a Communist was, but my father made him sound like a traitor. Looking for adventure, my father had gone on horseback to Russia, Herr Lehmann on his motorbike. What was the difference?

"Anyone against Hitler was shipped off to the labor camps. The trains took them there," my mother said.

That night I heard my mother's version of the glory and downfall of the Third Reich. She was nervous as she spoke to me. Always looking to the door, listening for my father's footsteps. Afraid. "Papa was a devout Catholic. He believed in the Ten Commandments and charity," she said. "He asked me to be the lookout while he snuck up to the train. He took our lunch, the loaf of bread and water, and handed them to the skinny arms of a woman. They couldn't see each other, but they talked. She was from Saarbrücken and had her twins with her. Papa spent a long time by the wagons. First the lady with the twins, then some of the other people gave him pieces of paper. They had scribbled addresses on it and asked him to contact their relatives."

My mother looked pensive, sad. I couldn't wait to hear the rest of the story.

"Papa was able to help four or five times in the following weeks. He always told me to be on the lookout. One afternoon, I did not pay attention. I was watching a zeppelin in the sky. Its huge banner promised us the ultimate victory: *Forward with courage! Today Germany is ours, tomorrow the entire world.* Two *Gestapo*…"

"Two what?" I interrupted her. I had to pee badly, but my mother's story was enthralling. I squeezed tight and stayed.

"The *Gestapo* were the secret police. It was their job to patrol the trains. They found Papa taking a note from one of the passengers. It was strictly forbidden to walk up to the trains, to give or to take anything from the people inside."

"What happened?" I asked. The pressure to pee was unbearable, but I was glued to my chair. "The *Gestapo* took him to their office in a nearby barrack. I was frightened."

I was afraid myself. Afraid to pee in my pants.

"What happened to Grandpa?"

"The *Gestapo* knew everybody's business," my mother said. Maybe they knew that I had failed *Völkischer Unterricht,* Ethnic Instruction, at vocational school? Maybe they knew that my brother often played hooky from the Hitler Youth meetings?"

I was about to burst and sprinted to the bathroom. When I returned I learned that my grandfather had not been a member of the Nazi Party. They were too un-Christian for his taste. He had often made fun of that little man with the funny mustache and listened to enemy radio. My mother's family had been friendly with their Jewish neighbors in the Hintergasse. The Nachmanns were kind. They often slipped the hungry Flommersfeld children pieces of matzo when they pressed their noses to the window of their grocery store. Grandma would light the stove during Sabbath in the synagogue until there was no more synagogue.

"What's a synagogue?" I asked.

"It's where the Jewish people pray. Instead of praying in a church, they do their praying in a synagogue."

"What are Jews like? What do they look like?"

"They are people like us. They look like us. They just have a different religion."

My mother got up from the table and wiped her hands on her apron. "I'll show you, I'll be back in a minute."

When she returned, she squeezed next to me on the bench and opened her palm. I looked at the tattered tiny black and white picture. It showed a group of people standing around a grave covered with flowers.

"That's the grave of Selma Weiß," my mother said. "The people on the left are her mother and father, August und Isabella Weiß, and on the right are her two brothers Max and Kurt. I always had a crush on Kurt. Isn't he handsome?"

I didn't care one bit about Kurt. "What happened to Selma?"

"We were friends."

"Did you meet at school?"

"No, all the Jews in the village attended the Protestant school; I went to the Catholic school. We met in the *Gesangsverein.* Selma had a beautiful voice."

"How did she die?"

"She was struck by lightning. A blessing."

"A blessing! How can you say such a thing? She was your friend. How old was she when she died?"

"Thirteen," my mother said. "When I think of what they did to the Jews later, it's better that she died a natural death."

"What did they do to the Jews?"

"Hitler hated them. He started by destroying their houses of worship, their schools and businesses and then set out to destroy the entire race."

"What happened to Selma's parents, to Kurt and Max?"

"During *Kristallnacht* they smashed the door and windows of their store and trashed everything inside. The bolts of fabric, the fixtures, the furniture, the cash register. Everything. They even pulled up parts of the floor. Selma's mother was asleep upstairs. People claimed they pulled her out of bed by her hair and pushed her down the stairs. She was still in her nightgown when they kicked her onto the sidewalk. My aunt Wilhelmine who lived across the street saw everything."

"What happened to her brothers and her father?"

"They were arrested and taken to the jail in Bad Kreuznach. The next day they were put on a train to Dachau."

"Dachau?"

"*Das Konzentrationslager*. You're nine. Too young to understand. I'll explain it some other time."

"What happened to Grandpa?" I asked. I suddenly remembered how he had gotten into trouble with the *Gestapo.*

"The *Gestapo* wanted to know why Papa was near the train, what he was doing there and what organization he worked for," my mother said. "After they questioned him, they let him go. I was relieved to have him back."

I was relieved as well. I did not want my mother to lose her father.

"The *Gestapo* knew that he hadn't joined the party. They knew he complained that the citizen's mobilization assemblies were held the same time as Sunday mass. Our family had *Dreck am Stecken.*"

"What do you mean?" I asked.

"We had intermarried with our enemy, the French," my mother said.

"What's wrong with the French?" I asked. I had heard my father say bad things about them, but never understood why.

"They ruled Langenlonsheim from 1796 until 1814, then again after we lost the First World War," my mother said.

She was getting ready to tell me about it, but I was not interested. I was curious about my grandfather's arrest. "What did the *Gestapo* do to Opa?"

"They threatened him with imprisonment if he continued to act like a traitor to the Fatherland. 'If you do not stop what you are doing immediately, you will end up on the same train and never see your wife and children again,' they told him."

All of a sudden my mother's body twitched as if a bolt of lightning had struck her. I had never seen her so pale. Her eyes were fixed on the kitchen table. When I turned I saw my father standing in the doorway. We did not hear him come in. Like a giant, his eyebrows raised, he towered above us. How long had he been listening? He looked so angry.

"Those Jews they had it coming to them," he said. His voice was strong and resolute. "They took our *Lebensraum,* but boy did we show them."

My mother lifted her eyes, turned to me and gave me her piercing *don't you dare say a word* look. I was confused. My mother's Jews were kind and not any different from us. My father's Jews were monsters out to destroy our country.

"What are you two up to?" my father growled. "Are you getting any work done? I'm starving. Have you forgotten about my supper?" My mother rushed to the stove and started to stir the pea soup. "It's almost done. I just have to add the sausage."

He had her trained. She obeyed like a dog obeys its master. Afraid of my father's temper, she never challenged his convictions. I busied myself, not wanting to provoke his fury. My mother placed a plate of soup, a bowl of pudding, a bottle of beer and three thick slices of bread on a tray to be delivered to him in the living room. "You're in charge now. Watch the pot. Make sure it won't boil over," she instructed me.

"Wait. Tell me what happened to Grandpa."

"I was so relieved to have my father back. So thankful to be back home, for all of us to sit around the kitchen table. I prayed for the people on the train. I never again complained about being hungry," my mother said. "I even learned to like *Einbrennsuppe.*"

While she was gone I wondered why she had married my father. Theirs was a long courtship. Had my mother been holding out, looking for someone better, a man not crippled, to come along? Did she marry him for the food? Did he lure her with those smoked ham, pork sausages, butter, and cream from his parent's farm during those ten long years of engagement?

I was just about to get up to check on the pot when I saw my mother standing in the door. She looked shocked, bewildered. "Emma. *Mein Gott*, can't I even leave you alone for a minute?" She yelled and threw the empty tray on the table knocking over my bowl of currants. Some of the currants landed on my lap, others on the floor. Then she rushed to the stove where the *Einkochtopf* had boiled over. A bubbling river of preserves was spilling onto the burners, making its way down the front of the stove and about to ruin my mother's spotless linoleum floor. "Hurry, get a sponge, a rag, anything," she shouted as she turned the gas off and threw two dish towels on the floor. I started to pick the currants off my lap getting ready to help her. "Don't waste your time." My mother's was frantic. I let the currants drop to the floor, dashed to the sink, picked up two rags, threw one at my mother and used the other to wipe the dark red mess from the stove.

The clean-up took more than an hour. "Look at us," my mother said, "as if we've been fighting a battle." My mother's hands and forearms were red; her clothes were splattered. The red mass had stained my apron, my dress and most likely my underwear too.

"How about some rhubarb-cherry marmalade?" My mother couldn't suppress a chuckle.

"Anything sweet is fine with me," I said while slowly licking the sticky residue off my fingers.

LORENA SMITH

CHRISTMAS EVE

On one night of the year we were fully, completely Swedish. All of us. My Sri Lankan cousins, our Sri Lankan staff, random acquaintances with no place to go for Christmas. We were all Swedish on that one night that was only my mother's. Every other day she moved about, more Sri Lankan than me really. She knew the customs; she knew what should be done in a certain cultural context. This was the country she had lived in for over 30 years. She had lived in Sri Lanka longer than in her native Sweden and she often said she felt more Sri Lankan than Swedish.

But on this one night, the night before Christmas we opened that cupboard that was only opened once a year. We brought out the blue and yellow flag and all the little Christmassy knick-knacks that she had brought over in her hope chest so many years ago. We set the table with white table cloths and red and green table runners that had little Swedish "tomtes" on them. There were the three little statuettes of the Lucia and her attendants in the middle. The Christmas goat made out of straw and tied with red ribbons stood under the Christmas tree. There were the advent candle holders with red candles in them. And there was the food. Lots and lots of it. Ham and potatoes. Janson's temptation, a strange potatoes and fish concoction. There were all kinds of breads and sausages and pickled herring. There were cheeses and salads. There were foods we never saw during the rest of the year. And all the mouths that were used to tasting curry ate and ate and ate. The dinner was always completely candle-lit in the huge stone dining room of the old English bungalow we lived in.

Towards the end of the meal when everyone was laughing and full and the glow of the Christmas tree seemed to reach out and enfold us all in a happy haze, my mom would put on the coffee and bring out the cinnamon twists and ginger cookies. And we would sit and talk and laugh and sing until late in the night.

I have later realized how important these nights were to my mother, when she got to celebrate in the way that she knew and remember her culture. And I have also realized that it was a way of honoring her when all these people from a completely different culture were able to come together around a meal that was not their own and celebrate life, Christmas, happiness and the things that people all over the world celebrate.

I think of her every time I lay the table for my own Christmas Eve Swedish dinner in Texas. People begin to gather around the table and I light the candles that sit in the same holders that my mom had. I know that far away in Sri Lanka my parents and brother and all the people they love have just risen from the table where they've eaten the same things that we're just about to eat over here.

It's the one night of the year when I feel the closest to them all.

COFFEE THE COLOR OF MY SKIN

Today I wore my knee-high boots.
I grabbed a cup of coffee.
Guatemalan Antigua. It is my favorite coffee.
When I pour the cream in I compare it to my skin.
When it is the same color then I know
It has been mixed enough.
I pull on my Saks Fifth Avenue hat onto my dark curls
And turn the heat on in my Japanese car.
It is very cold outside today.
Thank god for my warm coat
Made in Nepal.
My coworkers chat about the weekend.
What are you doing?
Going dancing I think, a new club, a new friend.
And you?
Don't know, maybe dinner, maybe a movie.
Lunch at Taco Bell.
I have learned to like tacos.
I didn't like them when I first moved here.
I didn't like the snow either and
Saks Fifth Avenue scared me.
I drift through the day like the snowflakes on my window.
Pushed here and there by the wind.
Conforming to the winds that flick it
is the only way to survive.
To ride the breeze.
Its late, its dark
But I promised my mother I would come by
So I sigh
And inside I feel warmth.

I know they are waiting
Ginger tea, warm smells of
Coconut and curry.
A discussion of the latest political news
At home.
And I know that
True reality, my roots dig deep
Down below, under the earth
Under the clothes
Under the coffee
They dip into a pool
Of tea and tumeric.

FAMILY

My family history is a fractured one. Half of it happened in Sri Lanka among fragrant blossoms and sea breezes and the other half happened in Sweden, icy lakes and midsummer sun.

Since I grew up in Sri Lanka that part of the family history was always vibrant and alive to me. My family was a big one, and since Sri Lankans like to adopt everyone as "uncles" and "aunties" it seemed even bigger than it was. And everyone liked to tell stories. I grew up knowing about Uncle Artie who liked to rip people off in the most imaginative of ways until he became a Christian and had to go around the little island nation apologizing to everyone. I knew about the funny memories. My twin uncles who would date each other's girlfriends. And the sad ones. My auntie Sheila who died of TB at 12 because my grandparents were too poor to afford medicine. I knew about Cousin Alex who backed my Dad's car out of the garage and down a precipice when he was 12. And about Auntie Dotty who was...well...Dotty.

Because I rarely went to Sweden that side of the family was a little murky to me. I knew Morfar had been a fisherman and an alcoholic and my amazing Mormor had brought up 12 children in a tiny house with no running water and very little money. I knew that my mother started milking the neighborhood cows at 5 years old for extra money and that my Uncle Arne would cry on people's doorsteps until they took pity on him and bought some of the fish he was selling. But it always seemed far away and not very real. Surely things couldn't have been that bad.

When I was about 9 we took a trip to Sweden. It was the first time I was old enough to form memories and understand a little better all that my grandmother had endured to bring to this world all those children and feed and clothe them.

The house was tiny. The kitchen, the living room and one room downstairs. A landing and one bedroom upstairs. It was beyond tiny. Our family of four seemed to fill it up. I couldn't imagine having 12 children in here.

My grandma was cooking and sent me down to the cellar to get a jar of lingonberry preserves. She still picked and canned them herself every spring. I walked down the steep cellar stairs, down into the damp and dark cellar. There were jars of preserves lining one wall. The other wall told the story of childhood. Names carved in the walls. Torsten. Arne. Stig. Jan. I knew that the boys had slept in the cellar. There were tic-tac-toe games scratched in the crude cement around the boiler and in my mind's eye I saw the little boys huddled around the boiler on the dark winter nights for warmth. Underneath the wooden shelf holding the preserves there were names carved too with little tally marks. Majbritt—3. Dagny—5. Greta—4. I wondered what the tally marks denoted. Maybe the number of jars they filled? Maybe the number of cows milked at the neighbor's farm. Maybe it was just a game the little girls had devised in a household too poor to buy them toys.

I was quiet during dinner thinking of how bleak it seemed. And wondering how people found the will to live when they were constantly cold and hungry. I shivered involuntarily and my mother put her arm around me to warm me.

My grandmother twinkled and smiled and dished out potatoes and sill. The conversation grew loud and lively. My uncles laughed and teased each other about how lazy they had been growing up. My Aunty Majbritt told the story of the once a year waffle day when my Grandma would sit all day in the kitchen making waffles for her brood of children who would run and play, then come back and eat the waffles and then run out again till the next batch was done. "Remember? Remember?" They asked and giggled like school girls. Stories of fun and love and sibling rivalry. Who stole whose bike and who covered for whom when they were out late.

"We could just run around and switch beds and there were too many to keep track of!"

"Remember when Stig stole all the potatoes and was sick in the attic?"

"Remember when Greta tried to milk the Bull?"

"I was only Five! No one told me!!"

They laughed till they couldn't breathe.

When we were leaving I held my mother's hand as we walked onto the porch and she turned to give my grandmother a hug. I heard her whisper "thank you" softly as she cupped my grandma's cheek for a second.

I knew what she was thanking her for.

MICHELE MARKARIAN

SHAKE

I hate Sundays.

The Sundays of my suburban childhood are boring, dull, dutiful, consisting of visits to extended family members who speak Armenian and expect children to be well-behaved and dignified, which we are. The loss of lives during the Genocide of 1917 has made even the vaguest of family connections genuine; in America, where scattered survivors have come from all over the world, every Armenian is a relative.

It is a hot Sunday in 1971. I am ten, my brother Joey is eight, and my baby sister Lucy, two. Fat Auntie Selpi has just had a baby, her first, a ten-pound boy named Bedros. We have to visit them in the hospital. After that, my parents inform us, we will be going to Logan Airport to welcome a new cousin into the family, who is coming from Beirut.

"Who is it?" Joey and I ask. If it's a cousin, maybe it'll be young enough to play and speak English with, like our Nakashian and Hazerjian cousins.

"Her name is Sharkey," says my mother.

Joey and I roll that one around our tongues. Sharkey. Sharkey. Certainly the funniest name we've heard in our family so far, and we've got some weird ones. Like Auntie Serpouhee. Or Araxi, my godmother. Even my brother and sister–Joseph Dikran Hagopian and Lucia Iskoohee Hagopian. Nothing as weird as Sharkey. Don't those Armenians in Beirut know that Shark is the name of a deadly sea creature?

"Sharkey is Arshod's younger sister", says my mother. "She is nineteen years old, and is coming here to live with Arshod and Anoush in Watertown."

Arshod. There's another one. He's our third or fourth cousin on my father's mother's side. God only knows how he got the address of my father from Beirut, but he did, asking him to help him come to America. My father, dutiful, kind, thinks he's the Statue of Liberty. When Arshod arrives, my father gets him a job with his third cousin's factory and sponsors him for citizenship. When Arshod wants to marry a chubby, phony woman named Anoush, he brings her to my father for approval. What could my father do? He approves. When they marry, my father is Best Man.

Here, on this Sunday, my father will show his support in welcoming Arshod's sister by dragging us all, including his sister Araxi, to the airport.

This time, I feel my father has gone too far. It's a beautiful August Sunday; the entire neighborhood had been out playing softball when we left for our visits. We are not allowed to play with friends on Sundays. We have just been inside of a stuffy hospital to smile at my fat Auntie Selpi and her ten-pound boy, and now we are smooshed in the backseat of a hot four-door Buick Riviera, headed towards a terminal with a funny name–Lufthansa–to meet a Sharkey.

I can't wait to grow up so that I can do whatever I want, I think as we drive towards the Lufthansa sign. Adulthood seems a fine fantasy as we finally peel ourselves away from the upholstery of the Buick and enter the terminal.

Arshod and Anoush are there. Arshod looks nervous, Anoush irritable. Arshod tells us the plane has just landed. Minutes later, Arshod is hugging someone and crying, and a Sharkey is standing for the inspection of her extended American family.

Her eyes are the first thing I notice. They startle me. They look as though they've been crying, deer brown eyes with red rims underneath. Yet her thick eyebrows are darkly knitted; she looks angry. She has fuzzy brown hair, not smoothly wavy and black like Arshod's, more like brownish steel wool pulled back in a ponytail. She is skinny–maybe 100 pounds–and I envy this because I'm chunky. She is wearing a dungaree mini skirt and matching jacket, with a red and white striped jersey. She kisses us all on each cheek and steps back, glaring. The grownups chat in Armenian for a few minutes, but my father sees that this is an emotional moment for Arshod and his sister and soon we all leave, relieved that it doesn't take long.

"She's *yaman,* that one," says my Aunt Araxi on the ride home, and they all nod sagely. *Yaman* is the Armenian word for savvy.

"No flies on that girl," says my mother, and everyone echoes, "No flies on that girl" and it's the first time I've heard that expression. I look at Joey, he looks at me. I picture the glaring Sharkey, flies buzzing around her but never landing, and it repulses me. Who is this Sharkey, with her horde of no flies?

Two weeks later, Sharkey comes to stay with my family for the weekend, a gesture of goodwill from my parents. Sharkey and Anoush aren't getting along too well, which surprises no one because Anoush is a bitch. My parents put Sharkey in Joey's room, and Joey gets to sleep on the den couch downstairs, because he's a boy. Sharkey doesn't say much, but is compulsive about jumping up and doing the dishes and scrubbing down the kitchen after we eat, which surprises and dismays my mother–Sharkey is the guest, after all.

After dinner, Sharkey watches TV with us, sometimes speaking Armenian with my parents, sometimes broken English, but the conversation is sparse and strained. My mother's very patient, but she can't help resent this latest intrusion of my father's–first he moves her to a neighborhood full of Catholics who think we're freaks, and now it's an awkward 19-year old cousin from Lebanon who is not skillful in the art of conversation. My mother is angry, but she appears charming and nice. Joey and I are too shy to say anything to Sharkey at all, which is unusual because we have been taught manners. Something in her commands distance, and we respect this, even though the weekend's Friday is tense with unspoken things. On this Friday night, I am happy to go to bed early.

Saturday afternoon I find myself feeling a little anxious. I haven't spoken to Sharkey, and I'm clumsy about it because I can't understand my lack of empathy. It's not as if I don't like her. It's just that I can't relate to her, don't know why the silence and boredom of our family life is better than Arshod's and Anoush's.

Sharkey is sitting stiffly on our living room couch. I can stand her mystery no longer, and tiptoe upstairs into Joey's room, where she has put her things.

The bed is neatly made up. Old fashioned black shoes, with little Cuban heels, round toes and thick black straps, look Old Country and out of place under Joey's round white table with the gray flecks. On top of the table is a photograph of Sharkey's mother and grandmother, looking craggy and deranged, like all my overseas relatives look to my ten-year-old eyes. Then I see it, a square of white with black letters, next to the picture.

BEDROSIAN, SHAKE reads her boarding pass from Lufthansa, which for some reason, she continues to carry with her.

Shake. Sha-ke. Not Sharkey at all, but Sha-ke. I know instantly that this is no mistake; this is how she spells her name in Lebanon. It looks very vulnerable, especially the KE part. Halfway round the world, from Lebanon to America, comes this funny name, probably unaware that Americans will mispronounce it, not understand it, and worse, maybe even think it odd. I look at this name, SHAKE, and start to cry. I cry for a little while, staring at SHAKE and eventually, I stop crying.

"Would you like to play cards?" I say to her in English when I go downstairs. I don't know if she can play cards, but it seems a safe bet, as I've seen Armenians much older than her play.

"Yes," she says, so eagerly it surprises me. She can play War, she says, and even though it's a boring game and we still have no idea what to say to each other, the ice is broken and we smile. We play War for a bit, then she teaches me a game from Lebanon called *Bonjour Monsieur*, which is like Slapjack, only more complicated and comical. We laugh loudly. Joey comes over and says he'd like to play too because it looks like fun, and soon all three of us are laughing and playing and feeling pretty good.

"I'm very proud of you for playing with your cousin," says my mother to me later on, as I'm going to bed.

"She's nice, Mum," I say. I want to tell her about the name, Shake, but I don't think she'll understand.

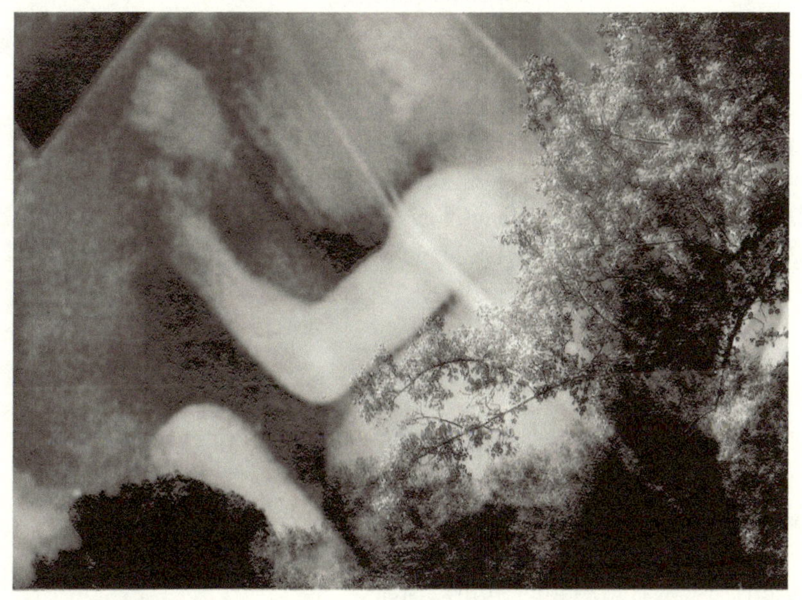

ELINOR BENEDICT

PAPER FLOWERS

Hall of Revolutionary Martyrs
Tianjin, China, January 14, 1980

An official hands out paper flowers. We pin them
on our coats, my daughter and I, following
our Chinese cousins into the Hall of Martyrs.
Cold flows from stone; an ocean closes behind us.
Our footsteps speak the only language we know:
Stop. Stop. We shouldn't have come.

*

In the anteroom we sip black tea. We try
to warm our hands on the cups while guests
fill the table like a jury. I bow my head, feeling
my daughter accuse me of mourning a woman I hardly knew.
Dear girl: She was my father's only sister.
You don't know yet, how that is.

*

The bald man beckons. We file into a chamber where
hundreds of gray flowers clutter the walls. From a hood
of black crepe her photograph gazes. I close my eyes.
Last time I saw her, the wind flew her hat like a kite
over the seashells, over the blue umbrella, at my father's
old house. She laughed when he caught it,
my father her brother again.

*

Four times we bow to her ashes boxed in a vault.
Men in gray suits collect all the flowers, stuff
them in cardboard for the next quick blooming. I'm dry
as the petals they crush, until someone touches my shoulder
like a sparrow perching: an ivory woman in black. She takes
my daughter's hand, reaches for mine. She says nothing,
but her cheeks are wet, her eyes alive with the shock of love.

IMMOLATION OF A STRANGER

for Ellen Liu (1937-1983)

It's jade, flawed with brown flecks,
rimmed with narrow gold and not quite
the shape of our usual hearts, those
valentines with twin scallops we send
to hide and seek love. This one,
cool as a lilac leaf but heavy
in my hand, grows a third curve
where the chain holds–an odd
catch of the heart.
I close my fingers
around the green stone, remembering
the chilly gift shop in Beijing
where bored young women sold
silks and bamboo offseason. They
hugged themselves in the bitter air
and turned their heater's flame so high
I imagined the fringe of my plaid
wool scarf catching fire for buying
something cheap to take home.

Ellen, my cousin and companion
that final day, watched me solemnly
as I made my small choice, guided me
with kindness through that gray city
she called home, looking even then
as though she were lost. Her eyes
and forehead–half foreign, half family–
made my face burn as I remembered
how my uncles, their necks flushed,
talked about their sister marrying
a Chinaman, disappearing for years,
only to come back at the end
to make claims on them.

But gentle Ellen,
who owned so little, claimed nothing
but what I felt from wearing
her mother's face.
Now three years
later this thin letter from Beijing
tells me how the same grim illness
and death that took her mother,
my second self, has finished her.
I think of journeys, kin, distances,
home. Foolishly I wonder what

she took with her. If I could
send her something, I'd say, Ellen,
take this, my flawed stone heart,
and keep it green.

GLIMPSES

It's nearly twilight as our bus rattles
from the airport through narrow streets
on the outskirts of Beijing, dodging
shadowy pedestrians and scattering bicycles
like mice in a gray pantry. We rub

frost from the window panes with gloved
fingers and beg my half-Chinese cousin,
returning in his Western suit, to tell us
what we see. He points out courtyards
smoky behind brick gates, small markets

choked with people waiting to buy cabbages
under yellow light. He says they hurry
to get home and dinner before dark. To just
such a market he used to rush, to wait,
to buy pears for his mother. We nod,

flutter our guidebooks and wave to children
in padded coats clustered like bells
beside doorways. Looking for familiar faces,
they keep their hands curved in their sleeves.
Workers stamp up and down in long queues

puffing the air blue with cigarets and cold.
At the curb a student ties green onions
to his bicycle, clutches a bag of pears.
He careens into traffic, trying to steady
an old woman against his back. Our bus

honks its way through the crowd. Cameras
click at the windows. But beside me
my cousin makes a low sound in his chest.

Turning, I find his face drawn, white.
He whispers, "In the market I saw–myself."

CARL PALMER

CORDIALLY YOURS

sitting on mother's couch
she has forgotten who I am
greets me like a stranger
treats this stranger better
than she ever treated me

I yearn for her glower
that glint of disgust
the biting sneer
refusal to say anything
nice to me at all

HAIBUN FOR PAPA

Unable to remember what happened yesterday, recall a name, date or telephone number, he will tell again every embarrassing detail of an event that happened back twenty years ago.

stories about mommy
when she was young
grandgirls laugh

SCREWDRIVER MATHEMATICS

Lying up under the car
on the floor of the garage
I saw his little feet arrive
the shadow of his head
bending down to ask
"Whattaya want, Dad?"
"Hand me that number two Phillips
off the workbench there, son."
I watched him switch his weight
from one little foot to the other
step away, start back, stop
turn around and then
scamper back to the car
"Dad, is the Phillips a plus or a minus?"

SHERYL L. NELMS

HEIR LOOM HOCKED

I always gathered
spring greens
with Gram
down by Mission Creek
we would climb
those steep banks
picking
dock
dandelions
lamb's quarter
sheep sorrel
poke weed
and nettles
using knowledge
handed down
from mother to daughter
from England and Ireland
now with Gram dead
and a mother who was too busy
I've become uncertain
can't quite
remember
how many times do I boil the poke
and was it the leaves or the berries

KERRY LANGAN

ETERNAL YOUTH

They say that of all the senses, smell is the one that can trigger memories of the past most easily. I believe it. When I was twenty, I was a perfume girl at Sheffield's, one of the nicest department stores in Toronto. Scents of all kind were a big part of my life then. Every week, I sprayed some new fragrance on the customers. Honey had the standard golden color of most perfumes, but it came in a little glass jar shaped like a bumble bee; you opened the lid by unscrewing the bee's wings. As clever as that was, the perfume itself smelled a little too much like bug repellent for my taste. Sunlight was a big seller. It was a topaz-colored fluid, a browner gold than usual, and it had a sprite, open-air scent. I was supposed to say, "Would you like a ray of sunlight?" and then wave the bottle in a circle before squirting a customer. I only did that when a supervisor was walking by; I didn't want the customers to think I was nuts. My favorite perfume of all was Rain Forest, a deep emerald elixir that came in a concave-shaped bottle painted with little gold vines everywhere and a beautiful long-beaked bird with fuschia and yellow feathers. It smelled like overgrown grass in August after a strong rain.

Not every one wanted to be sprayed with perfume. Women looked past me, avoided my gaze, suddenly becoming engrossed with the floor pattern or reaching into their purses to locate their car keys. I would call out to them, "Would you like to try. . ." but they'd say "No thank you," so abruptly that I'd stop talking mid-sentence. That kind of rejection can get to you after a while, so I learned not to hound the women who quickened their pace when they saw me. Other women stopped, eager to see what I was selling, and I sprayed their wrists, telling them to wave their arms a bit so the alcohol evaporated before they sniffed. Otherwise, the scent was too potent. For every ten bottles I sold, I got a teeny, tiny sample bottle. I would have preferred a commission, I only made minimum wage, but it didn't work that way at Sheffield's. As it was, I was always worried that if I didn't sell enough perfume, I'd be out of a job.

Nancy, my friend who sold Coach purses, always came to see me before she left at six o'clock. She usually had a date and, like everybody else who worked at the store, couldn't afford to buy the things we sold. I looked around to make sure no one was watching and then sprayed her wrists and the back of her neck. In return, she would talk loudly about how wonderful the scent was, trying to drum up business for me. She wasn't the only one getting something for nothing. Every now and then, I snuck over to the Estee Lauder counter and Lucille, a woman who'd been at the store forever, gave me a mini make-over. We couldn't get away with that too often. There was always the risk of Billy Sheffield, the boss' son, lurking about. He cruised the store trying to look important, making sure everybody was doing their job. I could usually tell when he was around because he sucked on smelly eucalyptus cough drops all day.

One day I saw him leave early through the employee exit, so I walked fearlessly over to cosmetics. Before I asked Lucille if she could do my eyes with pearl-gray eye-shadow and black eye-liner, she raised her wrist and said, "Smell."

The jasminey scent with the spicy, clove undertone filled my nose up to my brain. I recognized it, but didn't know why. It wasn't a perfume that I promoted. Without warning, a picture formed in my mind and I got that spooky deja vu feeling. A corner of my brain started to reel and it was like I was watching a miniature movie. I remembered myself in a bedroom standing next to a bed I was too short to see over. The bed had a white chenille spread and I was reaching up, rubbing my hand back and forth over the fleecy lines that felt as soft as talcum powder. There was a woman standing in front of an open closet, her back to me, the zipper on her dress waiting to be pulled up. Her brown hair stopped at the bottom of her neck and flipped up at the edges. I think it was night time, and the room was swimming with the fresh scent of perfume, of this same scent on Lucille's wrist. I assumed that the woman at the closet was my mother, but, in my mind, I only saw her from the back.

"What is it?" I almost demanded of Lucille.

"Shangri La. Nice, huh?" Truth to tell, Lucille was wearing too much of it, but it was a nice scent. Not as obvious as most of the fragrances we sold; lighter, more secretive.

"Where did you get it?"

She lifted a curved hand to one side of her mouth and whispered, delighted with her deviousness, "Ormonds," a store just around the corner, Sheffield's' biggest competitor.

"They've just re-introduced it," Lucille said. "It hasn't been sold for over fifteen years."

"Fifteen years?"

"Yeah. Ormonds ran a promotion the first day they were selling it. Half off."

The hanging fluorescent lights seemed to give up extra rings of hazy blue glow, and my left eye began to feel strained, a pinching just behind it.

"Want me to do you?" Lucille asked, unaware of how dislocated I felt. I distracted myself from the feeling by getting up into the long-legged make-up stool. I sat facing Lucille, my back to the customers passing by.

I didn't know enough about my mother. My father died in Vietnam when I was two, and my mother left me with my grandmother a few years later. I was almost five, ready to start kindergarten. We were living in Auburn then, a little town in upstate New York. I remember sitting in the back seat of a car, my clothes stacked in plastic laundry baskets next to me and some stuffed animals on the floor. The blue vinyl seats smelled like spilled nail polish, and a slight spatter of rain hit the windows. There was a band-aid taped awkwardly over the valley of skin between my thumb and index finger, and I remember tugging at the edges of it. We didn't go to the laundromat, however, we went to my grandmother's house even though she wasn't home from work yet. When we got there, my mother made me macaroni and cheese, my favorite meal. While it was baking, the wonderful aroma of milky cheese and slightly burnt bread crumbs filling the house, my mother took out a camera from her purse and told me to stand by the fireplace. She took three pictures, calling out to me to smile each time. It took me a long time to eat the macaroni and cheese because I had to wait for it to cool. My mother seemed nervous, sitting in a caned-back chair and bouncing the soles of her sandals against the rug. She got up and went to the window every time she heard a car. I wondered what we were doing at my grandmother's when she wasn't home, but I didn't ask. After I finished eating, my mother told me to lie down on the couch. I did and almost immediately fell asleep as I usually did after eating a big meal. The last thing I remember is my mother's hand gently brushing the bangs from my forehead and the scent of Jergen's hand lotion, a rich, almost cherry-flavored smell. When I woke, there was a different hand stroking my forehead, my grandmother's, and the fruity scent of Jergen's had been replaced with the pristine waft of rose milk. Grandmother was seated on the edge of the couch and she looked down at me proudly; I was her only grandchild. She asked if I had a good nap and whether I was hungry. She seemed sad, her eyes locked in a dead stare that didn't really see me. She ran her forefinger down my nose and tapped the end of it. "Don't you worry, Sarah," she said, "you and me are going to be just fine."

I knew instinctively that my mother was gone. I didn't cry. I felt confused more than abandoned, wondering where I would sleep in that big house and whether there was someone for me to play with in the neighborhood. My grandmother brought me into the kitchen and fed me Graham crackers and milk, and she told me she was going to put up a swing set in the yard. It preoccupied me until evening when I wanted my mother. Sitting in the bathtub, my lips started to quiver and I cried with the heartbreak of an adult. It frightened my grandmother and that frightened me more. She added more bubble bath to the water, pale pink crystals that smelled so potently feminine, motherly, until they dissolved in the water and relaxed into just another soapy scent. I cried until I got the hiccups and my grandmother got me out of the tub and into bed. She sat in a chair next to my bed until I fell asleep, her words sounding in my ears as I drifted off, "Don't you worry, pumpkin. We're going to be fine. *Just fine.*" When I think of those words now, I realize how fiercely determined she sounded.

When Lucille finished with my make-over, I walked around the corner to Ormond's and found the fragrance department. There were bottles of Shangri La everywhere on little tables. The first thing I noticed was that the perfume was lavender, that muted, romantic shade of purple. The bottle itself wasn't that impressive, just a simple glass cylinder with a gold cap, but the label was lovely, the word "Shangri La" written in an exotic, Arabic-like style, short, thick letters in cornflower blue ink against an ivory background, an elaborate pink rose dotting the "i".

A young woman about my age with a very short haircut came up to me and said, "Would you like to visit Shangri La, land of beauty and eternal youth?"

How could I say no to a fellow perfume girl, especially one made to spout such a goofy line? I smiled at her and held out my wrist. She was impressed when I waved my arm for the alcohol to evaporate with no prompting from her. Then I sniffed my wrist and waited for the memory to bob up. It surfaced immediately, bringing something new this time; the woman at the closet, my mother presumably, was leaning over to put on stockings. I think she wobbled a bit as she adjusted a clasp on her garter belt. In the store, my own legs started to wobble and I said apologetically to the woman, "It's beautiful, but I can't afford it." She nodded her head like she understood, and I said, "I'm the perfume girl at Sheffield's."

"*Ohh*," she said, smiling widely. "Wait here."

She returned with a couple tiny samples of the perfume. I thanked her and told her Sheffield's was pushing Moon Mist that week and that she should come by so I could return the favor.

Since my grandmother's death the previous year, I shared an apartment a couple miles from the store with two other girls. That night, I put the perfume sample on my night stand. I thought if I smelled it every night before I went to sleep and every morning as soon as I woke up, I'd piece together the memory and maybe it would tell me something about my mother. Aside from my own few recollections, all I knew about her I'd learned from my grandmother.

Grandmother. She had nurtured her anger at my mother through the years and often told me that if anyone asked, my mother was dead. While growing up, I had all kinds of questions which my grandmother didn't want to answer, but she did acknowledge a few things over the years. She told me my mother had a hard time recovering from my father's death and was reluctant to begin dating again. When she did, she discovered that she was very admired. "Could have had her pick," was how Grandmother characterized it. There was one man in particular, James, who was insistent on being the only man in Mother's life and, unfortunately, he was the one my grandmother cared for least of all.

For starters, he was black. He had also been to Vietnam. My

grandmother somehow felt this had something to do with my father's death. I don't know how. Perhaps she thought if James had died in Vietnam, her son would have come home instead. My father's military portrait hung in our living room, and I knew that my grandmother carried around the newspaper clipping of his obituary in her wallet. Every year, on the anniversary of his death, she had a special mass said for him. Growing up, I didn't know who was more of a ghost to me, my father or my mother.

My mother's dating James was a disgrace to my grandmother and, she argued, to my father's memory. I do remember the fights she and my mother had, my grandmother's hand slapping against the table, each of them shouting at the same time. My grandmother's high card was me. How could my mother disgrace her own child? Hadn't I gone through enough losing my father, and now my mother wanted to confuse me and lay me open to who knows what kind of abuse from people who also disapproved. My mother protested vehemently. If her husband's death had taught her anything, she said, it was that wars were fought because people didn't realize they were all alike. To this, my grandmother sneered. She said that she was nothing like Hitler, thank you very much, and my mother screamed back that James wasn't Hitler. Grandmother told me that she never in a million years believed my mother would leave town and marry James, but then she came home that day and found me on her couch and she didn't so much as blink an eye.

It's funny. James was in my life for such a short time, but I'll never forget him. I knew him for less than a year, but I felt I understood everything about him, and he understood me. He used to ring the doorbell over and over and my mother would let me run to answer it. Before he even stepped in the door, he held out two closed hands, but there was always candy in both. One time he brought me a paper parasol that he had brought back from Vietnam, and I broke it from opening and closing it too often. Another time he reached in his pocket and took out a few Mexican jumping beans that we watched jump off the window sill onto the floor. His voice was as deep as Brutus' in the Popeye cartoons, but it wasn't scary, it was funny. He laughed a lot, his "heh, heh, heh's" spilling out in sets of three over and over. And I remember that he called his car, an old blue station wagon, Maybelline. I thought it was the most beautiful name I'd ever heard, but I didn't understand why a car had a name.

I think my fixation with scents started with James. When he squeezed me around the waist and lifted me in the air, I breathed in his rich, sweet, smell, like grape jelly. I told him, "You smell like peanut butter and jelly," because I never ate jelly without peanut butter, and he said, "Yeah? You smell like Rice Krispies," or he'd say, "You smell like root beer." It was something different every time.

Young as I was, I had the strange knowledge that my grandmother wasn't the only one who didn't like James. Mother and James took me once to the soda fountain for ice cream and we sat in the cool vinyl booth for a long time, but the waitress never came over. We finally left and bought ice cream at the supermarket, taking it home to eat. Another time, James came with my mother to see a nursery school play in which I had a bit part, and the seat next to him remained empty even though people were standing in the back of the room and sitting in the aisles.

I started to carry a sample of Shangri La in my purse, taking it out to sniff several times a day. Then, two weeks after Ormond's promotion, Sheffield's followed suit and I was spraying it on customers. For days, I was surrounded by the scent, and pieces of the puzzle started to fall into place. I remembered more and more details about that memory, waking up one night with such a start, my breath stolen from deep within my chest, when it finally all came together. I still think about it. The thing about trying so hard to remember something is that once you do, you can't make it go away. No matter how hard you try, it'll always be there, following you around like some starving dog. So, for the rest of my life, I will remember this:

My mother is adjusting the clasp on her garter belt and I'm standing by the bed, reaching high so I can pat the mattress which rises above my head. The chenille ridges on the bedspread almost vibrate against my fingers as I run my hand back and forth faster and faster. My mother is humming a song, I don't know what, and replaces the cap on a perfume bottle. The smell of the perfume casts a pleasant feeling of anticipation over the room--James is coming over. There is a loud crash as something shoots through the window, blowing pieces of glass onto the bed and the floor. I watch what I realize is a rock fly across the gray carpet, blending in with it, and my mother turns around in slow motion and shrieks. Her face is something horrible, like someone scared to death in a movie. I lift my hand from the bed and am confused when I see the blood dripping from me to the white bedspread.

When my mother sees it, she hesitates for a moment before running to me, grabbing my other hand, and taking me into the bathroom. She sits me on the side of the sink and runs my hand under cold water that stings. She digs at my hand, making it hurt more and more, and I cry out and try to jerk my hand away. Finally, I feel my skin open up and she removes the piece of glass, throwing it into the waste basket. The cold water doesn't bite as much now, and I realize that I can't smell the blood any more. My mother presses a towel against the cut, finally taping a large bandaid over it. She is mumbling under her breath, and I can't make out what she is saying, but always, later, when I remember this night, I hear her say that my grandmother was right.

What does blood smell like? At the time, I thought it smelled like a strange red berry with no sweetness, instead a mineral odor like the nickel I had sucked on once in church while waiting for them to pass the offerings basket. Now, as I went to work each day, I remained haunted by the smell of blood. I asked myself why the scent couldn't evaporate from my mind like alcohol from perfume.

"She made her choice," my grandmother said all those years. I grew up thinking my mother preferred James to me and I tried to hate her. Hate her as much as my grandmother did and seemed to think I should. But I always had my doubts. You read about parents who abandoned their children showing up later at graduations or some other public place, watching their son or daughter secretively, anonymously, grieving for the choice they made however many years ago. I always believed that my mother would do that, or that she would have done it if she had the chance. Shortly after she left, my grandmother retired and we moved to Toronto and lived with her friend, a woman I called Aunt Selma, until we got our own place. I was eleven or twelve when I first worried that my mother was looking for me, but didn't know I was in Toronto. I wondered if she and James had gotten married, if they'd had children. But my grandmother, despite all her opinions and prejudices, was kind to me, and I liked living in a big city.

When my friends asked about my parents, I told them they had gone to Vietnam together and had died there, that my mother had been a nurse and my father a soldier, and they were both dead. I could almost believe it myself. Once, when my grandmother listened to me repeating this story to a neighbor, she looked at me directly and put her arm around my shoulders saying, "Yes, they're dead." She patted my arm as if she were comforting me. Afterwards, whenever she mentioned my mother, she said things like, "Before she left with your father for Vietnam," or once even, "I wish I'd saved that letter she sent me from Saigon." I didn't challenge her--what difference did it make? I had come up with the story she liked, and, in her mind, she changed history. She was happy knowing her daughter-in-law, like her son, had given her life for her country.

My recollection of that night so long ago bothered me for weeks. It made things messy, opened doors that had long been shut, locked. I asked myself all kinds of things. Had my mother left me with my grandmother out of fear of further violence, violence that could hurt me? I couldn't forgive her for choosing James over me, but the thought of her wanting to protect me ate away at me, softened me. And what if she had tried to find me all those years, but couldn't? What if she were still trying to find me?

My performance at work, such as it was, suffered. I didn't sleep well at night and I was tired during the day. I shifted my weight endlessly from one foot to another and hardly called out to the customers. One afternoon, Billy Sheffield caught me slouched against a display counter, one of my shoes slipped off, and he told me to straighten up and fly right or else. I hurried back to my position on the floor and realized a woman in her mid-forties had witnessed the reprimand and was now smiling at me sympathetically. I raised my bottle of Tulips, which smelled curiously more woodsy than flowery, and she politely held out her hand.

"Oh, that's nice," she said.

"It's available at counter three for just twenty-four ninety-five," I told her.

She smiled at me and I scanned her face, her clothes. She was a pretty woman with dark blue eyes and dark lashes. Her eyes were close together in that way that can be attractive. She was dressed in a polyester jacket and slacks. I knew right away that she couldn't afford the perfume.

"Maybe another day," she said and thanked me.

I saw that woman many times over the next several days. Sometimes getting on the elevator, other times just browsing the main floor. Always, she smiled at me, and one time, when I caught her eye as she just entered the floor, she waved at me as if we knew each other.

It occurred to me that I was the reason she was in the store so often. She was about the right age and her coloring was similar enough to my own. I had a couple photos of my mother, but they were so old, they had a non-descript quality about them. This woman seemed interested in me and I began to look for her each day. More often than not, I'd see her. She never came over and spoke with me again, but it was obvious that she looked in my direction every time she was in that part of the store.

The gamut of emotions I felt that week flung me up and down, left and right. Was I at last going to be reunited with my mother? Would I be disloyal to my grandmother by forgiving my mother for having left me all those years ago? I imagined what a perfume named Forgiveness would smell like, a neutral, honest scent that wouldn't be too strong or too weak.

On Friday afternoon of that week, the elevator bell sounded, and I watched the customers step out from the cubicle. I saw the woman; she was more dressed up than I had seen her previously. She wore a black, probably rayon, suit with a pink blouse that had a bow in the front. Her hair had been cut into a stylish bob and she looked younger. Our eyes met and she walked towards me. My heart beat became irregular and everything in the store became silent. I couldn't hear the people walking past me, the sales women talking, the music that was usually piped all over the main level.

As soon as she reached me, my ears flooded with the noises of the store and I strained to hear what she was saying to me. She was holding her hand out, introducing herself. Should I hug her? I was so confused, more so when I saw that she was already backing away, lifting her hand to say good-bye.

"Wait! Who did you say you were?"

She smiled and stepped forward again. "I'm Karen Tiffen. I was just hired as a part-time perfume girl, evenings and weekends."

"Perfume girl?"

"Perfume woman I like to call it," she said and winked at me.

"You were just hired?"

She shook her head yes and smiled broadly. "Mr. Sheffield hired me on the spot. Told me he thought I could increase sales with women my age."

She was kind, and I realized I must have seemed remote. "I've seen you in the store a lot lately," I said, trying to recover and sound friendly.

"You noticed," she said, nodding her head eagerly. "I was trying to get familiar with the whole store." She turned her head about, taking in the main level. "I thought it would help with the interview. I'm hoping," she said, glancing towards the accessories counter, "that I'll get to work in a real department before too long."

I nodded my head. My throat felt like a jar with a lid being clamped on it. "Good luck. Nice to meet you. What did you say your name was?"

"Karen. And you're Sarah," she said, reading my Sheffield's' name tag. She waved and walked out of the store.

I had to find my mother. The encounter in the store made me realize that if I did nothing else with my life, I would find her. I went to the public library and looked at all the phone books. There was no Marie Salyers in any of the directories I looked at, but, of course, if she had married James, she'd have a new last name. Or would she? Was my mother a feminist? I didn't have a clue. And I didn't know James' last name, probably never did.

I talked with the reference librarian, a woman about thirty who asked me lots of questions and wrote things down as I spoke. I told her I couldn't afford to hire anyone to look for my mother, I had to do it myself. She suggested that I telephone veterans' associations in the Auburn area and ask about James' whereabouts. The library had a collection of phone books on microfiche, and the librarian helped me find a huge list of numbers.

I spoke to at least thirty people before speaking to a man who thought he remembered James.

"Big guy with glasses?" he asked me on the phone.

Glasses? It was too long ago to remember. I told him all I could, that James was a tall black man, well over six feet, that he'd fought in Vietnam in the late sixties, and that he lived in Auburn just after that. I explained that he was a friend of my mother's, but that didn't seem to matter to him. I wanted to tell him that James smelled like jelly, but that was crazy. Then I heard a low murmur at the other end of the line, and the man cleared his throat hesitantly.

"Say," he said, "is your mother a white woman?"

"Yes!" I shouted, excited, realizing I had failed to tell him the most helpful piece of information of all.

"Sure, sure," he said. "James Williams. I remember him and your mother at a VA dance. They sure shook up that little town." He laughed and I felt peculiar, like he was laughing at me.

"How can I find out where he is now?" I said with coolness in my voice.

The line was silent a moment and then the man said, "Oh, he's got to be listed somewhere. The VA keeps tabs on people. Give me your number and I'll call you back."

He didn't call back for two weeks and I gave up hope. Maybe this man was like my grandmother, maybe he too had disapproved of James and my mother and had no intention of trying to help me. When he called back, I was sure he didn't have any information, but he gave me a phone number for a James Williams in Albany. He wasn't sure it was the right man, it was common name, but it was all he could come up with. I thanked him and he wished me luck. He seemed sincere.

I called the number right away because I knew I'd lose my nerve if I waited. I held my breath as the phone rang four times, wondering what I would do if a woman answered. Would I recognize my mother's voice? An answering machine came on and a woman's voice told me that the Williamses weren't at home, but to please leave a message. The voice was unfamiliar, a friendly, musical, black woman's voice. I hung up and sighed. Then, without thinking, I called again and this time I left a message:

"Hi. This is Sarah Salyers. Mr. Williams, I don't know if you're the same James who dated my mother in Auburn, New York in the late sixties. I'm trying to track her down and would appreciate any help you can give me. I'm living in Toronto, and you could call me collect." I gave him my home phone number and told him he could also call me at Sheffield's.

No one called back. I guessed that even if I had phoned the correct residence, James and my mother had probably broken up a long time ago, possibly on bad terms, and he probably had no idea where she was either. I had wild ideas about going on some talk show that reunites long lost relatives, my mother and I hugging on televisions all over Canada. But maybe she wouldn't come forward, and who needs that kind of rejection twice?

I went through all the things my grandmother had left me, boxes of old photos, books, pockets of clothing. I found my old grammar school report cards tucked into a copy of *Peyton Place*. I opened each of the books I kept in a box under my bed, fanning each page so the dust flew out. From "Profiles in Courage," two small, yellowed at the corners, envelopes fell onto the floor. I opened up the first, a flaking, brittle newspaper clipping with a headline that read: *Woman Dies in Car Crash*. The short blurb beneath the headline said: *Marie Williams is dead at 28 after having been hit Friday night on Clemson Road. The driver of the other vehicle is an underage youth whose name is being withheld. Police stated that the youth was driving under the influence of alcohol and that charges would be pressed. Mrs. Williams' husband, James Williams, also in the car at the time of the accident, sustained no serious injuries.*

I wondered why I wasn't crying. I wanted to, but my insides felt like an empty box, something stolen from it, the lid left carelessly off. I would never find her. She would never find me. She had died soon after she had left me at my grandmother's. I had spent years wondering about a woman who didn't exist anymore.

The second envelope was folded twice. I opened it flat and read the address of my grandmother's house in Auburn. The postage markings indicated that the letter had been forwarded to Aunt Selma's house in Toronto. I removed the letter and read the bold penmanship, the ink smeared in many places:

Mrs. Salyers: I hope you will reconsider having Sarah come and live with me. As you well know, it was my wife's and my intention to bring Sarah to Albany once we were settled here. At the very least, I want to see her and talk with her about her mother. That is not too much to ask. Mrs. Salyers, please, grant me this.

It was signed James Williams. I dropped the newspaper clipping and the letter on the floor. My mother's death came at me and hit me with the force of a car that killed her. Twenty-eight! All those years my grandmother had simply said she was dead, she really was. And she had taken my silence, my complicity, as acceptance, but she was wrong. "Wrong!" I shrieked out loud, but there was no one left for me to scream at. I suspected that in her strange way, my grandmother had held James responsible for my mother's death. If she hadn't moved to Albany with him, she wouldn't have been in that car crash. And if James had been killed in Vietnam, her son would have come home. She always had someone to blame, but I had no one.

I stayed in bed for four days. My roommates thought I was seriously ill and begged me to eat. I ignored them, nibbling on soda crackers and drinking water. I didn't want to leave my room; I didn't think it would bother me if I never had contact with another person again.

But I had to get up. That Saturday, the store was having its fall clearance sale and I had to be there. Billy Sheffield was just looking for a reason to fire me. I would be spraying probably a dozen different kinds of perfumes that would be set up on a little table right near the entrance to the store. I had to be there.

The commotion of the store helped to distract me. I sprayed so many different perfumes I started to sneeze. Women were impatient, not wanting to wait for me to spray their wrists, so they picked up the bottles themselves while I attended to other customers. Over and over I said, "On sale at counter three. But we're running out. Hurry." I don't know why, but when I sprayed Shangri La on one older woman, I repeated the words that the Ormonds' perfume girl had said to me, "Would you like to visit Shangri La, land of beauty and eternal youth?" As I watched the mist fly to her wrist, I realized that all my memories of my mother were in Shangri La, that every time I remembered something about her, it would be something summoned from my childhood.

At mid-day, I was very hungry, but Billy had told me I couldn't take a break until two. The heady mix of scents was starting to make me feel light-headed, and I wondered how long I could last on my feet. The doors to the store opened and a fresh throng of customers lunged towards me. Finally, at two, I replaced the cap on every single bottle of perfume. I started to lift the little table and carry it out of sight when a tall man in a leather coat stepped forward, saying "Let me help you with that, honey. You shouldn't be lugging heavy stuff around." As I said thank you, I studied his face. He smiled expectantly and held out two hands in front of him. Before I stumbled, falling forward and knocking two perfume bottles to the floor where they shattered almost soundlessly, James said to me, "You are the very image of your mother."

DONNA LEE RICHARDSON

MULATTO-COLORED PAIN

We were orphaned
but you chose not to see
how someone could help immediately
mom suffered pain and great loss
there was nothing in your power
was your wife always the boss?
gave to the church traveled with friends
but nothing on the children
who came to depend
on a welfare system that abuses the poor
they languished in a slum
even slept on the floor
they were no true friends
not a should to protect
we fought to survive
struggling to connect
sad to say this tell is true
want you to know I'm talking about you.

CHERISE WYNEKEN

IT'S TIME

Finally
he could stand the stress
no longer.
Black man
struggling in a white man's world
kids in college
sisters butting in.
Now this.
They say she has a tumor
on the brain.
So far no pain, but blind.
Where to find some peace?
It must be time to split.

Kids struggle on alone with Mother.
Fred, the oldest,
home between Philosophy
and Business Ad
from the campus at UC
to fry some spuds and bacon,
make the bed, wash up.
Tall, handsome, black and straight
he and my white one meet,
Flower Children classmates,
1968.
When Mother died they wed.

He's had a long, hard climb
back to his family
high here in the Berkeley hills
where we gather for a holiday at Fred's.
I think it's time we look beyond
this panoramic view and the sailboats
white capped on the Bay.
I think it's time to note
his eyes that plead, Forgive!

He looks so all alone and sad
I cross the room and kiss him.
I think it's time
to be at peace and live.

JOHN GREY

UNCLE RAY AND AUNT CHERYL

In nineteen sixty eight,
Ray married this girl Cheryl
from Birmingham,
had met her on a church retreat.
"Can you believe it,"
said Aunt Clara.
Uncle Ed was less discreet,
tossed around the "N" word
like confetti.

In nineteen seventy two,
there was family reunion
in the ballroom of the Hyatt.
Some wondered whether Ray
and that colored girl would show.
They didn't.

Three years later,
cousin Barry stayed a week or two
with Ray and that nice black woman,
and their two young children.
In the eighties, when Barry went to college,
he bragged to his friends
that his favorite aunt was African-American.

In nineteen ninety three,
Ray and Cheryl celebrated
their twenty fifth wedding anniversary
in their Georgia Islands beach house.
All the living family members came.
The dead ones stayed home.

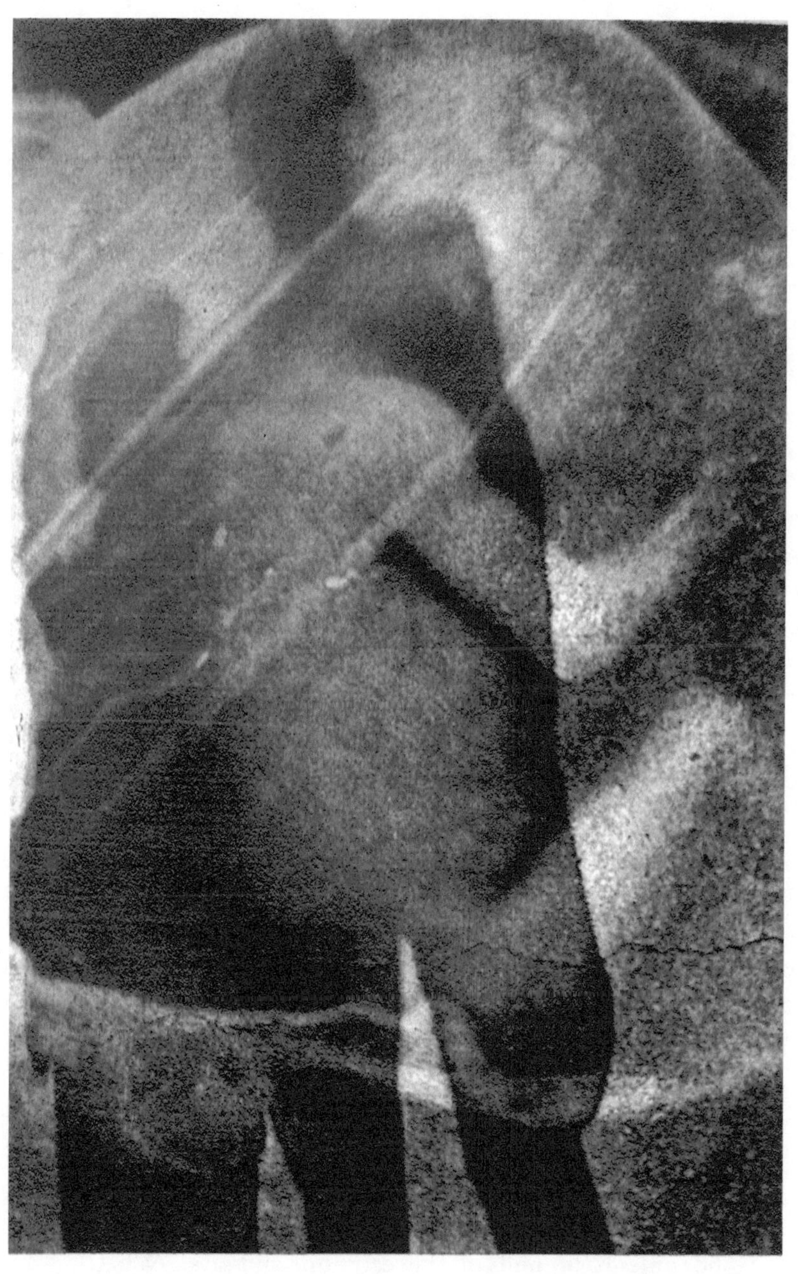

BENJAMIN ARDA DOTY

THE CONCERT

In a long cul-de-sac that calls itself Buck Crossing Drive, there are no bucks, only three-bedroom houses where families seem happy with their lives. My dad calls ours a mixed neighborhood. There are problems, sure. Mrs. Johnson woke up half the neighborhood at two in the morning kicking out her husband, who had slept with Mike's single mom. The guy who never cut his grass drove his car into his living room and then fell asleep at the wheel. We have a little too much credit card debt, and the cops arrested Mr. Reynolds, who paid me forty bucks to cut his small yard, which had little grass and lots of dead pine needles. It didn't surprise us he was a drug dealer, what with all the cars that drove up to his place. But, I mean this: people are okay. They barbeque on the holidays in their backyard; they lose themselves in TV in the evenings before they have to go back to school or work the next day. This is where I live, even though I get bussed an hour away to a magnet school where I try to draw with hopes of becoming a comic book artist some day.

The other person from my subdivision who goes to the same school I do is Cindy, whose dad is in the Army like mine. We used to hang out a lot when we were younger. We speak and all, we're friends. But at Donaldson Fine Arts School, she hangs with the popular kids. The bus picks me up at Raintree, our subdivision, and drives me to Laney High where I take a second bus to Donaldson in the city. Doris, Cindy's cheerleader sister, drives her to Laney to get the second bus.

When the bus to Donaldson gets to Laney, Cindy has headphones on and is bobbing up and down to her tunes.

"Hi," I say when I meet her in line waiting to board the yellow school bus. I raise my hand half way up to wave and smile.

She smiles back, pulls off one earphone and says, "What?"

I say it again.

"Oh, hi."

"What are you listening to?"

"The Killers."

"Yeah, they're good, awesome."

She puts her earphone back on, continues smiling and turns to the bus. It's boarding time.

I get the idea I'm going to get tickets to see the Killers, who are coming to Atlanta a hundred miles or so away. That is, I'm going to win them. I listen to the radio like I have nothing else to do. I listen when I have dinner, draw and do my homework. I heard a few days ago 102.5X will have a party bus going to the concert. I tell Andre, my close friend at Donaldson, about the plan, and he laughs. We both admit she's hot. Then Andre looks at me serious like an adult.

"You may not be her type," he says.

"And what's that?"

"You know."

I look at Andre, big as a football player and black as charcoal. My skin is not like that; it's in between.

"It's cool," I tell him. "She's not like that."

"You know what they say," he says. "The darker the flesh, the sweeter juice." He says it like he's being sly.

I take some of the money I've saved up and buy a radio to carry around. I already have a cell phone with prepaid minutes. The concert is almost two weeks away. In the mornings over breakfast, I listen to 102.6X. On the way to school, on the first bus alone, I listen. On the second bus, where Cindy sits with her friend Lauren three rows ahead of me, I listen with my headphones. I smile at her, she smiles back. Then in the afternoon after school, I tune in. When a certain Killers song comes on, I bring up the programmed number for the radio station's prize line and dial it. If it's busy, I dial again and again.

"Hello," I say.

"You're the seventh caller. Sorry," answers the deejay.

I dial so that I can be the tenth caller. The concert is October 10th. I'm not new to this; I've won before, but only CDs. And when I have a chance to win some other prize, I don't call; you can only win once a month. I am not the tenth caller. I keep trying.

I get good at knowing the words to every song that comes on the station. I know how many prizes they give away every day. I wear out the star key on the phone. My parents tell me to cut all the listening when they notice it's too much; it may harm my homework, they say. Andre asks me why I should care so much about the Killers and Cindy. I talk about their music, expecting I might say something about it that would explain it, thinking that if Cindy likes the music, they must be good. As days pass, I try and get busy signals. I consider buying the tickets, over a hundred bucks apiece, but have no way getting to the concert since I only have a learner's permit. I could get my dad to drive.

I leave my room after someone else wins the last tickets for the night—they only give out three a day—and go to the kitchen. My mom's friends chat away in Turkish. I understand some of it. But they talk about their other girlfriends, their families and people I don't know back there. Sometimes they talk about the craziest things, and now they're talking about diets.

"Look at your son. He's growing up to be a handsome man," says Hasibe in English, as I pull out a glass from the cabinet and take the milk out of the fridge.

"We're going to find him a nice Turkish girl," says my mom, grinning.

I try my best to ignore them. It isn't the first time she's made fun of me this way, and I don't know how much of her isn't serious. I say hello and leave them as quickly as possible to their talk of losing weight. My brother peaks his head out of his door and sticks out his tongue. I wave my fist in the air, so he gets the message. He quits. It amazes me that we are related. If one of us had to go into the Army, it would do my brother the most good.

When I see Cindy in the halls of Donaldson as classes change, I say hi, maybe I say more. And in social studies, we work together on a project where we identify where most of the oil in the world comes from with percentages and country names. I ask her about what her favorite Killers songs are, and many of them happen to be mine. I want those tickets and know I have to have them. Somehow I can't be happy without them. I put my money together and considered how I am going to ask my dad about giving me a ride. Less than a week to the concert, my luck turns, God answers my prayers, and I am the tenth caller.

At Laney High's parking lot in line to take the bus to Donaldson the next day, I wait for Doris to drive up and drop off Cindy. They are late, but soon they arrive. Cindy steps out. Her blond hair is in two long braids, and the ruffles of her blue blouse sway as she walks.

"Cindy," I say, "I've got tickets to the Killers concert."

"Cool," she says.

I'm full of butterflies, a nervous enthusiasm.

"Want to go?" I ask.

At first she doesn't say anything. I watch her face, impossible to read, but there is no smile.

"My sister is taking me and a few of my friends," she says, pausing and averting her glance. "Sorry." She looks up.

I don't know what words will come out of my mouth next. My smile is gone. But I find something.

"Oh," I say. "Cool." It's not much.

The bus must be boarded.

"Maybe, I'll see you there," she says, stepping up quickly into the yellow Bluebird bus before me.

I remain standing, locked in the direction of the fantasy that was there but now evaporates with the dew off the wild grass around the parking lot, breaking through the cracks. A couple of other kids take my rightful place behind her. I board the bus last.

That night I am angry, angry at her, at me, I don't know. It's mostly her. The radio is on out of habit. They play the Killers. It's like somebody, Fate maybe, has decided to twist and turn the knife Cindy jabbed into my chest. I vow to hate the Killers from now on, making them the object of my anger and hate. I feel like a fool. I race for refuge in my childhood, where I believe I'm like a Jedi having to forsake women for the Force.

Why do I still act like a child? I ask myself.

I go to the concert with Andre.

Cindy gets a boyfriend by the end of the school year. When I pass her in the hallways of Donaldson, I may smile, rarely will I say hello. When seats have to be taken in class, I sit as far away from her as I can. I want my avoidance of her to be taken as a sign that I don't need her, but she doesn't seem to notice.

One month before school is out for the summer, they let a new girl transfer to Donaldson. Andre watches her as she navigates through the lunchroom to find a place to sit among a crowd of mostly unfamiliar faces. She's black. She finds a seat with a few other black girls—Andre knows more of them than I do.

He shakes his head across from me and a few other friends in our lunch crowd.

"Women," he says, like he's wise, "you can't live with' em, you can't live without' em."

"My father says that," I say.

"Well, gentlemen, if you excuse me," he says, standing up.

He drops his lunch tray at the conveyer belt that takes all our mess away to a dishwasher and walks over to the table with the new girl. We watch him make conversation with the girls he knows, making his moves, he tells us later.

So that's how it is, I think, like I know what I'm talking about if I opened my mouth.

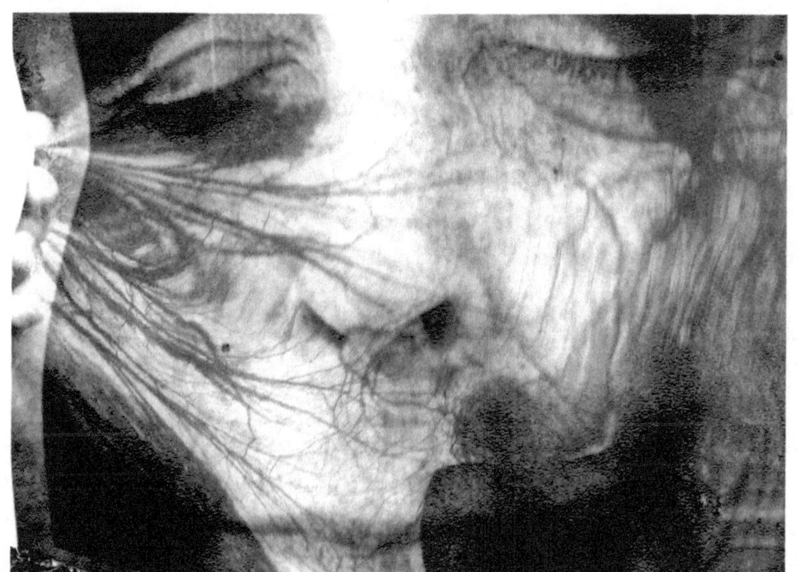

ANDREI GURUIANU

48th STREET AND QUEENS BOULEVARD

You could smell spices clinging to the thick New York haze even before you turned the corner at 48th Street and Queens Boulevard. Each street had its distinct scent of food, body odors, trash, and exhaust fumes. Across the boulevard divided by the raised tracks of the 7 train, you would find mostly typical South American cuisine because that's where most of the area's Hispanic population was clustered. On our street, the other side of the tracks, the smell of garlic and onions tended to overpower others. Those were the smells that marked the afternoons of my high school years from 1995 to 1998.

My parents chose that neighborhood and that particular building because they thought it would make adjusting to life in America somewhat easier. Romanian and other Eastern European families lived there, so that simply walking through the main entrance was like stepping into mother or grandmother's kitchen. The front door to the apartment building rarely stayed closed. It worked for a few days, then someone always jimmied it open, destroying any illusion of safety. Once through that door, the familiar greasy smells of fried carp, pork, sarmale thick with chunks of fat and myriad other unidentified ethnic dishes leaked along the hallways. They were the kind of smells that stuck to your skin and hugged your clothes so that you wore them with you for hours afterward.

Those smells were the reason I was embarrassed to bring friends home with me. Our two rooms did not smell like theirs, or what I imagined theirs would smell like, of juicy burgers, chicken, French fries, and pizza. I imagined their apartments wrapped in domestic smells that didn't make your nose wrinkle, aromas that were welcoming like those of wide supermarket aisles.

When mother cooked in our apartment, the odors from ground meat mixed with parsley and garlic or the burnt aroma of roasted peppers and eggplant spread from room to room within minutes. She kept the window open even in winter to allow some of the smell and steam to escape, but it wasn't enough. The kitchen would be wrapped in a warm, white fog that rose from enamel pots placed over low flame, while some of it left the kitchen under the propped door and through the top of the screened window. Sometimes it seemed like the frail gray ribbons of smoke and steam that fogged up the glass and drifted toward the sky were the only things that grounded us to something outside the world of our apartment.

Even when mother wasn't cooking in the kitchen, the smells didn't disappear entirely. Sometimes whole families would gather during the evening behind the building, setting up lawn chairs along a patch of concrete slabs and wild weeds in place of a backyard. There they fired up a round, red charcoal grill, and threw on thick slabs of meat that sizzled and hissed. The smells climbed along the fire escape from one apartment to another, getting stronger as the evenings wore on. Voices became louder, too, as Budweiser cans and glasses of cheap cognac were emptied in succession.

My parents tried to join in these backyard parties, to fit in, to have someone else to talk to and unwind after a day of work. I joined them on several occasions, but had trouble keeping up with conversations. I was used to the sounds I grew up with in Bucharest, the Romanian capital, while most of the others spoke regional dialects. They came from small farm villages and mountain regions where different forms of the language had survived, mixed over the years with Hungarian, German, and other languages. When they spoke Romanian, their words came out fast and they did not enunciate, they didn't have the same cadence as the speech I was used to hearing in our apartment. When a stranger spoke to me in Romanian, I often felt my tongue getting tangled up, and it took a long time for my brain to process what I wanted to say. My voice sounded deliberate and contrived. I felt unsure of myself. I could speak it fluently at home, in the surrounding comfort of family, but in the company of others my Romanian sounded like a foreign language, as if it wasn't the language I was meant to speak at all. I became self-conscious of what I sounded like to them, these people who used and wore the language like a badge of honor, so I began to speak less and refused to join my parents when they asked.

It was just as well, because in the back of the building discussions centered on things that didn't interest me. People talked of Romania as if life still revolved around what used to be. Their references to parliamentary figures and places I didn't recognize had made me feel even more like a stranger. They spoke of watching half-hour Romanian news programs when they came on PBS once a week, and argued about the country's economic and political struggles as if they mattered. It was like they never left and were planning on going back any minute, so keeping up with the latest developments was of utmost importance. Looking back, I suppose all of us have felt at one point that we were still there, although some feel the tug of home more so than others.

No discussion of Romanian news was complete without a comparison to American news. Everyone agreed that they trusted the Romanian media more. It told about how things really were. My parents sometimes would point out to them how sensational and contrived the news stories were. But their comments were dismissed as naïve. Anyone taking sides was not being loyal to the home country, no longer patriotic. Mother just kept saying that most of it was fluff, forced, and they dismissed her because she would rather trust the Americans. She should have told them that she doesn't really trust anyone anymore, never has. Maybe then they would believe her. Sometimes, I just wanted her to keep quiet and not contradict all the time. It made us seem pretentious.

But to mother their opinions didn't matter. Comments like those don't trouble her. She says she knows better. She knows where she came from and reminds me of the fact often as a way to keep reminding herself. Mother was the first in her family to make it past eighth grade, finish college, and complete graduate school with an engineering degree in electronics, the cutting edge of technology in the 1970s. She and father were educated in a way most Romanians at the time were not. She said that doesn't make them snobs, but it does make them aware of differences.

The men and women grilling in the backyard in Queens had been typical workers, manual laborers in Romania, which is what my parents have become. They're aware of that too. They work for others now, when back home others worked for them. That's why mother's pet phrase has turned into "Never forget where you came from." She means Romania, but she also means education. She wanted my sister and me to use education so we wouldn't feel stuck the way she feels now, the way those families could not talk of anything else but home. She wanted us to look back at where we came from not as an answer, but as a beginning.

When I visit Queens occasionally now for the rare long weekend, the apartment still smells sometimes the way it did during high school. But more often than not, it has no smell. My parents have become too busy to cook, so they rely on the quick fix of a Chinese take-out dinner, an already roasted chicken from the super market or a pizza pie if they're truly tired. When I'm there, we go out to eat most of the time. We choose Mexican, Indian, Italian, never Romanian, even though there are more than five Romanian restaurants within a ten-block radius of the apartment. They say their food just doesn't taste the same.

When we come back from dinner, we walk back through a rainbow of smells, some familiar, some strange. The Eastern European families have steadily been pushed out of the area by the influx of hipsters who can no longer afford to live in Manhattan, so they cross the river and drive up the cost of rent. Even my parents don't know how much longer they'll be able to keep up with payments that go up each year.

Inside the old apartment, we shut the door to save the furniture and clothes from those smells that once welcomed us into the building. The apartment looks like one big hallway as soon as you walk through the metal front door that's painted a shiny, somber black. My parents' bedroom doubles as living room, and has no door to separate it from the foyer/dining room. The only doors in the apartment are to the kitchen, which is broken, to the bathroom, and to the room I used to share with my sister.

On the rare occasion when I had visitors, especially if they were girls, I felt embarrassed having to explain why our apartment smelled the way it did, and why at seventeen or eighteen years old I still shared a bunk bed with my ten-year-old sister. I knew that I shouldn't have felt embarrassed, but I couldn't help it. A nagging voice kept telling me, "This is America. Things should be different here. We should have more," while inside I knew we were lucky to have what we had. After all, mother shared a room that had no electricity or indoor plumbing with her sister through college, and after I was born we lived in that same single room in the back of my grandparents' house.

Like a lingering, mocking remainder of that youth, the bunk bed is still there when I visit, more than a dozen years after we bought it. Not even the mattresses have been changed. The bottom half, which used to be mine, is in the bedroom, and serves now solely as my sister's place to sleep. Father has sawed off the narrower top half of the bed and placed it in the "living room" to serve as a couch. The mattress creaks when you sit on it, and the wooden legs wobble unsteadily. My parents don't want to replace either the bed or the couch until they get a new place. They've been saying that ever since I left in '98, so I try to convince them to move whenever the conversation turns in that direction, which is often, because they hate the apartment. They explain that they can't afford anything else, that they are short on money. They say, "We did it for you," the catch-all phrase behind our situation, the reason they came to America in the first place.

When I struggled in high school, father regularly scolded me for staying up too late, watching too much TV, using the computer, or playing music loudly. If they could sacrifice everything, at least I could sacrifice the small things. Didn't I remember that they "did it for me?" I did, day and night, and hated it. I hated that they took me away from everything I knew and now made me feel guilty for doing what other children my age took for granted. I felt guilty for wanting toys, games, clothes that were in style. I hated coming home to an apartment that smelled nothing like the America in which I spent my days, the America in which my American friends lived their normal lives.

"We did it for you" became the hardest words to bear, worse than being punished. They were a burden, a constant reminder in our household that things didn't come as easily as they did for others, that we had to work even harder to get anywhere. I was supposed to make the best of my education, become a doctor or a lawyer, and not waste the college tuition that they barely scraped together. I was supposed to join a profession that would earn respect and money, the cliché immigrant parent's dream, which for immigrant children is anything but cliché. It's a way of growing up. It's an ideal that few can live up to, and for me it never happened. I teach. I write. I feel as if my parents are still disappointed.

Although "we did it for you" comes seldom these days, when it does it always throws me back to the long nights in the apartment when there wasn't enough work and money was scarce. That's when my parents began raising their voices for the first time. They had never done that before. "We did it for you" became the reason and the excuse for the yelling. They blamed each other, blamed me, because there was no one else to listen or lend a hand. The people behind the building spoke of Romania and drank hard so they wouldn't have to listen to each other's problems either.

It was then that we all became tense and smiled less. When we did smile, it seemed forced, just another interlude between bursts of anger followed by uncomfortable silence and remorse. The situation got worse before it got better, and because it lingered we got used to it the same way people become accustomed to pain. We came to live in a comfortable state of tension and gloom. Because of that I still suffer days of melancholy triggered by an unexpected scent, a familiar sound, or the rustle of autumn leaves that reminds me of how my sister and I used to whisper to each other from our bunks. We whispered anything to keep up each other's spirits after heated family arguments.

I can control and appreciate those moments. I don't mind. What I mind are the days when mother calls and cries over the phone for the lost years, for her parents and the apartment in Bucharest she hasn't seen in almost two decades. She cries out of frustration, anger, a woman beaten by sacrifice. She doesn't say much through the sobs, can't find words to express how she feels. That's even harder to bear.

On those days I can't help but think that if I had done more and played less, then things would have turned out better. I could have remained silent when we argued and kept my mouth shut about the way her cooking filled the apartment with heady smells that coiled through the building. If I did, maybe she would still make those dishes she learned from her mother many years ago. Maybe she'd be happier. I know. She doesn't need to say it.

CHOICE

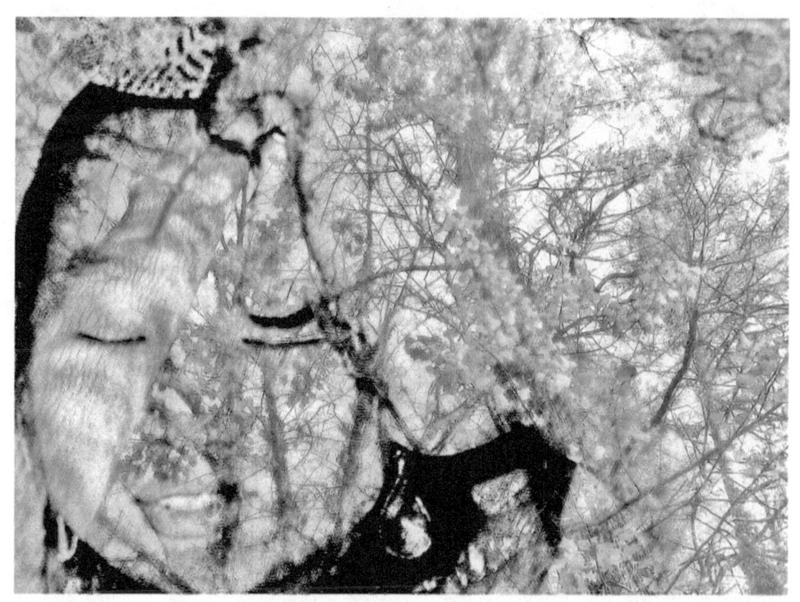

JANICE LEVY

BASEBALL AND BIALYS, THEY GOT RULES

A few hours after Izzy Epstein died, he spoke to his daughter at the mailbox.

"It's going to rain, you should put on a raincoat."

"Poppa?"

"You should listen what I'm saying. Trust me. Such a storm, Noah will be glad he got out early."

Leah heard the familiar laugh, deepening as it slid down the scale. By the time she had caught a flight back east, her father's heart had given out. It happened so fast—

"They needed the bed, there was no time to pack."

Leah hugged herself and sighed. All their arguments, then the long silence . . . There hadn't been a chance to clear things up, she thought. No time to say—

"You got married, you said good-bye plenty. Six months he don't let you outta the house? What am I, chopped liver? All of a sudden, I gotta make an appointment."

Leah felt her cheeks flush.

"Tell that *no-goodnik*, he comes to my funeral it wouldn't hurt to get a haircut, that *shmatte* around his head he looks like a drug dealer."

Leah covered her ears. "And the wedding pictures? What a *shlemiel*, with his fancy shmancy camera—every shot, my head's cut off. Everybody here's showing pictures, I got nothing to take out."

Leah jumped as a car drove by, its radio blasting a ball game. Today was Opening Day at Yankee Stadium. Her eyes filled, remembering each April—

"Every year I took you. That first time, you fell asleep."

Leah closed her eyes and leaned against the mailbox. Her father had picked her up from school early, still in his barber clothes and square black shoes, smelling of hot towels and lotion, brushing tufts of hair off his pants. "Don Mattingly at first," she had showed off. "Willie Randolph at second." Her father slipped the usher some bills as they sneaked down to the box seats. He leaned over the dugout, thinking everybody spoke Yiddish, and yelled *geb a kuk,* give a look, did you ever see such a beauty, until the manager, Billy Martin, flipped her a ball from his pocket. "Baseball, I like," her father always said. "They got rules."

They ate hot dogs *shmeered* with mustard, and sucked oranges, tossing the peels like confetti when a home run was hit. After the seventh inning stretch, her father fell asleep. Leah piled peanut shells on his chest. Later, packed into the subway, she buried her head in his stomach, as he held onto the pole in the middle of the car, his arms protecting her from the crowd.

Leah lowered her head, feeling a slight pressure on her back. She heard a heartbeat, maybe two.

Maybe she was losing her—

"Relax," her father said. "There's no question that there's an unseen world. The problem is, how far is it from midtown and how late is it open?"

Leah heard heavy footsteps. "Are you alright?" Brady called out. "Did you get lost out there?"

"Big mouth," Izzy said. "May all his teeth fall out—except one, so he can have a permanent toothache."

"Ouch." Brady held his jaw as he walked down the path. "My tooth is killing me. I think it's that old filling. Where did your old man keep the aspirin?"

Leah scratched her head. How could this—

"The how I don't know. The why is easy," Izzy said. "I love you. As below, so above."

Leah's fingers lingered on her lips, her cheek, then to the place between her eyebrows he used to kiss. Everywhere she felt flushed.

Leah asked the Rabbi if it was possible.

"In the Kabbalah," he said, "The Jewish mystics believe we have at least three lives, up to 1000 chances to make things right. The soul is a piece of God. Just as the Holy One sees but is not seen, so the soul sees but it not seen itself."

"Whenever I went out," Leah said, "Poppa waited up for me. I'd find him leaning over his prayer books and I'd ask what he was doing up so late. He'd say, 'When I pray, I pray quickly, because I'm talking to God. But when I read the Torah, I read slowly, because God is talking to me.'"

"When was the last time *you* talked to God?"

"When I did *Fiddler on the Roof* in college."

"Another *kibitzer*," the Rabbi laughed. "And what about going to *shul*?"

Leah's favorite service was the *Havdalah*, the ceremony separating the Sabbath from the work week. She would focus on the flame of the braided candle, inhaling the scents from the opened spice box, matching her breathing to her father's deep sighs.

"You can feel God," her father whispered. "He's the flame inside you."

When the Rabbi walked down the aisle with the Torah, Leah touched its cloth and kissed her fingertips. In Temple, her mind stopped racing, her worries slipped away. She felt connected to the past, hopeful of the future. Her father held her hand as they walked home.

"I'm a lucky man," he would say. "God has been good to me."

"So what did you pray for?" Leah asked.

"That *He* should only live and be well."

The Rabbi cleared his throat. "Where you live, there's a synagogue nearby?"

Leah didn't answer. Brady said religions created robots, that prayers were "hocus pocus." "Where's your proof?" he asked. Brady believed in only what he could touch with his hands. He didn't like rules.

"He's an artist," Leah had told her father.

"From this you make a living?"

Izzy stared at the red circle on the otherwise blank canvas. He looked upside down and squinted. "Do you know why they hang pictures like that? Because they couldn't find the artist."

When Brady appeared, in paint splattered cut-off shorts, Izzy pulled her aside. "This artist of yours, he ran out of thread?"

Leah raised her eyebrows.

"His face is ripped," Izzy whispered behind his hand, pointing to the safety pin in Brady's eyebrow.

“That’s his statement, Poppa.”

“I see. And on his thigh, that chicken-”

“Dragon.”

“Looks like a chicken. That’s also a statement?”

“Yes.”

“Go do me something. Tell your friend he should remember the camps, those tattoos are against our religion.”

“He’s not—”

Izzy covered his heart. “That statement I don’t need to hear.”

The Rabbi interrupted Leah’s thoughts. “*Kol netivotecha shalom.* All journeys that begin with Torah lead to wholeness. Perhaps your father’s still waiting up.”

Mrs. Bee loaded the dish washer and smelled the milk in the refrigerator, readying Izzy Epstein’s house for visitors after the funeral. She brushed crumbs on the floor, ignoring the jelly stains on the counter top. Leah’s father used to say the place was dirtier when she left.

“My father’s been talking to me,” Leah said.

“I ‘spect he would,” she said. “He be talkin’ to me, too, most times in Jewish which he *know* I don’t understand.” She shook her head. “Mr. Izzy, he sure do love an audience.” She reached into the pocket of her house dress. “This is for you. Mr. Izzy said this was a *mezuzah*? With prayers written down on special paper, rolled up inside? He said you supposed to put it on the door frame of a new house. Make the place holy so God would listen.”

She placed the small object in Leah's hand. "Even if you're on the right track, you'll get run over if you just sit there. That's what Mr. Izzy used to say." Mrs. Bee blew some crumbs off the table near Leah's elbows. "Seems you two got unfinished business to attend and me, I've got to dust."

Leah picked the onions off her bialy and pushed the plate away. She thought back to brunches in Bagel Buddy, where her father took her after Sunday School.

"This is my girlfriend. *Es dir oys s'harts*," he'd say to the bialy pullers. "Eat your heart out."

The workers in the back let her flatten the lumps of dough. She pulled high around the edges and pressed her thumbs to indent the top, then sprinkled on onions.

"Bialys are baked," her father said. "Never boiled. They got rules."

While they waited, Leah traced Hebrew letters in the sawdust floor. Her father cleaned his teeth with a minty toothpick.

"Are you sure you're the vaiduh I gave my order to?" he grumbled.

"What makes you ask?" the waiter grumbled back.

"By now," her father said, looking at his watch, "I expected a much older man."

As Leah poured her third cup of coffee, her hand shook. The liquid dripped down the legs of the table.

"Where *I* am, it's so clean you could eat off the floor."

"Poppa?"

"So, the *mezuza*h, what do you think? A little step like that, the artist won't even notice."

Leah's eyes filled. The air suddenly smelled sweet and sour, of herring and lox.

"Poppa, wherever you are. Are you comfortable?"

"I make a living, what about you?"

Leah laughed and wiped her eyes.

"Thank God. I was worried you forgot also how to laugh. You remember what Rabbi Hillel said: 'If I am not for myself, who will be for me? If I am only for myself, what am I? If not now, when?' *Ver veyst*," Her father sighed. "Who knows? You wanna find yourself, I got connections."

Leah stared into her coffee cup and sighed.

"Eat a little something, you'll think better. All over the world, people are starving. A little *nosh*, you won't bust."

"Brady, my father's still here."

Brady held up two ties. "Which one goes better?"

"He's been talking, telling me things."

Brady patted her arm. "The blue or the red?"

"This morning I smelled gefilte fish."

Brady kissed her cheek. "After the funeral, we'll go home. Can you help me with this?" He draped the tie around his neck. "My collar's stiff."

Leah imagined her father's scowling face, his arms folded like wings, refusing to dance at her wedding. He reread the marriage *Katubah*, looking for loopholes in the fine print. He drank shot glasses of *shnops* until he passed out in the coatroom.

Leah suddenly felt a surge of strength in her hands as she made a knot in the tie.

"Hey, you're choking me," Brady yelped, backing out of the room.

"Poppa!" Leah said.

"He who laughs, lasts."

At the cemetery, each person spoke, remembering Izzy Epstein fondly.

"Was a good man," said one, "Gave you the shirt off his back."

"Every time I needed money, he lent me," said another.

"Such a sense of humor," they all agreed. "He lit up the room."

"He never forgot where he came from," the Rabbi said. "He reached towards Heaven, but with dust on his shoes."

The Rabbi nodded to Brady. Brady pursed his lips. He rubbed his jaw, then his neck. Leah tugged his sleeve. Finally he spoke. "Izzy Epstein," he said. "He smoked a good cigar."

A gust of wind blew off Brady's hat. He chased it around the headstones, twisting his ankle as it slipped out of reach and landed in the open grave. Brady leaned forward, then jumped back as the sky trembled with thunder.

Leah stood alone. She ran her fingers over the headstone and touched her lips. She felt a tickling of eyelashes against her cheek. A tightness squeezed her chest.

"Poppa?"

"This artist of yours. He makes you happy?"

"He's my best friend."

"Outside of a dog, the Torah's your best friend. Inside a dog, it's too dark to read. I asked you a question."

"I love him, but sometimes I feel lost inside. There's a part of me that's empty -"

"Not for long."

Leah felt a flash of heat through her body. "Am I—"

"Twins. Seven more you got a team. For a reason I'm *hoking*, you think I like to nag? Listen, I'll tell you a story. Once there was a religious man, his whole life he spent studying the holy books. One night, he runs out into the street yelling, 'What is the meaning of life? I can't study one more verse without knowing the meaning of life.' Everybody thinks he's gone crazy so they send him to the head Rabbi. The man says '*Rebbe*, what is the meaning of life?' The Rabbi rises from his seat, walks over and boom, slaps him across the face.

"'Why did you slap me? All I did was ask 'What is the meaning of life?'

"'Fool,' says the Rabbi. 'You have such a good question—why exchange it for an answer? It is the answers which separate us, the questions which unite us.'"

Leah twisted her hands. "I've forgotten the prayers—"

"Piece of cake."

"And what if God doesn't answer—"

"You're a Jew. We got rules."

Leah wiped her tears.

A car door closed. "Honey, are you alright?" Brady called out. He took an umbrella from the car trunk. "It's going to rain any second."

"You'll talk to him, talk you can do," her father said. "An artist also makes something from nothing."

"I love you, Poppa," Leah said. "Rest in peace."

"Rest, shmest. I'm just cutting down on personal appearances. You want me, you'll get through. Everybody else, they gotta make an appointment."

The clouds broke. Leah let the rain wash over her as she listened to the laughter, deepening as it slid down the scale. She placed a small rock on the headstone. Then she reached for Brady, putting her arms around him as he held an umbrella over her head.

Leah fingered the *mezuzah* in her pocket. Later they would talk, she thought. Talk she could do.

DANIEL M. JAFFE

MARLA AND BILLY, A TRIPTYCH

The Mezuzah Wreath

Billy clicks the TV mute button, fiddles with the belt of his gold, terrycloth robe, turns green eyes to her and asks, "What's going on?"

"What?" Marla shuts the Hertz Bible, leans back on the sofa, stretches her white-socked feet onto his lap.

"You're. . .I don't know. . .distant tonight."

"Don't be silly," she says.

Of course she's been distant. A whole year living together and tonight, for the first time, Billy hung a wreath on their front door. "Just for December," he asked, "okay?"

She consented instantly—it was his house too, after all. However.

So, beside him on the sofa she's been leafing through upcoming winter Torah portions in reminder of connection and identity. Her attention has focused for some reason on the Exodus story, on the section about Pharaoh not wanting to let the Hebrews go. Why this section? Billy's heart, soft as lamb's wool, is nothing like Pharaoh's hardened one, although Billy would surely clasp hard if Marla ever sought to leave.

At the very moment she thinks this, he weaves the belt of his gold terry robe around her ankles. "You'd better undo those golden handcuffs," she says with forced cheer, "or I'll turn an umbrella into a serpent and summon the Ten Plagues. You're first-born, so you'd better watch out."

He gives a resigned chuckle, unwinds the belt.

She turns her head as if to watch HBO, clicks on the volume to mask her thoughts from him. She's never thought of leaving Billy, but now pictures herself tiptoeing out in the dead of night, her three Jewish star pendants clinking around her neck like armor.

How ridiculous. She adores Billy, his blond curls and Irish pout, and hasn't he always agreed that one day, after marriage, she can raise their children Jewish? "We lapsed Catholics just don't care," he said.

Thank goodness her parents live hours away and won't see the wreath. Her mother always laughed at the Kleins next door with their Chanukah bush—"assimilation pure and simple." And her father: "If I kept a wreath on my door every day of the year, I'd remove it in December." Never mind that the pine fronds of Billy's wreath match the green of Marla's doorpost mezuzah. Never mind that her mezuzah, containing quotes from the Torah, hangs there year round, his wreath now only one month. True, both objects are cultural symbols, but they just don't feel equal to her. Not at all.

Yet, why not?

She wonders about this as couples kiss and argue on TV, generic couples, couples lacking cultural past. That's it: mezuzah and wreath might be equal symbols if regarded side-by-side from today's eyes. But which Jew can look at anything today without seeing millennia of past oppression in the same vision? "With an outstretched arm, the Almighty rescued *me* from ancient Egypt," Marla's thoughts echo lessons from the Passover story read at *seder* every year. Certainly it wasn't Christians in ancient Egypt, of course not, but later. . .later the Christians were—sorry Billy, but it's true—were just as bad or worse.

Billy understands, she knows, the mezuzah to have been biblically ordained, to be an assertion of identity and pride by a persecuted people; but could he also understand that, for her, the wreath symbolizes one of the very cultures that has oppressed her own? Maybe he could. Maybe she should explain. He understands so much, after all. Doesn't he sometimes buy her Klezmer CD's? Didn't he surprise her for her birthday with a Chagall print, one of two lovers floating in air, bouquet of roses in hand? And still, after four years, doesn't he trace his tongue tip along the length of her nose, saying, "And the Lord bless every delicious Jewish centimeter."

Or maybe she and Billy could forge a new era of history together, one where mezuzah and wreath take on new, shared meaning. After all, if Egypt and Israel can make peace in modern times, who is she to define history only as the past? Isn't Israel teaching the world both to recall and move beyond the past in order to reshape the future?

Maybe she should keep her mouth shut this once, for if she imposes her values onto Billy, won't that turn her into oppressor? After all, who is she to decide that her separate past trumps their shared future? Just who does she think she is?

She turns her eyes from TV to her beloved. Yes, just who does she think she is?

Remembrance Day

Marla sits alone in the sanctuary, her long face dimly illuminated by electric candles set about the room. She has arrived early for the Yom Hashoah memorial service so as to contemplate private memories of the lost. Not that Marla can remember any specific person slain in the Holocaust, so long before her time, nor can she fathom the millions. But she can resurrect images taught by survivors: rabbis in one-room *cheder* schoolhouses placing honey candies shaped like Hebrew letters onto the tongues of boys learning the alphabet; audiences at Yiddish theater; neighborhoods where, rather than violate Shabbes by carrying from inside a house to outside, kerchiefed women handed pots of *cholnt* stew through kitchen windows to those gathering in summer courtyards. So much was lost. Stolen.

She pulls out the Hertz Bible from the pew's seatback in front of her, turns to the upcoming weekly Shabbes reading, scans the English translation until she finds the passage she's vaguely recalled to be there, the prohibition against tattoos. How many Jewish forearms did the Nazis violate?

Marla hasn't come to temple with any regularity, but today felt that she must. This morning, after setting coffee and croissants on their breakfast table, she was just reading in the newspaper about tonight's memorial service when Billy entered the kitchen. He knelt beside her, ran slim fingers through his blond hair, pulled back the sleeve of his red pajama top to reveal something he'd hidden from her the previous night, something new on his forearm, "Marla Forever" inscribed within a heart, a tattoo.

She traced the letters with her gaze, thinking—Jews don't get tattoos; but, Billy's not Jewish, so what's the problem? She looked into his eyes as he took her hand, pulled out a ring from his pajama pocket, proposed. They'd been living together for two years already, why was she surprised?

Before she could respond, he slipped the ring onto her finger, embraced her.

It was the suddenness of the proposal that shook her, his assumption of her "yes" that annoyed her, and that damn *goyishe* tattoo. She gently removed the ring. "Tonight's Yom Hashoah," she explained, showing the newspaper article. "I have to go to services, and Jews don't do happy things, like get engaged, when in mourning." She had no idea if this was really true, but Billy wouldn't know the difference.

"Jeez, I'm sorry," he said, clasping the ring in his palm. "If I'm marrying a Jew, I should learn these things. I apologize."

"No, no," she said. "Don't apologize." Please don't. Had he not promised, repeatedly, to learn about Jewish traditions so they could raise their future children Jewish? What more did she want from him except, perhaps, answers to questions he never knew that she posed to herself: was it possible to remain true to one's personal strand of history while intertwining with another's? Had ghetto walls been entirely a source of oppressive segregation, or had they also served as protective insulation?

In the sanctuary now, Marla pours over the Torah and, still seated, rocks with a *kavanah* devotion she has never before experienced, studies the prohibitions against paganism—idol worship, child-sacrifice, soothsaying, self-mutilation, marking of the flesh. Billy's Catholic, not pagan. And their children will be Jewish. And with Billy's help, she'll teach them about the Holocaust, what was stolen, about Jewish everything. And they will sit on their father's knee and he will. . . proudly display the tattoo of their mother's name?. . .And one day the children will read the Torah. . .will she explain their father to be exempt from the Torah's prohibitions?

She feels a hand on her shoulder, jumps. She looks up—it's Billy.

"Okay for me to be here?" he asks.

"Of course," she says, although quietly uncertain.

"If it's your suffering, I need to understand," he adds. "I need to share."

Marla takes his hand, presses her face into his palm, so cool and comforting. She pictures herself explaining to their children the extent of Daddy's love: "He even got a tattoo for me." Billy moves from behind and sits beside her, takes her hand.

Others arrive in the sanctuary; soon the service begins. Prayer and song. All the while, Marla wonders what lessons their children will take from Daddy's example of tattooed devotion, what they will learn about weighing the authority of the Torah against the power of love. She wonders what she, herself, believes.

Merry Wonderer of the Night

Marla's Catholic husband, Billy, sometimes reads the Torah so as to understand her values. And now, just as they're slipping into bed, he mentions this week's portion, *Ki Tavo*. "It just sounds so. . .so Christian," he says. "I figured the Jewish version would be different from what I was taught, but it's the same: If the Hebrews disobey the Lord's rules, then 'The Lord will cause thee to be smitten before thine enemies. . .and thou shalt be a horror unto all the kingdoms of the earth.' And the Hebrews' numbers will be diminished, they'll be scattered around the world, and subjected to vicious enemies. Kind of sounds like a prediction of all Jewish suffering to come."

"It does," she says softly, "doesn't it?"

"It also makes Jewish suffering seem like the Jews' own fault."

"What a horrible thing to say." Her voice is flatter now. "That's not like you."

"The portion reads that way, though. It reinforces what I've heard some people say over the years—that the Jews are destined to suffer. Biblical prophecy. The result of disobedience. The Wandering Jew and all that."

Marla sits up. "Shame on you!"

"I'm sorry. I shouldn't parrot that stupidity." His thin finger soothes her bangs.

Marla lies down on her side, breathes deeply. "I guess I should apologize for getting knee-jerk defensive. After all, some of the Hebrew prophets said the same thing."

"I disagree with them, too," he says. "Yes, the majority of Jews stopped observing all the ancient rules, and yes, the Jewish people have suffered throughout history. But one development hasn't necessarily caused the other."

"No, of course not." Marla has always viewed the Torah in historical context. So many ancient rules were obviously designed to insulate the Hebrews from non-monotheistic religions and to establish ethical values. But the world has changed, those ethical values have become universal. Doesn't that mean that many of the Torah's rules have grown obsolete? Doesn't every nation's laws evolve over time as the society matures? Isn't her progressive approach to Judaism—emphasizing compassion and good deeds over prayer and ritual—part of that evolution? Volunteer work feeding the homeless, private morning meditation instead of synagogue prayer, interfaith Passover *seders* acknowledging all forms of oppression whether Jewish or not. Much more important than lighting Sabbath candles or giving up bacon-lettuce-and-tomato sandwiches, right?

"Actually," says Billy, "even the observant get persecuted. I don't think Hitler asked his victims whether or not they worked on Saturdays."

Marla finds this historical fact perversely comforting in the context of their conversation. But she's troubled by a new thought, and rests her head on Billy's shoulder. "What if," she whispers, "what if we accept the possibility that the Torah's curse is real. Then couldn't it follow that Hitler was some divine agent fulfilling biblical intention? In ancient Egypt, it was the Angel of Death killing Egyptian first-borns; later it was Hitler against the Jews?"

"That's outrageous!"

"I'm just playing devil's advocate. And what if divine punishment is truly collective, not individual. So that all Jews suffer for the sins of some."

"You think?" asks Billy. "Then tell me how many New York Jews have to eat shrimp before Brooklyn gets. . .pogrommed? A hundred? A thousand? And what does your argument imply about the Orthodox—that their observances don't count toward redeeming the Jewish people?"

"I know it's all superstition, this curse business. Yet at the same time," she says, following an idea, "if we value certain teachings of the Torah, like those about being good to other people, can we dismiss other parts of the Torah just because we don't want them to be true?"

"Listen," says Billy, "how often did the nuns in Catholic school warn that if I didn't do this that and the other, I'd go to hell? Every organized religion predicts dire consequences for disobedience."

"You're right," she says, feeling a chill, nodding against his shoulder. Of course Billy's right. Because if he's wrong, if Jewish straying and disobedience have actually been the cause of persecution, or a contributing factor, then she—who does not keep kosher, who does not observe the Sabbath, who intermarried—then she has not, in fact, been helping Judaism evolve into a more progressive, humanistic tradition. No, if the curse of *Ki Tavo* is real, then Marla has been part of the historical cause of Jewish suffering.

"I'm sorry I brought up the whole subject," he says.

"Hold me, Billy." Marla presses close against him. "Just hold me tight."

DEBRA GINGERICH

THOUGHTS AFTER HEARING A LECTURE ON TRANSLATION

How is it that he loves me
through all of these languages,
through the check points
and road blocks of Serbo-Croatian,
German, sometimes Romanian,
the dictionaries he strums through
while I'm fast asleep, while
the introduction to his language—
the book I bought
with good intentions—rests
beside me on my nightstand
and the gift from his brother
in Paris—40 lessons to speak
French—sits shelved? My three
months immersed in French
are ten years forgotten
except *Je ne comprend pas.*
My dreams are content
in one language
while his wide-eyed mind juggles
four tongues. And this is his gift to me—
how he can love someone
so lazy, so rested
in American English—this language
of our love, this language
so far from his fractured home.

TO MY YUGOSLAVIAN IN-LAWS

If we could speak,
I would tell you that we have
trees here too, and rivers.
I know how to hammer
a nail. Transatlantic phone calls
are expensive, even for us
with our two cars, dishwasher
and American salaries. That he
will not get lazy or forget
about the ways he needed to make money
during the war, the merchandise
exchanged in dark corners of Turkey.
He is still thankful for good health.
He passes on every kiss
you tell him to give me.
I would admit that he misses
the stone beaches of the Adriatic,
he accepts the Atlantic's murky water
as part of the compromise. He thinks
Lancaster's streets are too vacant
at night and there is no place
to ride a bike. Also, that I wouldn't take
your name and will never
believe the wine in the cup
turns to blood. That he and I can't
agree on a slipcover for the couch.
That there is no perfect place
for anyone.

TWO MOTHERS AND A BABY

I listen to his sleep talk
in a language I say I'll learn
someday, about Albanians chasing him
through his elementary school
and, as dreams go, the devil
in an army uniform. It is years since
he walked the uneven streets
of Belgrade, one shoulder balancing
Serbia, Bosnia dragged by his right leg.
Solomon's counsel would have
cut his body in two, half flung over
the border, while I watched
starved men stare through barbed wire
into my TV and wondered
on which side the ones like him
ended up, the ones with blood
of enemies mixed together
in the cavities of their hearts. At least
he ended up on the right side
of my bed. And I, raised in a town
where all that threatened us
were flies in old cow feed, wake him
from his night thrashings and wonder if,
even as I say it, I understand.

MY HUSBAND BECOMING A NATURALIZED CITIZEN

He raises his hand, as if to say stop
to a man facing him with a gun.
And really, it is a shotgun wedding.
He's committing *I do* to this country
that can never be his true love.
He will always remember the country
that first rocked him in her bosom,
who in the end, turned her whole body away
with such violence that the force flew him
across an ocean. He's had a common reaction,
declaring his hatred for her, that he'd never
go back, even if she begged him.
But she is still the location
of his dreams in the candor of night.

Some party invitations are better left refused.
No one wants to witness the uncomfortable steps
of a newlywed who would rather be dancing
with someone else. Sooner or later he'll squirm
within her touch like a man
in a poorly fitted suit. Still, his legs
slowly sway to the music's rhythm.
He tries out a dip and flirtatious turn.
His nimble body settles into the moves
that will accompany the years ahead.

VIDEO FROM BOSNIA

There is a body bound
in white cloth on an outdoor cot
amid crying women
wearing *dimije* and scarves.
Even during communist times,
it was the same. My husband answers
my questions about the lack of casket
and the demure women—his mother,
the only Serbian Orthodox there,
stands out in pants with head uncovered.
But he prefers to point out
where a house once stood, the walk
to the stream for water, how gray
his father's hair has become, and that even
the imam smokes (he having given up
the habit years ago). He translates pieces
of the elegy on sorrow, going
to paradise, and thinking about life—
the same speech in any religion—
until the men proceed down the hill,
trading the weight of the body
every few steps, and my husband's father
lowers himself down the hole
to lay his friend into the earth
after a life of war and heavy drinking.
Then the video switches to weeks before
and the man alive sitting in the dirt yard
where he will later lie, surrounded
by family, shade trees, and plum brandy.
He laughs, his face red with high
blood pressure. My husband says,
Isn't the landscape beautiful?

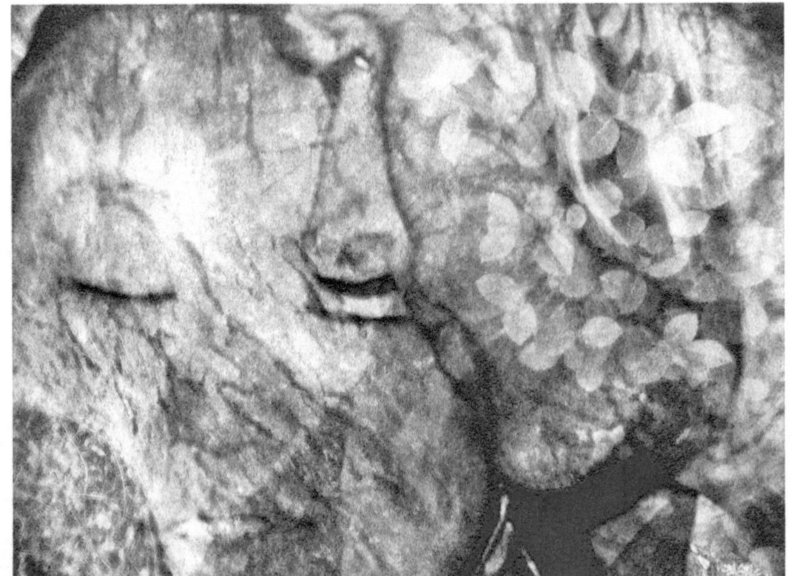

BONNIE WAI-LEE KWONG

TO SWIM DAILY

is to wing one's way forward.
to part water, wave water behind.
My mother stands facing me
with outstretched hands, wading
backwards as I breathe my way
towards her. Waves between us
bend light into tentacles on sand.
Her underwater body looms large.

My mother once told me a story
of two lovers, champion swimmers
fleeing communist China for Hong Kong.
They cast farewells in the sea.
The man lagged. The woman continued.

A refugee at six, my mother rode
the same waves from communist
mainland to capitalist Hong Kong.
What did she know of borders?
Did she ask where in the water
one idea ended and the other began?
She left no wake from her boat
for lovers or me to follow.

The summer after she landed,
she ran back into the sea once,
past the red flag on the beach.
The storm claimed her swim ring.
A stranger swept her ashore again.
At home, no one asked if the girl

who left was the wet one
who returned, or what
she was looking for in the sea.

I swim as if I have always
known the danger of water.
In the undertow of history,
we swim parallel to shore,
till the sea itself is tired.

COMMON FLOWER

You try to teach me the flowering
order of your garden in spring:
snowdrops, hyacinths, daffodils, tulips…
no, hyacinths, tulips, daffodils, snowdrops…
A forgotten rosary.

You would have me send down
your grandson's roots to drink the water
of this newly thawed Northeastern soil.

In the silence between us, a common flower
grows, a red hibiscus leeward from your house,
a transplant: flower of Caribbean winds
bearing word of your half-sisters,
flower of my childhood strolls
in the mushroomed woods of Asia.
Flower of blood. Nomadic, animal flower.

I note the growing caesuras
between your breaths, your paling skin.

In the silence after you, your grandson and I
will make love in yet another country.
I will forget to mourn you till I see a man feed
hibiscus to an iguana among Mayan ruins.
Scarlet, vegetable flower.

Our daughter will come to us
on the wild tongues of the Pacific,
the coast of your birth.

In a world where flowers travel,
it is impossible to be strangers.

JESSAMYN LUONG

LUNCH WITH MY IN-LAWS

They give me a fork and a spoon so I can swirl my noodles the way the Italians do. Everyone else eats with chopsticks and talks in Chinese with their mouths full; I can eat with chopsticks too but I don't want to seem too pretentious so instead I listen to the cacophonous sounds, rising like the mingling scents of garlic and ginger, pungent, indistinguishable. My mind wrestles with the syllables, arranging and rearranging them like shards of broken tile on a mosaic, looking for pictures, themes, concepts. My husband puts his arm around my shoulders and asks me if I'm ok. Little Joseph sits next to me, his spiky black hair bent over a game boy, his five year old brain flitting effortlessly between English and Chinese, putting one down, picking up the other, or using them together like a mouthful of lo mein washed down with a gulp of Pepsi.

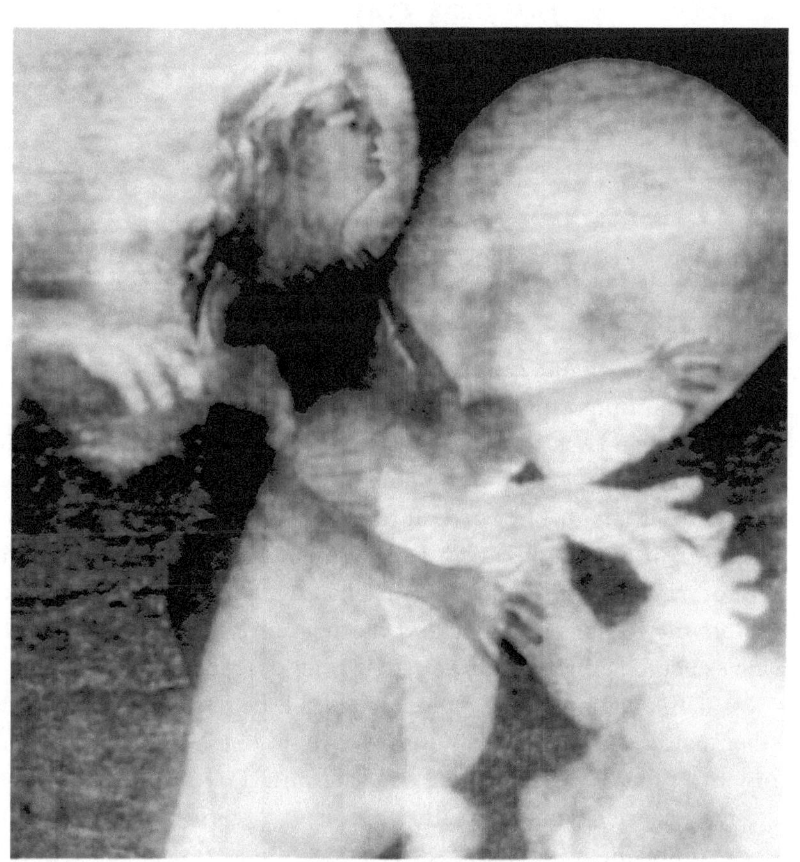

WENDY JONES NAKANISHI

A LIFE IN A DAY IN JAPAN

Morning

As an American living in Japan, as a woman inhabiting a culture that automatically designates her a second-class citizen, as an older woman whose children are sometimes mistaken for her grandchildren, I find that race, gender and age issues can preoccupy my life.

This morning I found myself saying, "I hate men. I hate men."

My husband was drinking his coffee and reading the newspaper. Ethan, our youngest child, looked at me anxiously. "Are you okay, Mommy?"

I don't want to blight the future of my three boys. I adore them. They are men in the making. Can I make them the men I want inhabiting my own future? I'm writing this account of a typical day in my life to confess and explore my feelings as a wife and mother and an "ex-pat". It may be a cathartic exercise. Perhaps, for example, if I can describe here my reasons for being less than enamored with the male sex, I'll be less inclined actually to voice them out loud. Someday my sons are bound to make the connection: if Mommy hates men, does that mean she hates me?

Experience has taught me the expediency of biting back any words of protest or complaint at life in this society, but I was sleepy. I had risen at five, ejected from warm blankets by guilt. I had walked only twice in the week; my self-imposed exercise regimen stipulates three. In minutes, I found myself plunged in deepest night, dawn a faint yellow glimmer of possibility in the east. Even at such an early hour, the road was crowded. Either as a cause or as a result of its population density, Japan is a country that doesn't sleep.

Huge trucks hurtled past, followed closely by tiny white pick-up trucks and by black sports cars. Farmers occupy the little white trucks and harassed men on tight schedules, the big trucks delivering goods, their drivers anxious to take advantage of the relatively deserted roads to meet deadlines.

But the black cars? Angry young men? The sex and age are impossible for a bystander to determine, but the anger is apparent—the cars weaving back and forth in evident frustration, their progress impeded by the trucks large and small, forbidden to pass by the yellow line dividing the highway. They want to go eighty kilometers an hour but must settle for sixty. Why do I assume they must be men? Because women don't have testosterone rushes?

But angry drivers can't disturb my equilibrium as I stride briskly forward, invigorated by the unaccustomed sense of release at my "invisibility": at such an early hour, I encounter only the impersonal machinery of motorized vehicles and the occasional old woman also out for a walk, bent double over a trolley which supports her—her perpendicular posture a legacy of years spent toiling in rice paddies. Nobody to stare at the pale foreigner.

At home, a quick shower. The morning tasks: laying out the children's school uniforms and the breakfast things, preparing my husband's coffee, then up to rouse the boys.

It's Monday. Predictably, they groan and grumble.

"It's still nighttime, Mommy."

"Please, just a few more minutes."

I tickle their feet gently. I stroke their hair. Finally, it's a tug-of-war. They cling to blankets and pillows that I pull inexorably away. Fridays are much easier. I can lure them from their beds with the promise of treats ahead: popcorn in the evening, all their favorite shows on TV, the weekend stretching ahead as a tantalizing oasis of free-time.

Ethan whimpers as he enters the warm, brightly-lit kitchen.

"Mommy, no pants."

"Sorry, baby." I rush to collect freshly-laundered underwear from the utility room.

Peter, Simon and Ethan are consoled for its being Monday morning by being allowed to eat breakfast while watching morning television.

Off the two youngest go, clad in their black shorts and black tunics and yellow caps, heavy school satchels strapped to their backs. I can't linger to say goodbye to our eldest, Peter, to see him on his way to the junior high. I must prepare for my first class, and the university is a good hour's drive away. My breakfast is an apple consumed in the car as I hurry to work.

But I am invested with a warm glow of satisfaction, remembering that on Saturday I had won the children a little treat. It was my only morning to have a lie-in. At seven I could hear my boys downstairs in the living room, immediately below my bedroom. Ethan was singing "My brothers are baaad . . .baaad. . .baad. I want to play my gaaame, my gaaame, my gaaame."

I buried my head under my pillow. Then I heard the thudding of tiny feet. Up the stairs. Towards my room! The last remnants of a delicious dream took flight as my door burst open. Ethan burrowed into my bed, under the blankets, into my arms. He pointed to his hair: he wanted it stroked. Then to his cheek. He wanted it kissed.

"Mommy, can you take us to the Harry Potter film today?"

I groaned. "Okay, sweetheart. Just let me see. I'll have to talk to Daddy."

I haven't been to church in years, not since the pastor delivered a stinging sermon denouncing abortion and homosexuality. But I found myself praying. "Oh, God, please let Kenji agree to take them. Oh, God, please let all the children want to go at the same time. Oh, God, please let Kenji and the children be able to get into the theatre, actually to be able to sit." I had heard nightmarish tales of huge lines in all the local theatres for the Harry Potter films. Of people turned away. Of disappointed children. "Please, please, please, God."

God might have been willing, but I found I must act as his servant.

I stumbled downstairs. "Oh, Kenji. . ."

I was struck by my husband's likeness to his father. He looked a remote, unapproachable figure bent over the newspaper spread on the kitchen table. Perhaps that subscription was a mistake. My husband and I had had earnest discussions about its advisability. We had used to pride ourselves on not having one, on our not "wasting" our time watching television or reading the news.

"For Peter," I had argued. "He needs to know more about the world."

Kenji was gradually won round. "I don't like papers. Only bad news. But maybe now Peter is in junior high. . ."

"Exactly! He needs to know about world issues. . ."

In the event, Peter evinces no interest in the paper whatsoever. My husband invariably fetches the paper each morning, left on a chair on the porch by a delivery boy speeding about the neighborhood on a scooter before dawn, and then spends an hour slowly perusing it.

I blinked. That could easily have been my father-in-law bent over the paper on the kitchen table, his speech limited to the occasional grunt in answer to any question or in acknowledgement of dishes of food placed before him. Two Japanese farmers: bodies lithe, faces made harsh by hard physical labor and lined by the sun.

"That film. . .Harry Potter. Would you take them?"

Silence. Then, "I can't. Peter doesn't want to go this morning."

"But it would be perfect this morning. It's raining, so you can't pick the oranges, so. . ."

"Peter won't go."

Upstairs, with dread. I knocked at his door. An office swivel chair scraped across the floor. "Mmmmm." A boy of few words: his father's child!

"Peter, won't you go to the Harry Potter film this morning?"

He sounded very cross. "No! This is my precious Saturday morning. There's lots of things I want to do. . ."

I felt unwilling to force him, knowing that his life as a student at a Japanese junior high school was stressful enough, with its severe regimentation dictating dress and behavior, with its intensively competitive system of exams administered every other month, and, even worse, with an emphasis on rote memorization which could destroy even the most inquisitive or bright child's love of learning.

Back downstairs. "How about this afternoon?"

"Impossible. I've checked the times. We'd have to go either at ten, for the eleven o'clock show, or at five, for the six o'clock show, or at eight, for the nine o'clock show."

With the ease born of long practice, I could supply the gaps in his explanation: "And the afternoon show is impossible because the piano teacher is coming then, and Ethan would be too tired if it was late at night. . ."

Back upstairs: pleading, cajoling, threatening, promising. Finally, success. Peter agreed.

Back downstairs, flushed with triumph. Ethan was bouncing on the dining room sofa, looking at me expectantly. "Mommy?"

Kenji roused himself with difficulty from the paper. "A decision? What are you talking about?"

I was approaching him with the coffee pot to replenish his mug and found I had to conquer an impulse to crash it down on his head. "Decision?! About the film, of course."

My husband groaned. "You really make such a fuss about things."

"I hate men, I hate men, I hate men." I couldn't repress that small indulgence.

"And I hate you," Kenji replied exasperatedly.

Ethan had been beaming, bouncing about more animatedly on the sofa. "We're going to gooo, to goooo, to goooo. . ."

He suddenly stopped, checked by the anger he heard in his father's voice. I intercepted his worried glance. My own angry words were swallowed.

"Yes, sweetheart, you're going, going, going, going."

Afternoon

My English colleague Tony comes to my office for lunch; we have bought sandwiches from a neighborhood bakery.

Tony wants to talk about next term's classes.

"The students have no motivation. We need to think about our goals in our classes."

I can't concentrate. Only fifteen minutes before my next lesson.

"Oh, sorry, the coffee! I wish you'd reminded me."

"I *need* it," Tony says. "I've been up since seven."

"Yes? Oh, sorry, how terrible. Aren't you sleeping well?"

"No. Not lately."

He smiles apologetically. I know he wants sympathy, gently probing questions. I am visited involuntarily by Virginia Woolf"s image of the dry, sterile male requiring sustenance and reassurance from the fruitful emotional largesse of the female.

"Anything wrong?"

He grimaces exaggeratedly. "Just the same old, same old. I've been staying up late, drinking more than I should, hoping that would help."

I replenish his cup.

"And when you get up?"

"I don't feel *refreshed* at all. Slightly hung over, naturally, but also just *low*. I tend to lie in bed reading the papers and listening to the BBC World Service. Finally I manage to stumble into the shower. Then breakfast. It takes me about two hours just to get out the door."

Tony frowns as he sees a copy of *The Spectator* magazine on my desk.

"Why are you bothering with *this crap*? Oh, it's got a few good articles, but that right-wing bias. Terrible Tories. But speaking of good articles, I read a very good piece scientifically discounting the possibility of any male-female distinctions based on actual brain differences. They've discovered that the lateralization of the brain that occurs when we pass the age of puberty. . ."

I see the room swimming before my gaze. I interrupt. "Sorry, Tony. Can I just get this clear. Do you really believe that there are no inherent differences between men and women?"

He smiles indulgently. It's an expression I recognize, sometimes using it with my children when they say something I think exceptionally silly. "But of course, it's common knowledge, those differences are only socially programmed."

I fight to control my temper. "Sorry, it's a matter on which we'll have to agree to disagree."

"But you really can't think. . ."

"I'm the mother of three boys." I extend my hands in supplication. "But let's not talk about this. We'll probably never agree."

Tony gulps down one more cup of coffee and accompanies me to my classroom. His attitude is softer, gentler. I know he wants me to draw him out. I feel compunction at what might have seemed rudeness.

"Sorry I was so abrupt earlier. Is there some reason you brought up that topic about male-female differences?"

He smiles abstractedly. "It's just that I suppose that I never have felt especially *male* myself."

I fight back the words that immediately rise to mind: "But you are very male! When I first heard of the manifestations of milder cases of autism, I thought you were the case study offered as a description. You like computers. You're always in need of sympathy and rarely give any in return. Only days ago I confided the secret of my stepmother's probably suffering from an incurable motor neuron disease and you've never asked about her since. Last month our youngest had first-degree burns on his legs after he'd spilt hot soup on his lap: again, zil, nil zilch! You're always needing comfort and reassurance about your girlfriend. . .you're lost in your own world. . ."

I can say none of this. It would be cruel and counter-productive. I love Tony. I murmur sympathetically. "Something about Misao?"

My spirits rise as I enter my classroom. A kind of sanctuary. I smile cheerfully at the students and turn to say good-bye to Tony.

I rush home. Stupidly, I've ambitiously planned to make pizza for our dinner. I'm rushing about the room hanging up the children's school uniforms, thrown with careless abandon around the dining room. A friend of Ethan's comes by. I remember how vehemently Ethan told me the previous evening that he disliked having to play with this little boy.

"Ethan, do you remember? We agreed we needed to go shopping this afternoon."

He's halfway out the door, looking miserable, his friend Hazumi clasping his hand, insisting he come to his house.

His face brightens. "Really, Mommy? What time?"

I look at the clock. It's four.

"Four-thirty."

My husband suddenly appears. He looks impatient. "But that means they can only play for half an hour. Let's say five."

"Five, then." But as I throw sticky dough into the baking tins to rise, I'm haunted by the look of desperation I had glimpsed on Ethan's face.

The pizza preparation goes terribly awry. The dough fails to rise as expected; the tomato sauce tastes sour; there is flour everywhere; the hot water unaccountably fails to come on, meaning I'm trying to wash sticky dishes in cold water.

Suddenly, it's five o'clock. Hazumi and Ethan walk into the kitchen. It's an incredible mess. Two pizzas are on the cooker. I try not to think of how unappetizing they look.

"Well, Ethan, we'll have to leave in a few minutes."

To my amazement, Hazumi, usually querulous, meekly bids us farewell and leaves. Ethan, it transpires, has no idea that the proposed shopping expedition was simply a ruse.

"Mommy, what are we buying? Can we get some more chocolate bread?"

Suddenly I can't bear my role of "angel of the house" a moment longer. I drag out the vacuum cleaner: surely it can make some inroads on the flour carpeting the floor. I drown out his voice; the cord gets stuck in the door. I jerk at the machine angrily, overturning a chair. My mother-in-law suddenly appears in the kitchen.

She looks surprised, as well she might. I try to be hospitable and my usual greeting rises unbidden to my lips: "Would you like some tea or coffee?"

Later Ethan tells me he wishes he had a Japanese mommy. He thinks a Japanese mother would never get cross with him and that she wouldn't make him try to speak English. Judging by the age of the mothers of my children's school friends, she would also, probably, be at least ten years younger, I think. I ask my husband if we can get a divorce so that the children can have a new mother. I see him thinking about it. Ever the practical individual, he asks me to introduce him to someone suitable. To my secret gratification, Peter and Simon, at least, look momentarily upset when we broach the idea in their presence. Would they miss me?

At the kitchen table, doing his homework, Simon asks his daily question: "Mommy, what happened today?" The children at the primary school are expected to keep a diary, recording the day's events.

"Today is the day Ethan broke my heart, sweetness. Why don't you write about that?"

Evening

Out with "the boys" tonight. My little treat to myself. We laugh and joke and tease each other and drink too much beer. We speak English with reckless abandon. We're all foreigners together: no need to accommodate our speech for Japanese friends. Worse even than having to speak slowly and with limited vocabulary is the necessity of being unvaryingly polite, no matter how much alcohol has been consumed. Too, I've come to conclude that sarcasm and irony are nearly incomprehensible to the Asian mind, who perceives them as simply hurtful.

When I go out with "the boys'" wives, it's another experience altogether. They are all beautiful talented women. In our own countries, "the boys" would have no chance of capturing such prizes.

Invariably, our conversations revolve around their complaints about their foreign husbands.

Michiko tosses back an impeccably-maintained mane of glossy black hair and abstracts a cigarette from her Louis Vuitton handbag. "It's his toys. That's what costs so much money."

Michiko's boy Takao is the same age as our Peter. I'm puzzled. "Your son still plays with toys?"

She laughs bitterly. "Not *Takao*! I mean Bruce."

I struggle to suppress a laugh.

"And he buys. . .?"

"Computer equipment, software, DVDs, videos, I'm not sure what. But the money goes. Or I assume it does. Everyone tells me about all the extra jobs Bruce is doing, all the places he works. He refuses to tell me about them, and he gives me no extra income. Then I find a new printer in his office. Or ten new videos stacked in the bedroom."

She stubs out her cigarette angrily. "Even though he won't tell me, I know he's *somewhere*, doing *something*! Certainly Takao and I see little enough of him at home."

Michiko's arm is grabbed by Azusa, who is nodding in apparent agreement. A quick flurry of Japanese, incomprehensible to my ears, ensues. They gesticulate in agitation and sigh. Then they remember my presence and turn to me with exaggerated attention. Azusa has rather different problems with her husband from Canada. She arrives at our meetings heavily made-up. It transpires that Kenny has a violent temper. Those black marks just visible beneath the powder are bruises rather than, as I'd imagined, the age spots that are beginning to mark my own face. I feel like apologizing for being a westerner.

It's difficult to reconcile my impressions of "the boys"—overweight, childish, engagingly comic—with the monsters described by their wives.

In our house, it may be me who assumes that role. February third is "cast out the demons" day in Japan. By common consensus, my husband and sons always think I should don the devil's mask and agree to be pelted with dried soybeans as I run madly about our front garden, dodging their assault while they shout "Out, demon. Go away, demon!"—ritual intended to cleanse a household of evil spirits. Is that how they all see me?

One of my fourth-year seminar students is writing a graduation thesis on attitudes to housework adopted by Japanese and American husbands. According to her research, the average Japanese man does six per cent of the family's housework while the American husband shoulders forty-five per cent. I know my own husband does more than most of his friends: he washes the dishes every evening, he helps the children with their homework, he washes the cars, and he keeps the log-burning cast-iron stove supplied with wood.

I think my husband's friends pity him. But he is also the object of some envy. Although it is his wife who is a university professor rather than himself, it is a position that carries considerably more social cachet in Japan than it does in the west. Shortly before Tony's visit to my office that morning, I had opened my door to a textbook salesman advertising his wares. It was the usual response: embarrassment and shock at suddenly being confronted by a foreigner. He mustered a few English phrases:

"So sorry. Look for Nakanishi-sensei, professor Nakanishi."

"I am Mrs. Nakanishi."

"Your husband here?"

I felt sorry for him and slipped into my rudimentary conversational Japanese, explaining that I was the college teacher and my husband, in fact, was a farmer.

Another shocked look. He pressed his catalogues into my hand and made his escape, bowing deeply and walking quickly away.

On leaving the bar that night, slightly tipsy from the beers consumed but exhilarated by the easy companionable conversation, I find that a slight rain has begun to fall.

"Damn, and I don't even have an umbrella let alone a raincoat."

The rainfall suddenly increases in intensity.

It's past midnight. On impulse, I scurry back into the bar and phone my husband.

Miraculously, he's still up. A man of few words, he simply grunts "Uhnmmm" at my request that he come to pick me up. He appears with amazing speed: a battered white van speeding down the deserted main road of the city, stopping jerkily in front of the bar.

On our way home, I am afforded the occasional glimpse of his face as illuminated by streetlights and by store signs. A harsh face; a kind heart. Doubly incomprehensible as a man and as a Japanese. Completely reliable. Inexpressibly dear.

YU-HAN CHAO

MAIL ORDER BRIDE

The only thing I have from home is a jade necklace that my mother had given me. I come from a small Vietnamese village, *My Lai*, where we had a small rice field from which we made a living. The river gave us water and a modest harvest. Then last year, mother died giving birth to a baby brother, a silent infant who died one day later. That was when father became an alcoholic, stopped working our part of the fields, and owed more and more money. I could not keep our land alive on my own. Some of our neighbors tried to help me plant the rice sprouts, but father, drunk on cheap cooking wine, would wave the glistening harvest sickle at them, threatening to kill anyone who meddled in our business.

There used to be young men in our village that wanted to ask for my hand in marriage, but now they were all scared away by my father.

"Anyone who touches my daughter will die," he yelled, and everyone heard him. Sometimes when he was drunk, he tried to hit me, but I would run and hide from him.

I missed my mother, and still loved my father, despite everything, but I was young, only sixteen, and wanted more. It was just a matter of time before I ran away.

My childhood friend Han gave me a lift to Saigon on his new scooter, and introduced me to his friend's cousin, a big deal business lady, Mrs. Rie, who worked in the city. She was the wife of a man who owned a special agency, an agency that sold Vietnamese girls to foreigners as brides. I had no money, couldn't even pay the fees, but Mrs. Rie persuaded her husband to let me owe it to them until I was successfully married to a foreign client.

She looked me up and down.

"You're not especially beautiful, the legs too thick and hips too narrow, face all bones, but I think someone will like you."

And she was right. They showed pictures they had taken of me with a lot of make up and beautiful borrowed clothing to their clients, and in three weeks they had sealed my marriage with a Taiwanese man.

"But I don't speak Chinese."

"He will not mind, my dear," Mrs. Rie smiled, nice to me all of a sudden now that I was bringing business to them. "He's looking for a wife, not a conversation partner. Just smile and look pretty and cook and clean. You'll be fine."

She was pleased that the Taiwanese man was willing to pay nearly half as much as an American would have for a Vietnamese bride. I never saw any of that money, of course, it all goes to the agency and they even claimed I owed them high fees for the arrangement as well as rent for the time I had slept in a cockroach ridden warehouse they let me stay in.

In Taipei, my new husband met me at the Chiang Kai Shek airport. He was holding a sign with my name written in English on it. Lei Lee. My last name would be changed soon; my husband was Mr. Ting. So I would become Lei Ting, Mrs. Ting.

All the buildings in Taipei are so tall and shiny, the people so happy, it is strange to me. Their faces are Chinese faces, not so different from us Vietnamese, yet their lives seem so different. The rice comes from burlap bags in supermarkets, not the fields. I don't know where the fields are here.

My husband, a retired soldier, has a long, stubbly chin, hollow eyes, and gray hair. We communicate with very bad English and some Chinese at first, mostly gesturing. I prefer nighttime, when no language is necessary. He gives me little medicine pills to swallow, draws an X with his fingers and makes the shape of a woman's round belly on me. He does not want me to become pregnant, and these pills will protect me.

We live on the eleventh floor of a tall residential building. Our apartment is a one bedroom place, smaller than my old hut in Vietnam, but I like it here because it is clean, bright, and has large windows to let the sun shine in, just like the outdoors back home, but with air conditioning.

The strange thing is that there is no fire in his apartment, no stove, nothing to cook with. Every afternoon, around five thirty, the busiest time on the streets, he used to go into the nightmarket to buy his special dinner. An *o ah jian*, oyster omelette from a food stand, and rice, vegetables and fish from a cafeteria in the nightmarket. He shows me the way once or twice, and soon it is my job every night to buy his omelette and some greasy cafeteria food for both of us.

From nine in the morning to three in the afternoon every weekday he sweeps the floor in a public library nearby while I have a walk in the neighborhood, clean the house, or watch Taiwanese television at home. We have Japanese cable channels, but I prefer local soap operas. I learn a lot of Chinese from them, especially since there are Chinese subtitles on everything. I had only seen television shows a few times when I was in Vietnam, but they had never fascinated me as much as the shows here. I especially like the period shows in which all the characters wear traditional Chinese clothing, flowing robes with sashes and wide sleeves. I would have liked to wear those clothes. But I still wear my plain blue gowns that begin at my neck and end at my ankles, even in this hot weather. It is important for me to still feel like I am Vietnamese, because even if I married a Taiwanese man, it does not change me inside, I am still Lei Lee. I will not forget my ancestors, it is important to honor them.

Gradually, as I get out more during the day, I make friends. Most of them are maids and nannies from Vietnam. They tell me the latest gossip. One woman, Taiyun, has a neighbor who got a mail order bride from Russia. Russia! It was such a big deal because a Russian woman is a white woman, and white women are like goddesses in Asia.

"How can you possibly buy a white woman?" I ask.

Taiyun smiles slyly and makes the motion of rustling money in her right hand.

"Money," she says. "Lots and lots of money. And do you know what, that man's family treats her as if she were a princess instead of a mail order bride no offense, Lei Lee."

"What do you mean?" I ask.

"They are afraid that she will be bored, so they find her little students so she can teach them English, even though her English is so bad even I will laugh at her. But they don't care, they think she is so wonderful to marry their son. Rich people, of course. They are insane. And they can't wait till she gives them little foreign looking babies, beautiful and creamy-skinned."

"Well, I certainly wouldn't want to teach English, I don't envy her that," I say.

"The point is, they try so hard to please her," Taiyun says. "From what I can tell, your husband treats you like my employer treats me. Like a servant. Because they bought us. They know it and we know it."

"Well, I don't think of it that way. I want to please my husband because if he is happy then I will be happy because he will be good to me," I reply.

"Right, right," Taiyun scoffs. "You are perfect material for a mail order bride. Exactly what he ordered."

"That's not a nice thing to say."

"Let me ask you, if you go out to buy his dinner in the nightmarket and come back, say twenty minutes later than usual, will he be mad?"

"Maybe, if he is hungry. Once I walked a little slow, and. . ."

"Ah ha!" Taiyun interrupted. "That's exactly what I mean. He treats you like a servant. A man will not scold his wife like a child for being late. He will only scold a servant."

I didn't say anything. Half of me saw Taiyun as being jealous of my legal status as a wife here, my freedom to stay in Taiwan as long as I like without having to work or bribe officials for a visa. Another half of me understood what Taiyun said. After all, my husband, Mr. Ting, had purchased me. That itself made him feel like I was something he owned, which he could order around. He has trained me to respect him like that--I cannot think of him in my mind as Hsia, his first name, I only know him as Mr. Ting. My friends are used to it and no longer laugh at me for calling my own husband by Mister, but I still feel a tinge of embarrassment about who he is to me. My husband? Lover? Owner? Master?

I was still thinking of what Taiyun said today as I left the house to get dinner.

It takes fifteen minutes just to walk to the omelette stand, and there is a long line. The owner notices me today however and nods; he knows I come every day, and he happens to be in a good mood. He gestures to the cook to give him the next omelette, catches it in a styrofoam container as the cook tosses it to him, and sprinkles coral colored special-recipe sauce on it. I hand him four ten NT coins and he gives me the container in a little red and white striped plastic bag.

"Just one, not two?" he asks, flirting. "Buy one get one free, only for you, number one customer."

He knows I am buying Mr. Ting's omelette, he knows I am a Vietnamese mail order bride, and leers, as he often does. I shake my head and walk away as politely as possible.

I never eat any of Mr. Ting's oyster omelettes, I think they are disgusting. I ask Mr. Ting why he will not get a stove, I can cook all this food for less money than we are paying the vender and cafeteria owner.

"Can you make *o ah jian* just like the stand? Eh?" he asks me back.

"I could learn," I say.

"Forget it, I don't want the smell of cooking in my home," he says. "It is a small space, and I won't have it smelling of grease and oysters. Just go buy the food and stop questioning your husband."

I feel the heavy ring of keys in my pocket as I drag my feet in cheap sandals in the direction of the nightmarket. Because of moments like this that come back to me over and over again, when he ends the conversation with scolding me or sending me off to run an errand, I have built up some resentment for him. But I vent it in small ways, little by little, so that I can still like him. I spit in his omelettes and his coffee in the morning; he'll never know and it won't hurt him, anyway.

Recently, I even stopped eating the little contraceptive pills. I decided that even if Mr. Ting didn't want a child, I wanted a son, a boy whom I could love, and who would grow up to be tall and strong and who would take care of me. I don't believe that a man would really not want a child once it is here--doesn't every man want a boy, a small version of himself? It will make him feel more manly, to have produced another human being, especially in Mr. Ting's case--he is forty-five years old already. Eventually, when I become pregnant, I'm sure Mr. Ting will change his mind and love the child. It's human nature.

At the cafeteria, the *la ban nian*, female owner of the store, smiles and nods when I come in. She works hard and is polite to all customers, adult or children, mail order brides or not. As she hands me two paper containers for the food and a plastic bag for the rice, I open my mouth to speak, which somewhat surprises her because she has probably never heard me talk before. She must have thought I did not speak Chinese.

"Can I have *su pi nong tan*?" I ask.

I had seen other customers eating it here before, and could smell the fragrance. *Su pi nong tan*, crisp skin thick soup, kind of a creamy western style soup cooked in a small crock pot with a layer of golden puffed pastry baked on top. It would be the ultimate luxury; I could imagine the crisp skin contrasted with the smooth creamy texture of the soup on my tongue. I would eat it so eagerly my tongue and the roof of my mouth would burn but I would not be able to stop because it was so delicious.

"Why, sure!" She smiles broadly.

She is happy for more business, especially since *su pi nong tan* is not cheap. One hundred NT for a bowl of soup, but it's completely worth it in my mind.

"But it is too hot for you to carry home. And if it spills, you will be burned. You see, the bowl is baked in the oven."

I think about this for a while. "It's okay, I will eat it here then," I decide.

The *lao ban nian* smiles and calls to her chef, a short handsome man who looks half Taiwanese, half some kind of Caucasian. "One *su pi* soup!" Then she turns to me courteously, "Please have a seat and wait here."

"I'll get the food first," I say, and walk towards the steam trays full of green, brown, red, white, and yellow dishes shining with grease.

As I pay her in advance for the soup and the food I had put in the paper containers, she looks at me with concern. "Are you sure it is okay if you make Mr. Ting wait?"

I nod my head. It's too late now. I've paid for the soup and am all ready to eat it.

The soup seems to be taking a long time. The *lao ban nian* turns to me at the table and apologizes every few minutes. "Sometimes the oven is slow," she explains. I smile and say that it is no problem.

The handsome chef finally comes out with my beautiful soup with a rounded pastry top shaped like a breast, golden and perfect. He holds it with oven mittens and an extra rag. The *lao ban nian* rushes to put a coaster down before me as he sets the bowl down.

"Enjoy," says the *lao ban nian.* "And be careful, it's very hot!" she adds as she returns to the counter to accept money from another customer.

I look at my *su pi nong tan.* It is absolutely perfect--I can hardly bear to break the perfect crisp skin at the top, but I do, my husband is waiting for this food beside me at home, and is probably grumbling already. I make a small hole in the pastry skin, which breaks immediately and some pieces crumble into the soup. Steam rises from the hole in the puff pastry, and I smell the fragrance of creamy mushrooms and chicken. I make a larger hole with my spoon and reach into the soup, picking up a small piece of pastry that had fallen in. I blow on it to cool it down, then put it in my mouth. Delicious. I savor every bit of my soup slowly, blowing on every spoonful but still burning my entire mouth. I'm sweating even though it is winter and twenty degrees Celsius, cold for Taiwan; the soup warms me up and satisfies me completely. This is one of the best moments of my life; I feel free, like I am defying the universe by sitting here, enjoying *su pi nong tan* as my husband waits hungrily at home for his dinner.

I want to linger in the store, with that cute little crock pot in front of me, enjoying my wonderful *su pi nong tan*, but there is no more. I did not even leave a scrap of mushroom at the bottom of the bowl. I smile at the *lao ban nian* and wave cheerfully as I pass her on my way out.

As I walk home, some men look at me. They see my red cheeks and red lips from the soup; they must think I am in love. I turn my head down and walk as quickly as possible. After all that waiting, the omelette must be only lukewarm. I do not want Mr. Ting to be too disappointed, or upset.

When I open the door Mr. Ting is standing right behind it.

"Where were you?" he asks.

"In the nightmarket," I reply.

"Why were you so late?"

"I just. . .walked more slowly."

"You are forty minutes late and you say you walked more slowly? What kind of lie is that, what were you up to?" He raised his voice.

"Nothing." I say, trying to walk past him to put the food on the counter.

"Don't evade my questions like that."

He feels more and more free to scold me in Chinese since he knows I understand it well enough now. He seems more angry than is appropriate for my being late, though, even if he is hungry and worried.

"I'm not, I'm really sorry. Here, let's eat now," I say, using my most soothing voice.

"After you explain this," he says.

He holds something out in front of me. It is a blue and white foil and plastic thing with twenty one little pills in it. He had found the contraceptive pills I did not take and had hidden in my underwear drawer.

"I. . .I forgot all about them," I stammered, sensing his anger.

"Forgot? You lying woman, how dare you lie to me twice in so short a time, did you forget I bought you from your country, gave you a good life and home here, you ungrateful wench! How dare you disobey and deceive me!"

I back towards the door as he advances towards me. I suddenly remember that he used to be a soldier, and that my mother had warned me to stay away from soldiers. They were prone to violence, she had told me; they were not balanced people.

"I'm sorry, I'm sorry. . ." I say over and over again.

"Sorry is not enough. Where have you been? Have you been sleeping with someone else? The cafeteria cook, that mixed bastard? Do you want his child, is that why you are not taking the pills?"

"No, no!"

I try to push him away as I open the door to run out, but he pushes it shut with his right arm. He is strong, and much bigger than me. He uses his left arm to twist me over to face him, then lands a punch in my abdomen with his right fist. The pain is sudden and fierce, and I fall to the floor. I did not know this was what it was like to be hit—my father had never managed to land his hands on me—it felt like having all the air knocked out of me and I lost my balance. He pulls me up again and punches my stomach again, like I am a punching bag.

Tears stream down my face as I try to catch my breath, I feel my consciousness leaving me; the pain is like a screw in my body, screwing tighter and tighter. The last thing I think of is that if I wasn't a mail order bride this would not be happening to me. If I was Taiwanese, like him, he could not feel so much more superior, or if I was a Russian mail order bride, then I would be tall, strong, and beat him right back. With the last strength I have I lunge towards him with my fists and try to punch him back in the abdomen, as he had done me, but it takes him only a slap to land me on the floor again, where I curl up into a C shape, groaning. I can feel myself bleeding, I think in my womb. He lunges and lands on me, but I kick him hard in a vital place, and it is his turn to fall to the floor.

I open the door and run out, into the street. I do not know where I can run away to this time, but I know I must run, keep running.

RIFT/REPAIR

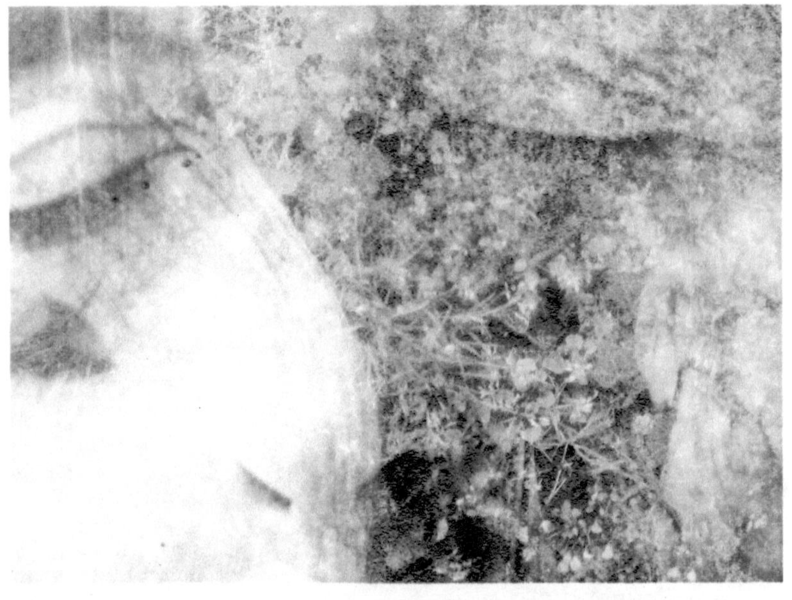

CHERYL HICKS

A SUDDEN WILLINGNESS TO SLEEP

Some nights I almost die in my sleep. I keep the muzzle pointed at my head, and though tentatively I am tethered by bed sheets and promises of the good life, my saving grace is reality and knowing that the end is only a figure of speech.

When my brother and I were young, it was not unusual for one of us to find my mother passed out, usually on the kitchen floor.

How would you describe the dizziness that you felt before fainting? Did you feel light-headed, off-balance, or like the room was spinning?

I don't know what caused the fainting. I thought it might be because she was pregnant, but even after she gave birth to my red-faced sister, the fainting continued. It must have been a reaction to the violence in our house.

She and my stepfather fought sometimes. It was the kind of fighting that started with yelling and often escalated to him hitting her. On at least one occasion, she pulled out a butcher knife to back him off. I'm pretty sure it was the time she told my brother and me, in the heat of the argument, that he had "slept with" our maid, Juanita, (a term I didn't exactly understand at the time) because times had been tough and he had heard it would change his luck. Looking back, I've often wondered why she didn't go for the knife *before* he hit her...but I was never the kind of kid to ask such questions.

It was usually the day after the fight scene that we found her on the floor.

When you regained consciousness were you aware of your surroundings or were you confused?

The first time I saw her crumpled on the white tile, she was on her stomach with her hips and lower body turned uncomfortably to one side. Her arms were loosely curled about her head, slack hands palms down, and her right cheek was flattened against the pale, horizontal plane. I thought at first that she was she was asleep, but her face didn't have the tensionless look that sleep brings. And when I tried to wake her, she didn't seem quite able to open her eyes. (I had just started taking swimming lessons, and imagined her posture, the way her torso was scrunched up and turned sideways, as being similar to my dead man's float. According to my swimming teacher, this was not good form and I needed to relax more….)

Two and a half years my senior, and obviously more experienced with such situations, my brother knew to get a cold washcloth and blot Mamma's face until she came back to us. This pattern of discovery and resuscitation went on for years, and other than the occasional black eye or bruised jaw, she showed no lasting signs of wear or tear.

Did you experience chest pain or heart palpitations when you fainted?

Maybe it was because I sort of got used to seeing her that way, but sometimes when we found her, I almost felt like she was pretending to faint in order to get attention. We did feel sorry for her when she fought with my stepfather. She didn't really ever seem to be at fault, and we thought he was mean to her. But after a while, we wondered why she didn't just pack us up and leave him. (She had been married before to a man who beat her and she had left him.) In the end we weren't sure if the fainting was an attempt to keep the tide of our emotions predictably surging in her direction or if she was just trying to keep everyone afloat a little longer.

But they didn't fight all the time. And we were always reassured afterward that things would be okay. We learned with time that this was merely *parent talk*, a coded message sent not so much to keep us from worrying, but to keep us from telling anyone about the fights. I guess you could say my brother and I grew up in a house of secrets. It was as though each member of the family lived in an iridescent bubble of potential sealed off from the rest of the household, and most decidedly from the rest of the world. I grew up not completely understanding the dynamics of the situation, yet somehow convinced there was no real point in asking questions. Something told me I had all of the answers if I could just be very quiet and listen for them. So I stayed quiet.

The only one I ever really talked to was my brother. Being older than me, Bubba was naturally more confident, and I looked up to him worshipfully.

He didn't like to spend much time alone, and our household wasn't the kind where our friends were welcome without making an appointment, so to speak, by way of our mothers. So by way of default, I was Bubba's primary companion, and at least on the weekends, he was my primary caregiver.

We lived in a beautiful, new house that had recently been showcased in the Tyler Parade of Homes, and everyone had his or her own bedroom. But I liked Bubba's room best. And when he didn't have anything better to do, he was willing to spend time with me. We were strongly discouraged from messing up the common areas of the house, such as the living room, the family room, the glass-walled atrium filled with artificial plants... and my room was much too frilly for adventure. Besides, Bubba had his own TV, so we usually ended up playing there, and as long as we didn't make too much noise, we were pretty much left alone. Except for naptime.

During the week I usually laid down with Juanita for a half hour or so, and often dozed off as she rubbed my head. And usually on Saturdays, when Bubba was home from school, we were required to take an afternoon nap. Neither one of us really felt a pressing need to sleep in the daytime, but we were still forced by Mamma, or the maid, or whoever was on duty, to "just lay there for awhile and rest."

My room was bright with sheer white curtains that let in most of the sun. And since I didn't like my room much (it would have been tolerable if my bed had a canopy, but Mamma said they attracted too much dust) I tried to convince Mamma that I was completely unable to sleep there during the daytime. (I had learned at a very early age that if I complicated the issues enough and just kept talking, I could convince her of almost anything.) I would propose elaborate scenarios and chatter on about things like remodeling my room. In a detached voice that told me she was paying more attention to putting on her makeup than she was to my plan, she said we couldn't change my curtains because they wouldn't match the rest of the window treatments on the front of the house. So I proposed putting tinfoil on the windows (I had recently discovered this technique and, believing it to be a necessary step toward the space age, was fascinated by the reflective possibilities....) Mamma practically swooned.

I told her she could buy me one of those satin sleeping masks, the kind that movie stars wear. At that point I stretched out on my back on her bed, crossed my arms over my chest like a corpse, snored like a stooge, and played out the act of napping in my imaginary mask...then I sprang up dramatically and warned her there was always the chance I would forget to take it off when I awoke and somehow wander out of my room out of the house into the street and "what good would all of those years of naps do me if I got hit by a car?"

When I would go off on these practically unpunctuated tirades, my mother would try to ignore me at first, but I could be relentless in a quiet, dogged way, and almost always got what I wanted eventually. So, though I wasn't allowed to alter the atmosphere in my room, I was allowed to take my naps in Bubba's room.

His room was darker and much cozier than mine. Whereas mine had bare, white walls, snowy linens, and pale, glass-protected, French Provincial furniture, his had rust-colored corduroy, dark oak paneling, lots of book-filled shelves, and a subdued atmosphere like that of a perpetually rainy day. But the best part was his headboard. It was a cabinet of sorts, a rectangular box that stretched the width of the bed, and it had two sliding doors across the front. When both doors were pushed all the way to the center, they neatly overlapped, leaving just enough room on each side for us to squirm our heads and shoulders into the openings, and just enough light for us see each other's faces at opposite ends of the "tunnel." It was a crawl space for secrets. And it carried our whispered words back and forth from one end to the other as effectively as if we were two tin cans connected by a string. When we were in there, I always felt as though we had stumbled upon a communication invention as conversely primitive as it was amazing.

As equally amazing was the fact that Mamma didn't seem to care that we liked to cram our heads into the headboard. She would come in to check on us, turn the radio on almost silently to the "piano music station" to provide us with a little ambient sound (she was always one for setting the right mood) and pull the door almost shut behind her, leaving it was open just a crack. "In case I want to take a peek at you; that way I won't wake you."

Mostly we talked about silly things at naptime like whether or not we really brushed our teeth, or what we would take on our next trip to the woods. Sometimes we pretended we were characters from television shows. Bubba's favorite was Rin Tin Tin and Rusty, but I wasn't crazy about that one because I always had to be the dog. When it was my turn to choose, I always wanted him to be Maxwell Smart, so I could be Agent 99. I especially liked to pretend we were in the "cone of silence."

Sometimes we were more ambitious and made plans about things we would do when we got older. Bubba wanted to be a fireman or a policeman. (He would someday become both.) I guess he liked professions that offered the bonus of a uniform. I just couldn't seem to lock myself down on any specific vocational plans. I couldn't decide if I wanted to be an astronaut, a ballerina, a stewardess or an accordion player. But the limited circumstances of my life up to that point were definitely helping me narrow the spectrum of my career choices. I didn't really know enough about the space program to adequately fuel my imagination, and my mother couldn't seem to find the time to take me to dance lessons. While I definitely liked the idea of being a flight attendant, I had flown a couple of times and was beginning to think it might get boring after a while. But I was truly hooked on the notion of playing the accordion.

I had been virtually steeped in the Lawrence Welk Show since birth, and for a while, wanted desperately to become one of the Lennon Sisters. (But, as my brother pointed out, I was way too young and would probably not stay blond forever....) Besides, I was truly enthralled with the kinesthetic energy that accompanied the accordion. I had accumulated quite a collection of polka records (given to me by the sympathetic music lovers in my extended family), so when I was forced to play in my room, I would lope about the pristine space to a 2/4 beat, playing a pretend accordion I had fabricated out of two shoe boxes and a wad of duct tape. With my right hand splayed across the cartoon face of a smiling Hush Puppy, I manipulated imaginary keys, while the fingers of my left hand pushed crayon-drawn buttons and I rhythmically squeezed the instrument's crudely constructed bellows. Not surprisingly, no one seemed to understand my obsession, and my mother assured me quite emphatically that not only was the accordion impractical, it absolutely was not an instrument suitable for a girl. She must have been right, because I have yet to possess a squeezebox....

Bubba and I eventually outgrew our headboard conversations, but we still spent time talking about the future. Sometimes when we were upset by one of Mamma's and Daddy's fights, we ached to leave home. And though we still felt more sympathetic toward her (he, after all, was the one we were most afraid of), when she failed time after time to follow through on our evacuation plans, we decided we could live without her, too, if we had to.

Still, she fainted every once in a while. Bubba said he thought it was because of the pills she was taking. I had seen the twin yellow moons set each morning by my stepfather against the backdrop of her breakfast plate, but because of the v-shaped cut-out in the center of each pill, I assumed they were like the vitamins he gave us. I learned years later that the little yellow pills were Diazepam, more commonly known as Valium, a psychotropic substance often prescribed for chronic anxiety disorders. Mamma began taking it right after it came out in the early '60s, perhaps as an alternative to barbiturates. It was supposed to be safer and less likely to lead to an overdose, but was later found to be highly addictive. (Evidently Valium has also been used at times by military snipers to relax muscles and slow breathing for increased firing accuracy…It's probably just as well that Mamma didn't know this at the time. You know, with the knife and everything….)

Bubba had the idea that the pills were somehow supposed to keep her and Daddy from fighting so much. If so, they didn't work very well. No matter how much we talked about our lives and how they might change, I could never draw a clear picture in my head of a safe, quiet place that I could see myself going to at the end of the day. I was upset when my parents fought, but to be honest, I was almost as upset when they got along. It was as though when they were in agreement, they were still in opposition to me.

The only thing that helped me get by during those years before I went to school full time was the fact that John (I had come to think of him this way instead of thinking of him as Daddy) worked out of town most of the time. I'm not sure what he did exactly, and I never bothered to ask my mother. I almost never asked anyone direct questions. I had developed a tendency to limit myself to the information I could take in directly through experience. In a strange way, this put me more in control of my environment. In other ways, it left me vulnerable both mentally and emotionally. I was like a mirror, able to reflect only those events and ideas that passed directly before me. At times this dubious ability protected me, but at times, it made me open to things I wished I had never witnessed.

For example, one night, not long after my sister was born, Bubba and I had to ride with Mamma to the nearby town of Troup to pick John up at the train station. He had been away on a business trip and was returning by train instead of plane because of some bad weather in the area. It was well after our bedtime, so Mamma, having left the baby with my grandparents for the night, put us in our pajamas and packed us in the backseat with pillows and blankets to make the thirty minute trip to the depot.

It was rainy and dark and almost unbearably cold, and the defroster on Mamma's car wasn't working right, so she took the cloth "emergency diaper" out of the glove compartment, and every half mile or so, she would make a swipe across the inside of the windshield to clear it of vision-impairing fog. Even though she cautioned us repeatedly to sit back, we couldn't keep from leaning over the back seat, chins propped on our arms, as though we could somehow help her see where she was going.

Every time she mopped the windshield, we could see the rain-drenched scene before us, but only for a few seconds, then the road would begin to disappear in the inevitable fog. At one point the traffic on the two-lane highway suddenly stacked up. We slowed down almost to the point of not moving, and I could see the cars in front of us, one after another, stopping, starting, then finally stopping for good, as their brake lights flared and faded, flared and faded, and then stayed lit. Down the road a bit, I could see a row of headlights pointed toward us, stretching over the hill into invisibility.

Mamma was preoccupied with keeping the windshield clean and moved her car only in response to the movements of the line of cars in front of us. After fifteen or twenty cars swished past in the oncoming lane, it was our side's turn to go, so we proceeded forward impatiently as though we had somehow earned the right to do so.

Suddenly Mamma said, "Oh my god!! You kids sit back!" We braced, expecting her to brake suddenly, but when she continued to creep forward, our curiosity made us stretch even taller to see what was going on outside the car. I was in the seat behind her and couldn't see much, so I turned to the triangular window at my left. It was covered with convex water droplets, pregnant round dots that constantly grew heavier and ran together in small, clear tracks down the pane. Beyond the veil of the speckled glass, I saw lights, red, blue, and sometimes yellow, flashing, almost painfully bright, a warning that something dangerous or criminal had happened nearby.

In that moment, I was convinced that John's train had crashed, that he had been killed, and that there would never be any more fights or fainting spells at our house.

Then I saw the bodies. At least, I assumed they were bodies, various human-shaped forms draped in rain-soaked white sheets, laid out randomly on the side of the highway.

Since Mamma had just said we were still several miles from the station, I couldn't figure how they had gotten off the train. I imagined a fiery explosion and screaming people being thrown through the air, flying like aliens. Then the traffic stopped again. I saw more police cars with their strobing lights. And then I saw another car, a mud-streaked white one, upside down in the ditch and caved in on the top. On the back corner, one yellow-orange light flickered off and on in an unpredictable rhythm.

Bubba touched Mamma softly on the shoulder and asked, "What happened?"

"It's a car wreck," she answered, and this time when she told us to sit back, we did. That's when it hit me. It was a car wreck. Not a train wreck. John wasn't dead. And our lives were not about to change.

On the way home from the train station, I heard Mamma telling him about the wreck. She pointed out the section of the road where the bodies had been temporarily laid to rest. He thought for a moment. . .and said matter-of-factly, "The curve is too flat. It should've had more bank to it."

Mamma was silent. From her seat on the passenger's side, she leaned toward the left and wiped the fog from the window.

"Were the kids upset?" he asked.

Mamma peered over her shoulder to the back seat where my brother slept and I pretended to. . ."I don't think so," she answered quietly.

Later that night in my street-lit white room, I pulled the sheet over my head and lay very still. I wondered what it was like to die. I wondered if people would line up and look at me some day, a faceless mound held barely tethered to the earth by a clinging sheet. I tried to imagine the faces of the people who had died that night, but I could only imagine their tiredness... their sudden willingness to sleep. . . .

I wanted so much to be able to sleep. At an early age, I had developed an ongoing relationship with insomnia. I came into the world afraid there was a monster under my bed and a bear in my closet, and more often than not, I would wake up in the middle of the night screaming for someone to come save me. My mother had been worried for a while that I wasn't getting enough rest. As I got older the problem would become exacerbated to the point that she would eventually take me to a sleep specialist. A few electrodes later it was revealed that I was a "hyper" sleeper, cycling through R.E.M. sleep in half the time of the average specimen. (Studies have shown that it is during these periods of relatively light sleep that memories are formed. It has also been hypothesized that disruption of R.E.M. sleep can improve depression. I guess on some level, even at an early age, I was attempting to control what my brain took in, how I stored it, and how I would deal with it later.)

The day after the trip to the train station, when it came time for our naps, Bubba and I were worn out from the night before, and we didn't argue. But we didn't put our heads in the headboard either, opting instead to lie like mirror images, facing each other with only inches separating our faces. With Mantovani playing softly in the background, I told him how I had imagined the train wreck, and I admitted without shame, my disappointment when I had realized the truth. He didn't say anything, but his eyes agreed. We never talked about it again.

As we grew older, there were lots of things we stopped talking about. Some things it just doesn't do any good to hash out. They're beyond our control, and for that matter, were never a matter of choice to begin with. Like being born. Some of us try repeatedly to wish life away. Most times I try not to think about things like that. . .or about the other brother I never knew, the one who lived only three days. . .or about the fact that I was born less than a year after he died. Or about the stories I've heard about the purple shadows my father's fingers left on my mother's fair skin, and how she went into premature labor on that wet day in late October . . ..

My other brother lived no stories and he had no name, so sometimes I write about him. I write about wanting to feel close to him, like the space of one minute on the face of a clock must, out of inescapable necessity, be close to all of the others, no matter how minute the connection at the center of the circle remains. Sometimes I pretend, that since I came after him, I was his replacement. I pretend that I burst out of a wasted womb and onto the scene like an enthusiastic stand-in. And I make up stories. Enough for two people.

I never did find out for sure what it was that made Mamma faint. Maybe it was the Valium, or the natural aftermath of the violent episodes, first with my father...and then my stepfather. Either way, I guess there were times she just couldn't go on in an upright position. Maybe it was the promising coolness of the hard floor that pulled her down, the flat, grid-like tiles so different from her warm, round, vulnerable body.

Is this the first time you fainted?

I think Mamma wanted to escape to a place where the boundaries were clearly defined, and that she saw the squares on the floor not as limits or fences, but more like a map, a guide, presented in predictable, manageable pieces.

And I think there must have been times she just needed to lay there for a while. . . and rest.

KAREN ASCHENBRENNER

LOVE FROM A TO B

I love my younger brother, Kevin, more than anything. He loves me that way, too. He told me so, last fall. I waited nineteen years to hear it.

Kevin helped me move back home to Milwaukee after my college graduation. The turning point in our relationship happened along I-43.

Kevin's tanned hands gripped the steering wheel so tightly a long line stroked up his dominant arm, defining thick muscles. Comfortable in his muscular six-foot-two, 170-pound frame, he spends his summers using every muscle in his body. Roofing, siding, flooring, building. If he can, he does it. He glanced over, opening his mouth. Silence. His blue eyes deepened in frustration.

I didn't help. I looked out my window and wondered what I could say to someone who's refused to speak with me in four years. My own hand, pale white, thin, fragile, and deformed, gripped at the passenger side armrest. My right arm, outstretched towards the window, cuts off at the palm. I angled it on the window frame.

The tense, uncomfortable silence broke when Kevin's phone rang. As he talked with friends, he smiled. He could balance a phone and steer a wheel on a speedy highway, knowing full well where he was going. I could stare at a map for hours, glancing back and forth between points A and B, and never figure out how to get from one to the other.

To distract myself from spiraling thoughts, I asked him if he was excited for his own upcoming graduation.

"Not really. High school was lame—"

I interjected, unable to contain my exasperation. "You did fun stuff all the time. What about all your funny stories?"

On weekends, he earned his popularity by being everywhere and there for everyone. Kevin and his friends were inventive with their fun. They'd "kidnap" cute girls by pulling up to their houses and asking them if they wanted to be kidnapped. If the girl of the evening said sure, they would drive her over to pick up her friends and take the girls out to McDonalds. One of his friends lived on a wooded lot where his parents planted rows of seedlings to grow Christmas trees. Kevin and friends would dig up a few of these trees at a time, pile them in the back of a truck, and replant them randomly in the middle of other yards. 'Treeing' was a sporadic summer pastime.

Kevin's voice lowered and broke up, "I'm not talking about the funny shit."

I looked at him, seeing his own vulnerability for the first time. Maybe, I thought, a perfect body doesn't give you a perfect life. He looked at me through raised eyebrows, reading in my face my confusion and frustration in all I didn't know. He seemed so capable. I wanted to lean on him, but I finally saw he wasn't solid.

It took twenty-two years and a college degree before I figured that out. My pain was visible in my face. Kevin squared his shoulders and took great pains to meet my gaze. He had not been there for me in a long time, but his eyes said, he'd be there now.

When he was younger, Kevin was always available to hold on to. As a little boy, he thought he was born to make me smile while charming, cajoling, and entertaining all those around him in the process. He trusted me completely, no matter how ill-natured or conniving. We were unnaturally close siblings.

He relied on me for entertainment. My world—my friends, my knowledge, and my vivid imagination—made life a game worth playing. We'd sit on the kitchen linoleum with Lego boards spread out before us. I'd stay still and stare at the cityscapes we built, seeing an imagined universe. Kevin would poke my arm to bring me back to the floor, Lego boards, and his high-pitched chatter. "What do you see? Karen, can't you tell me?" He'd pull on me. I wouldn't move, patiently waiting for him to give up with a defeated, "I wish I could see what you do."

When I was six, Kevin played with one of my old toys, a wooden duck on wheels that pulled along on a string. Ducky fell down the basement stairs, landing on cement. One of the wheels shattered. Ducky lay on his side, broken. As I watched my dad get a garbage bag, I grabbed my right arm. Kevin saw my cradled arm and the broken wheel. His face contorted into misery. We cried for things that couldn't be fixed.

Kevin's early happiness was falsely enhanced as a counter or balance to my unhappiness. He lived to see me smile. He would talk about anything, everything, nothing. He was little and cute; he knew it, and he used it to wriggle into people's hearts who needed him most. Intuitive, he was older than his years and comfortable with that. He understood that bad things can happen even when your parents are there to protect you. He was prepared to clutch his plastic sheriff's badge and make the world ordered when it didn't want to be.

He wasn't prepared for a clear spring evening when he woke up alone in the bedroom we shared. Peeking out the door down the narrow, dimly-lit hallway, past his playroom and the bathroom toward the stairs, he couldn't see his parents' room on the other end. In between the corner bedroom and the opposite end of the hall, I lay with my shirt torn open, pallid and silent on the floor. Four shouting paramedics with their cords tangling and machines beeping hunched over me in a circle. A uniformed police officer standing off to the side jotting notes on a pad, and our parents, shocked but focused, stood over the paramedics, yelling my name along with them, as if the louder they spoke the better chance they'd have to drag me back from wherever I'd gone.

Kevin, uncharacteristically, didn't say anything as the stretcher maneuvered its way down the stairs and out into the sharp spring air towards the ambulance parked in front of the house.

Two mornings later, Kevin visited me. Before reaching my door, he paled at the stench of disinfectant and the overabundant plastic tubing. He didn't have anything to say. He needed to sit down, close his eyes, and pretend he wasn't there, I wasn't there, he wasn't lonely, I wasn't hurting, and we weren't so helpless.

Death's whisper, no matter how fleeting, leaves its imprint. A grief process, once started, is difficult to stop. A person is irrevocably altered, "blessed" with all of the insights that come with profound loss. Life continues. A shadowed life, trailing behind all of the broken pieces swept under the rug. A child, in particular, has trouble comprehending, processing, and so the child's body makes the decision for him/her; it numbs itself past feeling, living out a lie until ready to wade through the thaw. Kevin froze himself to me.

He couldn't be vulnerable again. He had friends, but he didn't care for them the way most children do. He patrolled the cul-de-sac he lived in on his plastic green tractor, flaunting his shiny plastic sheriff's badge as he tried to right the wrongs of the world. He stood on his short but straight and healthy legs in the schoolyard, hands on hips, perfectly aligned, and yelled up at kids twice his age. White blond locks whipped in all directions as he delivered his angelic message—Don't even look at my sister. I'll fight you. I will! By the time he turned nine, he had tossed his badge and all it signified.

There was no justice. At nine, he sat in an empty hotel room picking at the cotton on the bedspreads. No matter how loudly he blasted the television, he couldn't block the yelling from the lobby where my parents and I sat in a triangle arguing over what was right. Diagnosed with scoliosis, I wore a thick Boston brace for the first time that weekend and was reconsidering the alternatives. Our parents had thought to take us on a weekend vacation to retreat from the reality of the new situation.

Kevin retreated to the woods. A nature lover, he delighted in tracking deer, walking nature trails, baiting squirrels into live cages and later releasing them, camping, and playing with his new puppy. He treasures, to this day, the magic and wonder of October and November, a dusting of the surreal he's convinced himself is sprinkled lightly over every leaf and pine wood forest in Wisconsin's north woods. He collects guns of rare makes for their scented wood and professional carvings, but he doesn't hunt to kill. He hunts to feel the leaves crunching under the crevices in his boots, to be with the air, with the ground, with the animals. Part of a whole. Wholly part.

The summer Kevin was fourteen, he was looking forward to the excitement advertised on every TV channel as the high school years. He'd sat in the stadium bleachers at his new high school in mid-June as I received my high school diploma, doing what some people, in cruelty, had predicted I'd never be able, and others, in ignorance, had feared I'd never have the opportunity to do. He took a risk when he took my hand in his and squeezed, vulnerable again.

A few days later, Kevin stumbled into the kitchen as Mom and I ran in. I had appendicitis and would be going in for surgery. I packed a bag as Kevin turned away, walked into the family room, and plopped onto the couch with the dog. He flipped through the channels so quickly it was impossible to focus on any detail.

He stayed there by the TV from noon past twilight. Alone in the darkened room, he clutched the phone to his ear as his aunt told him my mom had called her from the hospital. Something had gone wrong.

The boy who never confided in anyone called his pastor and confided what was happening. In that silent two-story house, Kevin prayed aloud to the empty space, echoing the words of the man on the other end of the line. With his dog nestled in his lap, Kevin prepared to hold night vigil.

Early morning, Kevin got the phone call I was stable but in ICU. Only time would reveal the damage done to both of us.

Three weeks after my disastrous surgery, I left for college with a bandage around my neck and flagging spirits. I reached out to Kevin because I truly needed his companionship in our shared pasts and, hopefully, intertwined futures. He couldn't look at me.

"I made up my mind. We could never be close again, because I knew I could lose you," Kevin explains to me now when he recalls that time. "Pretty much everything I did in high school was connected to those times when you almost died, but didn't. It was like you had, to me."

Kevin seemed to thrive in high school. He knew he looked good and could be popular but he didn't play the game, dating and dancing his way through his teenage years. My existence never allowed him to be that carefree, but for all his wisdom, he felt no distance from his peers and was the clichéd life of the party.

But by his junior year, Kevin was on a collision course with everything he hadn't dealt with in life. He made decisions according to his reckless abandon in regards to his own life. Though he never acknowledged my existence, I was forever in his mind. My daily struggle haunted him. He wanted to die young while living to the physical fullest, so that he wouldn't be in pain.

He played a dangerous game. It doesn't matter, looking back, what he did, what he tried to do, or what he said about it. We don't have to describe the depths to know they're there.

No one could get close. He dazzled girls but didn't want a relationship. Even the friends who hung out with him night and day would be asked to leave him alone at unexpected intervals. He'd go to parties and drive back home in the middle of them to regroup because people annoyed him.

Part of him struggled to achieve academic success, making high honors and all those merits you need to earn scholarships that make college a possibility. The other part loved to sabotage by blowing off big assignments. He wanted nothing to do with me. He wanted to be like me.

When I left for graduate school, I encountered the full force of my physical limitations which triggered anxiety about jobs and helplessness that

I'll ever be able to achieve my goals as a disabled academic in an able-bodied world.

I called Kevin late one night. I didn't qualify for educational funding because physical disabilities do not, in scholastic reasoning, affect cognitive learning. I would, however, qualify for 'disability' if I could not make it through the education system long enough to get a job I am fully capable of performing. I'd just realized the hypocrisy of it all and I searched my phone bank for a receptive ear. To my own surprise, I scrolled down to my brother.

Instead of blowing me off with his usual "Don't throw yourself a pity party," Kevin listened, becoming satisfactorily outraged. He voiced his adamant belief in my writing ability and the tangibility of my professorial dream, his confidence that I would be able to publish the stories I wanted to. He told me he had always thought I was the one with a goal worth pursuing and that all along I was the one who had known where to go.

He started talking slowly, sparsely. He told me what happened in high school and the years before them. He was the one to tell the story of how the greatest pain in both our lives was that we love.

ANNABELLE BAPTISTA

LOVE'S VENOM

"If you're finished with that magazine, can you put it in the magazine rack," I said, tapping my barefoot against the linoleum. Deborah rolled her eyes and turned up the television. I exhaled disgust as I retrieved my social studies book out of my bedroom to work on a paper I was writing for extra credit over the summer break.

It was on Lucy, *my black Eve*, I thought as I reverently flipped to her picture in my book. Her full skeletal remains were found in Ethiopia. She was black, small forehead, big lips. "My ancestor," I said, rubbing my hands over the glossy page and touching my hands to my lips. We are all compact and low to the ground, like Lucy, she was the first woman, the beginning.

I let out a sigh looking at my sister's thin frame, shoulders curved over her large chest. Her scaly feet hanging over the edge of a cushion as she polished her toenails, watching Soul Train.

"Can you turn the TV down?" I asked biting the end of my pen. Deborah rolled her shoulders and swiveled her head, a habit that she took from watching *I Dream of Jeanie*, which I absolutely hated.

The telephone rang; Deborah and I both stared at it for a moment.

"Don't answer it…what if it's Mom calling to see if you pick up?"

Deborah had been on punishment for a week for chasing boys and I was stuck in the house with her.

She sucked her teeth, and looked bored, "You're trippin," she said, picking it up on the fourth ring.

After a pause, Deborah said, "What's up, Ebony?" and I exhaled with visible relief. She held the phone on her shoulder at her jaw line as she continued painting her toenails. Driven by curiosity, I listened. Deborah began pacing the floor, tightening the phone cord around her wrist, her voice getting louder and shriller until I was sure the neighbors in the apartment across the hall could hear her. I hand signaled wildly for her to keep it down as if she were summoning a police raid.

"He said *what?*" The big mouth must have repeated it because Deborah let out a bawling scream, as if she'd been kicked in the stomach.

"I never let him do that. Oh no, not her, she's always been after him, the tramp. Don't worry; I'm coming to the park, right now. I'll see you there." Deborah hung up the phone, closed the nail polish and carefully slipped into her flip-flops. Reaching under the macramé planter that hung over the television set, she produced her car keys, which she had hidden there last week to keep mom from taking them.

"Aggie, I've got to go. I'll be back in 15 minutes," she said, pulling cherry lip balm from her back pocket and applying it in the mirror that hung over the sideboard in the dining room.

"No, you're not, because we aren't suppose to go outside," I reminded her.

"Aggie, if you tell…I won't take you to the drive-in with me," she said.

"We're not allowed to go out anyway because of you, and now you're going to make it worse!"

"Don't be a jerk," she said walking to the bathroom and returning to the mirror with mom's make-up bag. I watched, as she put on liquid eyeliner, in thick bands.

"Do you want to be on restriction forever?" I asked, throwing my hands up in exasperation.

She ignored me, so I tried another tactic. "So that boy doesn't want to date. Good riddance…*you're both too ugly to mate.*"

Deborah looked at me with a fire in her eyes. I could tell she was struggling to keep herself calm.

"You are so immature. One day you'll understand what it means to love somebody."

I stared at her unfazed.

"You…Hoover, you're not so mature yourself. Boys just use you." I said leaning my back against the unsteady sideboard.

"Oh, What do you know! I'll only be out of the house a couple of minutes tops. Come on, go with me. Don't you want to get some air? It will do you good to go out for a little while. It's so hot in here. How is Mom going to find out unless you tell? She won't be home until six. Come on," she said, smiling at me. The scent of Love's Baby Soft perfume, wafted over me like a summer's breeze filled with anticipation. I weakened.

"Well, maybe, we could go for a minute." I said, but inside, I was dying to get out of the house and Deborah's excitement was catching on, even if I didn't want to admit it. I picked my notebook up off the table. Deborah pressed her advantage and grabbed me by my arm and dragged me out the kitchen door, without my shoes. I hopped from one foot to the other stepping on patches of dried grass to avoid cockleburs, trying to breath, as the humidity devoured the air.

The car, was a green Dodge Dart, from our Uncle's junkyard. Deborah had been driving it since she got her permit. Mom trusted her to drive me around when she couldn't drive me somewhere herself. But that was with her permission.

Deborah angrily floored the gas. The engine had some kind of leak in it and was always hard to start, but Deborah was determined not to sit for half an hour. She cocked her head to one side, and revved the engine, shifting out of park and jerking us both forward as she peeled out over the grass. I moved over as far as I could to the jammed window, trying to force it down further. My thoughts turned to eating an ice cold Popsicle. A Mr. Misty would be a good idea…Dairy Queen, I reasoned, thinking in terms of blackmail. Deborah was tapping the wheel and I knew she was fired up and just waiting to tell her mind to that boy. My stomach was churning as we coasted into the parking lot at the park.

"You're just going to talk, no yelling. We've got to get back home, and before that I want you to take me to Dairy Queen and buy me a Mr. Misty," I said crossing my arms.

"Okay, okay," She said, nodding her head as she walked toward the park. Deborah's quick temper is a school legend, so I imagined yelling, and drama. Maybe that's why I agreed to go. I wanted to see her make verbal breakfast sausage of this boy quickly and then we would be on our way, no more late night calls, and with that the end of our punishment. My heart dissolved when I turned and saw what must have been a telepathic crowd trampling the resilient grass. I was sure it was thanks to Ebony, who I spotted talking to a girl in the outer ring of the circle.

Jamo, Deborah's "boyfriend", was in the center of the crowd, with his arms around some girl that I didn't know. She had her arms crossed as if she wanted to hear what Deborah had to say for herself. The crowd howled as Deborah approached, and the ring opened.

"You tramp!" Deborah said moving towards the girl. Jamo quickly placed himself between Deborah and the girl.

"What are you doing?" Deborah said, looking at the thin, light-skinned girl who stood behind Jamo. She was everything Deborah was not, tall with long legs, and hazel eyes.

"We are just talking, like you and I was just talking. There is no more to it than that," Jamo said, but his arms were tense and he shifted from side to side as if he were hiding something.

"You said," Deborah started and then as if she couldn't bear to repeat his words out loud she changed gears, "I'm on restriction because of you, and now you're telling everyone…"

"You coward!" She yelled. He turned toward the girl as if preparing to leave but Deborah grabbed him by the arm.

"You are a two-time loser and I wouldn't want to be caught dead with you." He kept walking and Deborah kept goading him as the crowd followed along.

I grabbed at Deborah's arm and tried to pull her back as she danced around him and the girl, taunting them. I thought her yelling was just a bluff. The next thing happened so quick, I stared wide eyed as if my eye-lids had been pulled over the back of my skull. Deborah punched him in the jaw. The blow slipped off the left side of his face, toppling the black baseball cap. I caught my breath suddenly in the middle as he turned around. I stepped to the sideline, yelling Deborah's name but they were both screaming and the crowd was yelling encouragement. He attempted to hold her back; I yelled her name again as loud as I could. She ignored me or didn't hear me; I wasn't sure which. At that moment Jamo swung at her and caught her full on the temple. She took the blow, lashing out, her fingers curled into hooks. It felt like I had been hooked up to electricity. Even the mosquitoes attacking my sweaty skin were shocked. Deborah and Jamo wrestled, slipping off one another like clothes during the rinse cycle, at the laundry mat. Deborah's eyes were lowered, she kicked and clawed like someone possessed. Her womanly body, disheveled and heaving made me feel lightheaded. Only the crowd's clamor, as it moved in tight bands, kept me standing.

He leered at her, stepping back, taking up a cocky stance, "Now hold up girl. You have to admit, you are one ugly ass!" he said, laughing. The crowd let out another collective howl. Deborah looked at me; I had jokingly attacked her with the same insult just moments ago. I hadn't meant it. I felt as if I had betrayed her as if I had put the words in Jamo's mouth. The words drew blood like a parasite, destroying quickly, but brutally. I tried to back away, to get some distance, but I was pinned in.

Jamo and Deborah paused as if not sure what to do next. Everyone looked to Jamo, who stood his ground. The scratches on his chest were open and flaming red. We were all standing there as if waiting for a family portrait, and then the band that bound us together loosened and everyone began to drift away.

Deborah seemed deflated, empty. She didn't look at me as we walked back to the car. A fresh purple golf ball size lump had risen on her temple from the only strike Jamo had lifted against her. She gunned the engine, beating the steering wheel in frustration, but the car wouldn't start. We sat there stalled. Deborah looked back, but no one was in the park now. Fear subsided and adrenaline oozed from my pores and soaked the back of the torn leather seat that bit into my back.

"You looked like an Amazon! I still can't believe it. You kicked his sorry butt. The chump! Good for you," I said, pumping my palms together with respect for how she went at him, strong and fearless. There was something lifeless in the car with us, I could feel it but I couldn't name it.

"I loved him and he used me," she said wringing the steering wheel, between dry pants.

"He won't come neee-aar you now," I blared like a trumpet through my nose.

She swallowed hard, sweat clogging her vision as she sat up close to the windshield, her hands trembling. The sun set the air on fire and the heat pulsed, threatening to turn the airless car into a kiln.

"I'm beautiful too, aren't I?" she asked, her voice caught, the muscles in her throat seemed to be closing. I wasn't sure what it was she was asking of me, but my blood began to boil.

"Why are you so hung up on that, I snapped. You're not and I'm not. You just have to accept it. Stop trying so hard, it's pathetic."

Deborah looked at me her face clouded over with rage.

"I don't mean you're pathetic…but they talk about you and use you and then tell everybody, how cheap you are…I don't mean you're cheap," I started again lost in the viscious poison that was spewing from me. Deborah lashed out at me, slapping my face. The blow caught my ear and sent it buzzing. I grabbed the door handle and almost jumped out. The slap stung, but I also felt my compacted heart wrench free from the bands that held it in place as I grasped for the first time our self-hatred.

"I—…I—…I'm so..sor..sorry," she spattered. Her jaw dropped open as if she were in shock too. I sat on my side of the car, quiet. She sobbed between ragged breaths, as if she had just come to rest, and saw the unfairness. My throat was tight, as if something had lodged itself in my lungs and I couldn't speak. A murder of pigeons dived from the gutters of the pink and white houses that sat across from the park. Beautiful houses. I placed my hand on Deborah's leg and let her cry.

PRECIOUS MCKENZIE

STILL LIFE OF BUCKEYE TRANSPLANTED

Reminiscing about home since Aunt Anne had a nuclear size feud with (or I should say at) my mother (in the presence of the entire extended family), I can't help but wonder which forces of nature made the women in this family so strikingly bizarre. I never really thought much about it before. Sure, as a child, I knew that there had been some quarrels, but now those issues were water under the bridge. Jean, my mother, is an expert at creating a serene, sheltering microcosm—not quite June Cleaver but working-class close.

As a child, it never occurred to me just how poor we were. There was nothing that we wanted for (thanks to credit cards). Jean was, and still is, magical with children. Patience to the nth degree and the domestic skills to put even Martha Frickin' Stewart to shame (I inherited absolutely zilch of those genes). She sewed us clothes for our baby dolls (and the cat), led the Brownie troop, illustrated our emergent stories with her colored pencils, hugged and kissed our aches and pains away. She gave herself completely to the three of us.

She didn't work outside the home until I was in eighth grade and Matthew was well into elementary school. That's not because my father was some big shot attorney or neurosurgeon. He is a telephone man. Somehow, through careful budgeting, they scraped by. She occasionally babysat neighborhood kids to help with the bills. Sometimes Dad worked two jobs. When Jean did go back to work, she chose the public school system. She would leave the house early in the morning to cook five hundred children breakfast and lunch and then return home to her brood by 2:30, sweaty, food-stained and exhausted. The days of our well-balanced meals came to an end—those were the frozen pizza days.

She is a talented artist but she never went to college. Does she regret it? She's not the type to mope. She did confess at one time she dreamt of being an art teacher. Elaine and Edwin wouldn't pay for college for a girl (in the 1970s!), although they could have afforded it. Instead, Jean married a man that made, makes, her laugh and created a safe, stable world for her children.

As children, transplanted from northern Ohio to southwest Florida, we spent vast amounts of time out of doors. Mom loved to get her hands in the dirt and plant things, so naturally we traipsed about behind her, pestering each other. She can identify and diagnose any garden disease. She could have been a botanist the way she recognizes and classifies plants. She planted hedgerows behind the house, palm trees, cactus beds with decorative rock borders in the front, banana in the back, a vegetable garden in the corner (oh, her tomatoes). She grew aloe cacti. These she would cut and peel open with a pocketknife if our fair skin was blistered from sunburn.

Like her mother, Jean always had a dog. This dog was never a problem—loyal, sweet, charming, low maintenance, like Jean herself. It was the rabbits and the chickens that she guarded her home against.

The chickens came next. They were Easter gifts from the feed store. They lived in a large cardboard box with newspaper on our screened porch. Who am I kidding—they were hardly ever in that box. Most, of the time, we were in the backyard, rolling around the warm grass with these chicks. I taught mine how to come when called by name, like a dog (chickens are smarter than they look). We had a nice bond going on until I brought a chicken into the house and let her run down the hallway. The next day, Grandpa McKenzie drove them away to the chicken farm off Rock Road. That was the unfortunate day the chickens left the suburbs.

Then came the rabbits. Free, with cage, to a good home. Dad enforced the rules: NO RABBITS IN THE HOUSE. It was soothing to gaze upon a solitary rabbit nibbling weeds in the early morning hours. When word spread, our backyard became the Humane Society for unwanted rabbits. We topped out at six. Dad built a long hutch with nest boxes for each one. We shoveled rabbit poop all summer (my children will never have rabbits). Why didn't Jean say "no" to this suburban farm?

Our home was not a showcase, not a mansion. Her walls were heavy with family photographs and her own embroidery. Her furniture was inexpensive and squishy. When things went threadbare or stained, she sewed sofa covers or invested in throw rugs (if the carpet shampooer wouldn't do). She always said that expensive furniture was a waste of money with three children in the house. Why pay $500 for a sofa, only to have kool aid and ice cream spilt on it, she'd say. A shelf built into the wall of the dining room was jam-packed with encyclopedia sets, dictionaries, children's books and novels. All of our friends had to go to the public library to complete research projects for school. We had immediate access to knowledge. When she sold those encyclopedia sets at a garage sale many years later, I cried.

Elaine is my mother's mother. Elaine is first generation Polish-American. She is the daughter of grape growers from Dunkirk, New York. Elaine married a stuffy first generation German from Dunkirk. I can only speculate on the attraction. He was a military man. She had large sparkling blue eyes, wavy dark hair, a milky complexion and a trim figure. Any looks in the family gene pool come from Elaine. She is not a high maintenance kind of beauty, not the hours in front of a mirror beauty. But the easy, light, non-threatening beauty that many Polish women carry about with them. It is a beauty not thought of, not flaunted, not vain, but friendly, open, honest. I can see this reflected in my mother's smile, the wrinkle at the corner of her eyes, the sparkle and warmth that are deep inside her yet bubble out freely with those she feels comfortable. Elaine and her second born daughter are alike in that respect.

Elaine quickly had five children with Edwin. They relocated to northern Ohio. He became a railroad executive. When home, he would spend his time woodworking in the garage behind the sprawling white house on Kilbourne Street. She, with five children, would spend her time cooking, cleaning and washing clothes. She would put her children to bed before the sun set so that she could go outside alone, with no children hanging off of her, to dig in the earth. My mother resented this. I understand it. I can forgive it, my mother cannot. Her yard was an elegant creation that she nurtured and controlled.

Our summer visits to Ohio occurred every three years. We would drive two days in our beat up green station wagon to see relatives who coolly tolerated each other. In those two weeks, we were supposed to catch up on three years of lost time. Those were the summers that I wished we had never moved to Florida. It seems the relatives did agree to hide the feuding from all of the children. I enjoyed the attentions of a slew of pampering relatives and late nights running under the stars, catching fireflies.

Grandma's house was all that our house was not. Her home had two stories, with a remodeled basement and an attic that you could play in, a huge, painted front porch with rocking chairs and cool, moist stone pillars.

She had lush, new carpeting, and formal upholstered antique loveseats. She had fine china and wallpaper—class. It was a privilege to be allowed inside. We drank our pop on the porch.

Her kitchen, at the back of this home, was unlike any other room. Here the gas stove, the meat grinder and the laminate-top table dwelled. Only in this room, did we glimpse Elaine the farmer's daughter. I had no idea as to the amount of baggage that accompanied this façade.

As Edwin climbed the Norfolk and Western ladder, Elaine had to follow. As the children grew, they were expected to work for the railroad. The two boys did. Charmaine married a railroader, a Polish railroader, much to the delight of the entire family. Jean was engaged to an up and coming railroader but then dumped him for a white trash telephone man, from, quite literally, the wrong side of the tracks (he grew up two doors down from the railroad tracks and the grain silo).

Certain things are expected. If your father is a big shot with *the* railroad, you must carry on the tradition. I am sure this is not the mafia but something very close to it. The manicured yard and the staunch, noble white house on Kilbourne did not appreciate the dilapidated home on York, even though this home was in the shadows of the tracks and within walking distance of the carryout. When Jean met Lon and fell for his merry blue eyes (he was much slimmer in 1973) and wild ways, her future as the wife of a railroader came to an end. Elaine and Edwin threatened to disown her as she broke her engagement to Mr. Railroad. She tried to reason with them. After all, Lon's father worked for the railroad.

It wasn't good enough. The McKenzies were a Nickel Plate family. Not just that, but a large Scotch-Irish, poor Catholic family. A railroad switchman for a father-in-law was not good enough. Jean and Lon married, to the dismay of her family. Edwin burned his daughter's wedding photographs and the curse began—because of the railroad.

When the time came for Lon to make a career decision, he opted for Ma Bell and moved south, away from the railroad wars. This aggravated matters. The curse went something like this: "No good will ever come to you if you marry/move with that Irish/Nickel Plate/ white trash man. You will be sorry!" They moved.

Everything about my mother's Florida home was different than her mother's. Finances played a large role in that matter. We went without air conditioning for five years because we could not afford it; we sucked ice cubes during the sticky tropical evenings. At Grandma's we didn't put our feet up on the furniture to relax. At mom's we did. Grandma's German shepherd was chained outside the back door. Our menagerie threatened to break neighborhood code. Alligators, turtles, diamondbacks, sea gulls, egrets and anhingas visited our slice of the glades (it was much more primitive in the early 80s, before the multi-million dollar homes and golf courses invaded). Perhaps mom's house was an act of blatant rebellion against her family, her way to snub her nose at them.

Jean never told us of the curse. She did not want us to know of it or to live with it. When the three of us graduated from college, she became the only mother of college-educated children on her side of the family. She hoped to make her mother and father proud. It might have but Edwin died too soon. Elaine came around after his death. In fact, the McKenzies got her, too. Years after Edwin's death (he was probably rolling in his grave) she traveled to Europe and New Zealand with a good friend of my father's grandfather (admitted to the McKenzie clan through dedicated friendship and carousing on the Nickel Plate).

Jean cannot forgive her father, even in death. Finally, my father has been welcomed into my mother's family, after thirty years. He takes pride in the railroad, nation-building men that came before him. As we walk through the Bellevue Train Museum, he proudly tells his small grandsons about the boxcar that used to be their great-grandfather's tool shed at the hump. We climb into that boxcar and touch the wood, hoping to take with us a bit of Grandpa H.'s soul, for a time. He is proud of his father-in-law's legacy to industrialization. My mother grimaces and thinks about the lost time that she will never regain. Time that she could have spent with her father; instead he was at the rail yards. She grimaces about the grumbling, prejudiced, stubborn man that crushed Elaine's exuberance, the exuberance that Elaine should have been able to give her children. Lonnie then proudly shows his grandsons, my boys, the hammer and lanterns that used to be his father's that rest behind cool glass in the same museum. No placard proclaims our legacy to the world. But we know. We retell the stories. We return to Ohio, to revisit those memories in the museum. We traipse out to the corn and wheat flanked cemetery on 269. My father's parents rest beneath the cool breezes and wildflowers of St. Michael's church. I've picked my plot there (though no one knows that and no money has been exchanged). It is quiet and cool among the blowing wheat. Edwin is buried in the cemetery in town. He is surrounded by iron fences and staunch, solid tombstones. Elaine's name is on the marble, patiently waiting. Uncle Bill rests behind him, sharing time, sharing history. This town, that could be any town, holds my history—great aunts, uncles, cousins, and great great great grandparents that I never knew yet somehow genetically influence my past and future. As we walk about the grounds, my father points out distant relatives he knew and friends who died in Vietnam. He tells these stories and makes these journeys so that we continue.

As I look around my adult home, I try to find my history. This home in North Carolina was not my choice—much too urban, much too far from the salty Gulf water. The yard is not my country. The plants and flowers die in the winter (where are the hibiscus and cactus?), the clay and even the bugs are alien. How do I cultivate such foreign land? My roses do grow here, that is one comfort, though they do not bloom quite as frequently as I am used to. I migrate to Wrightsville Beach quite often, to walk and smell salty air. If I close my eyes, I imagine I am standing at Wiggins Pass among the whispering Australian pines, swimming in the Gulf of Mexico. I can forget, for a little while, that my father now has high blood pressure, my mother has the onset of arthritis, my sister has cancer.

The interior of my home, as I like to believe, is a blend of the best of my mother and the best of my grandmother. The comfortable sofa with the table to put your feet up on, the quilts and family photographs that are scattered about are my mother's, as are the calico cat and the mutt of a dog. The porcelain teapots and silver napkins rings are reminiscent of Elaine's home on Kilbourne. The toys that I buy for my sons are my grandparents' heritage—the trains, the track, even the curtains in their bedroom come from our railroad past. I look at those trinkets and remember that I am a child of railroaders, a mighty inheritance that links me to the foundation and the prosperity of this nation.

What is *mine* in this house then? Somewhere, dancing through my veins is the blood of the executive, the switchman, the Polish farmer's daughter, the vineyard owner, the telephone man and the cafeteria worker. They are with me forever, proud. As I tuck my children in bed tonight, I bend to kiss them and whisper a blessing. I pray in silence that they will be strong, loving, and most of all, forgiving.

DANIEL R. MARTINEZ

MILITARY MEN

My brother is a military man
like my father,
stern hands and trumpet voice,
discipline.

But with what I know,
who am I to judge,
or praise,
or condemn,
since I am always running from my father,
leaving my brother behind.

BOY

We fixed the sprocket and forks
on his bike the other day.
He isn't my son,
but he is my boy,
and that day I became his old man.

POEM FOR A DISTANT DAUGHTER

I dreamt of you many times,
silent,
in a crib fixed along some wall
in the dark of an apartment bedroom
five hundred miles away.

Was it that way?

Our first meeting
trails in the vapor of a possibility
of what we wanted the other to be like.

We each had dreams and expectations,
smiles and hugs just as meaningful
as the fears, welfare lines or bigotry
I allowed to come between us,
but not as strong as any of the words
we still can't find to explain
how distant we are now.

PATTI SEE

FAMILY STORY

Each summer since I turned thirty I've commemorated with a change beginning on my birthday. At thirty I started wearing lipstick, and at thirty-one I started running again. At thirty-two I made the decision to leave my husband. Almost thirty-three, I was stumped over what to choose. This was the age they got Jesus or when Alexander the Great wept because there were no more worlds to conquer, and two birthdays after Sylvia Plath put her head in the oven for the first or last time.

The night before my birthday, I sit at Griffin's kitchen table drinking beer. His teenage son shows me his newly pierced eyebrow.

"Cool," I say, a word that never goes out of style.

Griffin says, "We were in and out of the piercing shop in ten minutes. This very tattooed woman shot my son with a piercing gun. It took longer to pay than to do the actual deed."

Since Jack and I separated, Griffin's kitchen is the only place I feel at home. My apartment is temporary, two large rooms where I sleep and sometimes eat. The *Mary Tyler Moore* theme in my head—*gonna make it after all*—wore off quicker than I expected. We decided that it's best for our ten-year-old to stay with his dad and his house, a nesting arrangement that allows Sam to be with both parents every day but has turned me into a visitor. Jack and I still like each other, a relationship way too overtly non-traditional for our families. Since I moved out, all of them distrust me or fear me or maybe just don't know what to say.

Ethan suggests I pierce my belly button. I shake my head. I say, "I gave up piercing almost fifteen years ago." I show them the five earrings in my left ear.

"Maybe it's time for a new one," Ethan says. He disappears and returns in minutes from his Rasta van with a navel/eye brow piercing kit, still in its original packaging. He lays its contents on the table before me.

Griffin says, "Sure, most fathers expect a hidden stash of crack or

Ecstasy in the glove compartment. My son has piercing paraphernalia?"

"What?" Ethan says. "I got it free with my dread kit."

The needle appears to be hermetically sealed in an oblong tube. I work up a joke: *This might be what astronauts would use.*

I spent twelve years in Catholic school where it didn't take much to stand out in a crowd. By the time I was sixteen I'd pierced my ears ten times. What might a woman on the edge of thirty-three say: *I was doing cartilage before cartilage was cool.* I nearly tell this to Ethan with his three gold studs in each ear.

I know a pierced navel will certainly not make me any more or less that *goofy Rachel Unger*. I have been a marked woman for some time now.

I hold the belly ring, still in its plastic. I start to unscrew the tube. "Can I?"

"Sure," Ethan says. "Take a look."

He tells me that his girlfriend Tina pierced her belly button with a safety pin.

My toes curl inside of my running shoes. He says, "She had to take her ring out after about a month so her mother wouldn't see it."

As a teenager, I was so expert at hiding my piercings behind my long hair that my parents didn't notice all of my earrings until they saw my graduation picture. They know less about me now.

I pull out the three-inch needle. "That's the widest needle I've ever seen," I say. I couldn't even prick my own finger when I had to test my blood for glucose. I pick up the clamp, a vice grip for skin, and attach it to the fleshy part above my navel.

Griffin raises one eyebrow. "Perhaps for this birthday you can just look at the needle and pierce next year."

Ethan answers the phone before two rings. Ten p.m., his girlfriend. I've been here before for his thirty or ninety minute conversations.

I let my t-shirt cover the clamp. Surprisingly, it's not uncomfortable, less than a clothespin stuck to my finger. I read the kit's numbered directions.

> *1) Clamp the flap of skin you want pierced between the holes on the clamp. 2) Press the piercing needle through the holes on the clamp, piercing the skin clear through to the other side.*

Blood rushes to my face. It's the beer or the directions. These words are too complicated for me, especially since a thick needle through my flesh is in the middle of all this.

3) Now with the needle still piercing the skin, open the Ball Closure Ring and thread it through the hole behind the needle as you remove the needle. 4) Once the needle is removed and the Ball Closure Ring in, close the ring with the ball.

In minutes Ethan is back. He says, "You ready to do this?" I know from his eagerness that he's got to call back Tina.

"Let me see the needle again," I say.

Griffin says, "Don't do it if you're not sure." He is not an aggressive man, or perhaps surviving to middle-age has meant he learned when to back down.

"No, I want to," I lie. "I can do it. I gave birth, you know. What's a little pin prick? I cut my son's umbilical cord before I passed his placenta."

I imagine Ethan's toes twitch in his sandals. He hands me an ice cube for my belly, which I hold against my flesh until it turns white.

We all wash our hands. For the first time it strikes me how comical this is. I should tell them I lied about cutting Sam's umbilical cord.

I say, "This is going to be nothing." I rub the ice cube on my flesh caught in the vice grip. "I just have to keep Tina's mother from seeing." I laugh. This needle before me is making me giddy.

Ethan holds the needle like a pencil or a fork. His hand shakes. He says, "I think it's better if you do it yourself."

"Sure," I say.

He swabs over my skin and the clamp with alcohol, which appears out of nowhere. I hold the needle to my flesh and put the sharp point into my skin slowly enough for a tiny drop of blood to form. I don't feel any pain; the needle is that sharp.

The phone rings and Ethan scoops it up. "Nope," he says. "We're just about to." He sets the cordless phone on the table in front of me.

I hold the needle, inhale, look at my stomach. Since I was thirteen I've done 500 sit-ups a day. Twenty years of daily exercise based on my fear of getting fat or at least soft. Right now, I don't think of infection, the initial or later pain, the scarring of this piercing. Instead I ask, "Do you think I'll still be able to do sit-ups in the morning?" This may be my way out, explain to a buff sixteen-year-old that I want to continue to be my version of buff.

Ethan says, "Hard to say. It takes an average of three to six months to heal. You pierce an eyebrow or a tongue, the body fights to heal it. The belly button the body doesn't really care about."

I'm on my fourth beer so it sounds like Ethan has done his research. I hand him the needle.

"No," he says, perhaps more sure than he's been sure of anything this week or month. He says again, "No." He hands the needle to his father.

Griffin stands over me with the needle. He shakes his arms like a conductor, like some 50's comedian getting ready to perform an onstage operation.

He asks, "You're sure?" I've had this clamp on for half an hour. Of course I'm not sure.

I say, "I gave birth."

"You said that before," Griffin says.

"Yes," I say, "I'm sure."

This is one of those moments everyone has: the time you almost held onto a rope tied to a car on icy dead end streets; the time you almost tried cocaine. Your mother called you home or a phone rang and you changed your mind.

I am thirty-three years old tomorrow, Bastille Day. Perhaps this is my tri-life crisis, as if mid-life looming out there isn't bad enough. This would be a better story if I pierced my navel and it changed my outlook on my next sixty-six years, if I awoke reborn on my birthday as a tube-topped, chaps wearing, spit into the wind Harley babe who no longer pines for a family to accept her.

Griffin says, "You're sure you're sure." He drags out all of the R's and pokes the needle through in one thrust. He has pulled Band-Aids and plucked slivers from three children and two wives.

"Mother fucker," I scream.

"Through," Griffin says calmly.

Ethan picks up the phone, whispers. "Okay, Tina, the needle's through. Now we just have to get the ring in."

I say, "Let's take a break for a minute." Ethan nods and walks into the living room, murmuring into the phone.

"You did great," Griffin says. "One push and it was through."

I look at the needle through my flesh. No pain, no blood. My swollen belly button with this needle through it looks like a hotdog skewered sideways on a roasting stick. I laugh.

I say, "I can't believe I said *mother fucker* in front of a child."

Griffin rolls his eyes. "Two children, really. Tina listened to the whole procedure. Ethan's narrating like this is the goddamn golf channel. *He slowly approaches the abdomen.*"

I laugh until my stomach feels like I've been punched. I say, "I couldn't pierce it myself. Thanks for doing this."

"Nothing," he says. "I was a Boy Scout for one meeting. Though this was a little like shooting morphine into one of my children."

I get overly dramatic, think that this piercing seals us: a family connected not by birth but by choice, or perhaps best of all, deliverance in the hands of a lover.

Griffin looks at the needle and says in his best *cool guy* stance, "It was nothing. No problem."

Ethan returns and puts the phone in front of me on the table. "I'm sorry I swore," I say, loud enough for Tina to hear.

Griffin pulls the ring from its zipped plastic bag. His hands shake. He says to his son, "You'll have to do this." He hands it to Ethan.

The waistband on my shorts is doubled over to my underwear line. Ethan's wrist settles on my belly as he works. I haven't had a sixteen-year-old's hands on me since I was sixteen. I am tipsy enough to overlook this weirdness, sober enough not to mention it.

Ethan releases the clamp and tries to feed the ring through the hollowed end of the needle. He squints. "You okay?" he asks.

"This doesn't hurt," I say. "Surprisingly." After more poking with the ring, Ethan's fingers are covered in my blood.

Griffin pulls the top of the needle while Ethan inserts the ring.

"I can't see anything," Ethan says. His upper lip is wet with sweat.

Griffin goes to the kitchen drawer and returns with a flashlight. He aims it at my belly.

When I see my blood spread around by so many hands, I have to turn away. To calm myself, I watch their reflections in the four-foot windows beyond the table. They stoop over me. Griffin's cigarette smolders in the ashtray beside a bottle of bourbon. This image reminds me of a late night western: two outlaws pulling a bullet from a comrade.

"Almost there," Griffin narrates for me or for Tina, wondering, five miles away. "He's almost got it."

"You know," Ethan says, "if you'd have gone to the piercing shop downtown this whole thing would have been over in thirty seconds."

"Uh-haaa," I say. He's not my kid but there's still a lesson to be learned from this.

"Through," Griffin exclaims.

Ethan screws a tiny bead to my belly ring and picks up the phone in one swoop.

I say to all of us, "Sure a piercing shop would have been easy, but what's the story in that?"

BRUCE TAYLOR

HER

Things kept disappearing, the first few days after his wife moved out, like in some time-lapse comedy short, one moment it seemed he would reach for something and it'd be there, the next it was gone. A favorite carving knife, the sunflower potholder she had hung over the crack in the wall above the stove, a half a bottle of soy sauce, his children. The kids, at least, would reappear from time to time, only to disappear again. The plan, such as it was, was to let the children be where they wanted to be whenever they wanted to. Either with their mother at the apartment she had rented, nearby and large enough for all of them, or with him at what he assumed they would continue to regard and therefore favor as their home.

He bought a cell-phone and a Palm Pilot. He fired the cleaning woman he could no longer afford and who scared him anyway in her black tights and knee-pads. He found what struck him as a manly mop, something black and chromed, and an industrial sized dustpan. He started clipping coupons. He became haughty at how much money he could save. He remembered his wife used to say her momma used to say, "If you have to look at the price, you can't afford it." "If you can't find it cheaper," he began to hear himself saying, "you just aren't trying."

He bought a lot of stuff at the Dollar Store he found in the "As Seen on TV" aisle—"Tap Lights," "Wonder Broom," "Egg Wavers," the complete set. Each, he was sure, was the answer, or part of the answer; "the right tool for the job," or was it "work smarter not harder," or just the usual boy/man imperative, "be prepared," though no one ever says for what. He bought a pistol at the local pawnshop. He had always all his life wanted to own a gun but never could before without having to explain to someone. Three months later he bought some ammo. He resurrected the Bible from his sixth grade confirmation and placed it squarely on his bedside table. He wondered if it was too late for Rogaine and Pilates, Botox or Jesus. He retrieved his childhood teddy bear with one gnawed off ear from the attic, and the broke-backed, much worried, worn and nearly unreadable copy of the AA Bible, "Twenty-Four Hours a Day," his father had carried after his divorce the last twenty years of his life, one day at a time.

There were also those things he got rid of, or at least moved. All the kitschy crap in the kitchen, the refrigerator magnets, "Queen of the Kitchen," "Nurses need love too," and all quotations by Deepak Chopra. Pictures of the two of them together—the one with him in his 70's perm and her in her signature white dress and a waist you could wrap your hands around. The other of him in his beloved Yankees cap and brown leather bomber jacket looking as hip and unconcerned as a guy could only be with this sweet thing draped all over him and grinning—he was sure he wouldn't have ever said, even back then—like there was no tomorrow. These went into his six-year-old daughter's room because he knew she would treasure them for the next few years, and then for a long while not, and then again she would.

For six weeks after his wife moved out he nearly was washed away by panic. He did not even know his kids' doctor's name never mind their health insurance numbers. One, he remembered hearing somewhere, was allergic to eggs and one to peanuts. Which one was it liked the peanut butter on the same side with the butter and which with the jelly? Was it starve a cold and feed a fever, or the other way around? He never could do a dish that had not needed to be redone by his wife. When he thought he had made the bed she thought he had just "pulled it together."

Never mind his lack of any math skills beyond long, sometimes on his best days, division. His studied unfamiliarity with such institutions as, P.T.O., Sunday school, WMCA. His ignorance of Pokémon, American Girl or Blink—or was it Boink—101. He didn't know their teachers' names, their friends' names, last ones anyway, who their parents were, or where anybody lived. Christ, he thought, he could carve a better father out of a bar of soap.

He had been consigned to the peripheral, distanced, summarily or voluntarily but eventually X'ed out. His butt in his Barco-Lounger whenever he could manage it, his naps prioritized, his face always in an important book, his flat peasant hand wrapped around another double bourbon. Escaping the annoyance of children, their constant clutter, tuning out what he thought then was the noise, though he has realized since they have been gone, it could have been music.

Was it not so much that he made the wrong choices, but that he made, really, no choices. As with the rest of this life he merely lived through, not really lived at all. Maybe it's a roller coaster—all those predestined or random and rapid ups and downs—but it might also be at least a bit of a bobsled run, a bit determined by, if nothing else, which way you lean and when.

When his wife left she said she was the one who ought to move out because he had more stuff that would be harder to move– meaning, she said, the tonnage of his books and all the plants he worried into the yard. At the time, he also figured that his staying in the more familiar surroundings would give him an edge; a dad after all could never be a mom. As it turned out his wife left him with the decaying, if still charming, old house because she didn't want anymore the work that came with the ten rooms, the yard, the driveway, the failing roof, the increasingly impotent furnace, an incontinent water-heater, the very bones of this old house sinking into its own face like abandoned luggage. Neither evidently did she want anymore the cooking, bragging, nearly, as she did that in the pseudo-modern white-walled sterile over-priced and tasteless apartment complex she ended up in and seemed proud of, no real meals were made. So of course he went the other way, or tried to, at least for a while.

"Some of our best meals," she said, "I remember were Campbell's soup and sandwiches." She meant after her mom divorced her dad. It was not the first time he realized he should have, perhaps, been paying closer attention to how her mother had turned out and at what point his wife might have seen there was not that far for him to go to become her father? And then hating him for it, but this time able to say so and do something about it.

Finally after many leathery roasts, gruel-ish stews, casseroles and hot-dishes undistinguishable and unpalatable, he realized he would never know which children would be with him when or for how long. That, after all, was the plan, no plan at all. So he resorted to Rice-a-Roni, boxed mac and cheese, TV dinners—though to his children treats beyond measure to him tokens of shame. There were many breakfasts for dinner and soup and sandwiches, never Campbell's, a moral stance his kids often complained about. He always sprang for the good stuff.

Right about then began the second-guessing, the pathetic unstated shameful and shameless competitions. Why were they, the children together or separately, with her when they were, rather than with him? Who did they like better and why? So the oldest boy liked the rides to school, rather than humping the school bus in the morning. And the middle boy would go wherever whatever video game he was into at the time could be played on what system he had left where. And the youngest, his darling, the only girl, had to be mostly with Mommy because that was how Mommy raised her. Or that was how he, in his dumb complicity, allowed it all to go down. When he thought about children, before he had to really think about them at all except in the most abstract if proprietary of ways, it always seemed simple —Flintstones and bike helmets—give them a vitamin every morning and make sure their heads were protected. And while their mother was there, that theory held up pretty well.

And while his wife was still with them he never really wondered, guessed he didn't have to, what his kids thought about him. Since she left, however, it worried him considerably. It was one thing to be thought of, as he was sure the kids had, as part of a couple—Mom and Dad—something else entirely to bear the burden of their judgment never mind their memory separately. He knew, or supposed anyway, the kids saw some of the blatant differences between them all along. Mom the good cop, him left, he always felt, with the other role, one he never would have imagined himself having to be cast in. Mom: math, church, science, headstands, roller-blading, lullabies and homemade desserts. Here he suspected he was short-changing her, misunderstanding again probably.

Him—he wasn't sure—maybe drinking and smoking, laughing and talking loud with lots of friends around the kitchen table. His goofiness, he hoped, his loving teasing and his willingness to play. Or was he and would he remain forever in their memory this loud, sloppy, old man, nearly always smothered in ashes, always smelling of something distasteful and foreign. A fat guy with bad teeth and a fondness for weird music. Maybe they think he's an asshole, the way he heard his wife told people they did. Wasn't that how he thought of his old man at their age, wasn't that how you were supposed to?

Dancing, first in his den, while her mother was still in the house — usually asleep by now—then back to the smooth expanse of kitchen floor his wife's leaving had opened up for both of them. Saturday nights, the local public radio station locked on to jazz and swing. "Let's do our moves," his daughter would say.

A simple jitterbug cross-over, a basic box step, your standard fox trot, your basic waltzing for the ages. An exaggerated dip, an overstated *pas de duex.* His smile when they did that, the small abandon and trust of her body

—that realization—here, of course, was the perfect girl for him, but with the kind of a guy he'd never let her near.

One morning, a Wednesday—Tuesday night being the only time he was sure to have her each week—he found himself one on one with her in the downstairs bathroom. She was adamant about changing her pierced earrings before she went off to fourth grade. *Woman's work*, he did not have the time to think right then, if there ever were any. She had already taken one earring out and was desperate and abandoned enough to ask him to put the new one in.

Now if a hundred angels could dance on the head of a pin, then this earring was just one of the earrings just one of those angels might have worn. He had never felt anything so small, so beyond his grasp never mind manipulation by his meaty, manlier than ever fingers. Worse yet, each of his timid thrusts brought first a small yelp of pain, then a flinch – some of which were not from him alone.

Yet somehow, thanks to her brave coaxing and, he had to imagine, the Chaos Theory of the Universe, the damned thing eventually went where it was supposed to. Somehow now, trembling increasingly, beyond tears, which meant he knew he could not cry them, his job now, he figured, was to convince her that wearing two mismatched earrings was the fashion's rage.

A sliver of soap stuck to the sink. The hand towel that remained crammed grotesquely behind the towel-bar he knew without even checking was rancid and damp. The stain in the fine cracks where the linoleum met the base of the toilet bowl he had watched go from yellow to brown, to something approaching lime-green.

She already had the second earring out, folded the replacement into his sweaty palm. Her eyes were his mother's, which meant his, her skin his olive tone also, but her voice at that moment was her mother's, "You did fine with the first one. You can do this one too."

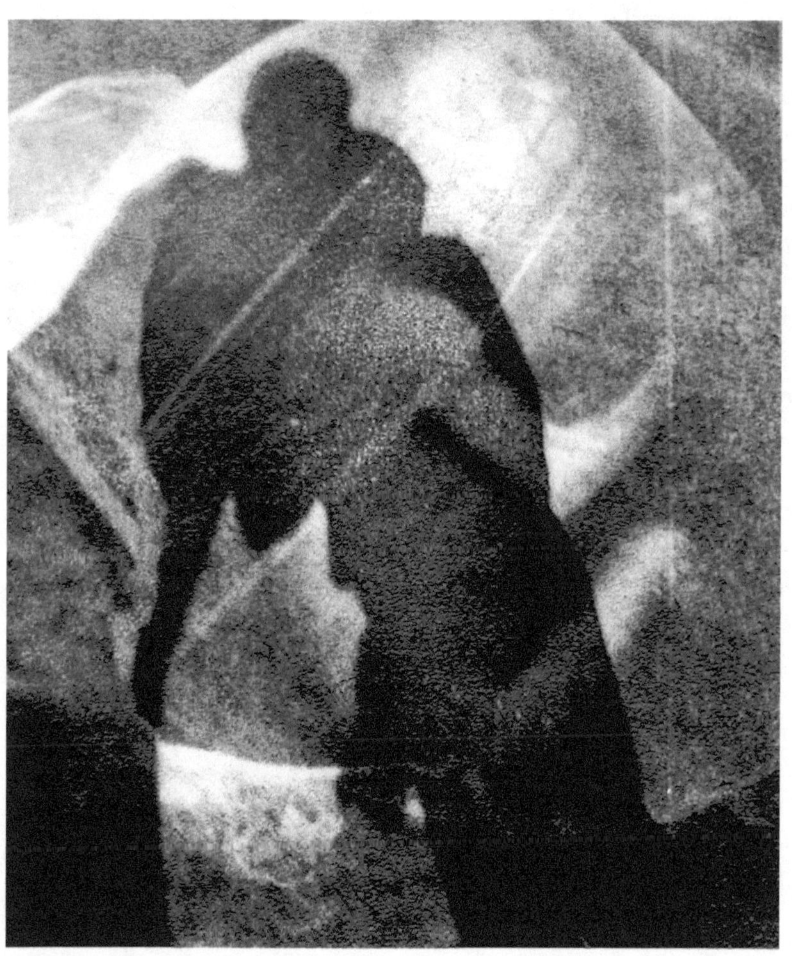

CATHERINE R. FIORELLO

INTERFERENCE

Forgive me, my dear daughter
for using everything as grist for poems,
even our arguments
which, by the way, I don't understand.

When I called you today,
to mend our yelling match,
your father's background remark
made you hang up

on my call.
My peace-making, conciliatory call.
I didn't know whether to cry or hurl the phone.

Bonds are so fragile these days,
flung across sound spectrums
that bounce from tower to tower –
our attempt at detachment.

Even face to face,
messages are encrypted.
But why fret when,
though I can't decode you,
I still find you perfect?

THE BLUE HERON

I was in Costa Rica when my grandson drowned.
I'd called home to say hello,
resting a crumpled bag of vegetables on the ground near the outdoor phone,
heard Alexa screaming, "The baby fell in the water,"
ran back to my Spanish hostess shouting,
"Must fly home."
The woman rocked me while she made arrangements.

Suddenly, I could speak perfect Spanish
as if the Spirit gave me tongues to grieve.
A cab driver lifted the rosary hanging from
his rear view mirror and pressed it into my hand
saying, "Para el niño."
Standing in line and on the plane, I told my story,
calling family in each city,
like prayers offered up
at the stations of the cross.
Charlie met me at the airport and we drove to
the Children's Hospital where he lay
hooked up but dead,
his blood like paste,
my daughter's clothes still wet.

I rubbed his stiff little hands 'til they were soft again,
but life didn't return.

The next day we saw the blue heron
standing on the dock where he'd fallen in,
heard a huge wind tear at the trees
while my daughter, drunk on misery,
shook her fist at God.

TERESA TUMMINELLO BRADER

AGE APPROPRIATE

Her wet hair weighs heavy on my palm. I move my hand up to hold her head steady as I run a comb through the tangles. Zoe, my husband's granddaughter, wants me to use a brush, and I explain how wet hair doesn't break with a wide-toothed comb. She seems interested, and I imagine when she gets back home she'll tell her dad she needs a comb like this one.

I can discern the different shades in Zoe's hair when it's wet: honey yellow, sandy beige, pale brown. It'll dry into a tumble of dark goldenrod, looking much as her mom Karen's hair does in the childhood photos of Karen and her twin sister Tina. My stepdaughters—I seldom think of them that way, since they're only ten years younger than I—aren't identical, neither in looks nor in the way they're wired. Tina lives nearby with her husband and three children. Karen, in and out of rehab, sent Zoe away before her fifth birthday. Zoe's almost eight.

"Who are the people in these pictures?" Zoe asks. She sounds annoyed. We're sitting on the bed in the extra bedroom. Her two front teeth are coming in, and they give her upper gum a flattened look. She's gazing at a portrait of me at five years old with my younger brothers. My mom gave me the painting after her house flooded, after the levees broke, saying she could no longer risk attachment to objects.

On the adjoining wall hangs a black-and-white photograph of my dad's law school class at Tulane. Before the photo was salvaged from the family home, it hung in my dad's study since before my birth. The one woman and the one black man in the group—Dad graduated in the mid-fifties—are what the adult eye notices. I don't have space for these refugees elsewhere, and the guestroom seems a good site for memorabilia.

I believe Zoe's holding back a second question: What are these people doing in my room? I head off that potential exasperating question by answering the one she did ask. As I explain each picture, her eyes glaze over; she's quiet.

Though for most of her month-long yearly visit, Zoe is settled in at her aunt Tina's house where she's surrounded by cousins, my husband Dave insists on telling her that the guestroom is hers. Zoe's oldest cousin sputters in disbelief whenever Zoe calls it her room; the younger ones believe her—for now.

For the sake of the grandchildren, I've left up the family photos that include Nancy, Dave's first wife. During the early months of my marriage to Dave, I encountered their engagement photo while sorting out a cedar chest. The sight of their young, fresh faces gave me such an ache that I buried the photograph at the bottom of the chest to stop myself from pulling it out every day.

Dave and I had been married less than a year when Zoe was born. He waited at the hospital for hours, same as he did for the births of Tina's children. My son Greg and I stopped to see the newborn before I dropped him off at his high school for summer football workouts. Dave placed Zoe in my arms and turned to talk to Karen. Before I grasped what was happening, Karen's boyfriend Lance, like some kind of avenging angel, rose up from the chair by the bed and took the baby from my arms.

Stung by Lance's wordless rebuke, I stood up and turned to Greg. "Ready?" Dave looked at me, his eyes squinched together quizzically. He hadn't seen Lance removing Zoe from my embrace, and I knew he'd blame our brief visit on Greg having to get to practice. I wondered how far back Lance and Karen had planned the snub.

Karen and Lance blamed me for the conflicts between her and Dave during the short time she lived with us. After listening to her complaints, Dave would patiently tell Karen, 25 years old then, that I was his wife, that this was my house too, and that I could refrigerate the butter instead of leaving it on the counter if I wanted.

When forced to speak to me, Karen didn't refer to Dave and me as a couple.

She spouted phrases like "Dad's house," "Dad has toys for the kids," even at those times when it didn't make sense to use that singular paternal moniker. Dave employed first person plural whenever he could; he'd done so from our beginning. Ten years before I met Dave, I shed my first husband like a worthless skin. A lone wolf, I needed time to become accustomed to someone who wanted to attend Greg's football games with me and was interested in my career.

We met when Dave hired me to plan his firm's holiday party, called a Christmas party before political correctness came to his practice. Semi-retired, working as a legal consultant when his health permitted, Dad recommended my event-planning services to Dave during the break of a seminar on construction litigation. Nancy died two years before and I quickly realized that Dave, happily married for many years, was lonely. I tried to ignore my own loneliness by keeping busy with my job and Greg's activities. Dinners and drinks with friends of friends disappointed, not seeming worth the effort. Dave's inability to be untrue to himself allowed me to relax and to carve out the same kind of niche for myself.

I enjoyed buying birthday and holiday gifts for the grandchildren, a task Dave didn't care for. Every Easter I selected age-appropriate items, including books, for the grandchildren's baskets. By the end of one holiday afternoon, the books were glanced at, scattered like autumn leaves in a yard and forgotten by all of the grandkids, except three-year-old Zoe. Karen, already broken up with Lance, granted her daughter "two more minutes" of playtime before departing, and Zoe started to gather the discards, crawling under the big maple dining table and under the low-slung armchairs in the den to retrieve them. The stack cradled in her arms grew until there were no more books to harvest. She toddled behind her mother on the way to the front door until Karen, turning, noticed Zoe's newfound treasures. Shaking her head and referring to Zoe as "my daughter, the thief," Karen helped her sister Tina redistribute the books with no complaint from the little girl. I smiled at Zoe, wishing I could tell her that she was a rescuer and not a thief. Before they left, both Karen and Tina instructed the children to "thank Grandpa for the Easter baskets."

Though Dave and I saw more of Zoe after her parents' break-up, she had trouble remembering my name. Once she asked us if I was Grandpa's mom. Dave and I laughed—I'm ten years younger than he is—and told each other that Zoe didn't understand the concept of husband-and-wife yet. Privately, I believed Zoe's confusion was due to Karen pretending I didn't exist. After Zoe moved away, I mailed her books, cards and letters, signing everything in big block letters with 'we love you and we miss you, from Grandpa and Jane.'

A month before Zoe was sent away, though unaware of the impending day, all of us celebrated Dave's birthday at O'Henry's. The grandkids started chasing each other around the restaurant until Tina's husband Wayne corralled them, shooing them back to their seats. Zoe ran off again, scooping up peanut shells from the floor and tossing them in the air. Without a word, Wayne hoisted Zoe from the back, his arms around her waist, her feet kicking into his thighs. She made herself a dead weight in his arms, as he waddled back to the table with her. If the expression on Zoe's face betrayed her thoughts and those thoughts could've been activated, Wayne would've been transformed into a toad or some other slimy creature conjured up by a four-year-old. Sitting across from me, Karen gazed at her crawfish-and-corn bisque as she brought the soupspoon to her lips.

The day we found out Zoe was leaving, Lance had already sent his mother Elizabeth from their Philadelphia home to collect her. Zoe was at our house, swimming with a pregnant Tina and her two children, when Karen called to tell Dave about the arrangement. Elizabeth had driven through Meridian by then, less than three hours away. Tina, Dave and I stood at the edge of the pool, worrying, speculating, and watching the children splash around in their orange and blue swim vests. Elizabeth had visited once, but we doubted Zoe remembered her.

Keys in hand, Elizabeth entered through the gate and trod through the backyard toward the pool. Somewhere between my and Dave's ages, no-nonsense but pleasant, she bent down and told Zoe she was taking her to her mom, which was technically true. They would pick up Zoe's clothes and some toys before heading east. Unbeknownst to us, Karen had been packing for Zoe all morning.

Trying to hide my trembling, I brought Zoe inside. Karen had told Dave over the phone that Zoe would be with Lance and his family for the remainder of the summer, only a month. We figured she was lying; we knew Karen's latest boyfriend didn't care for children. Before the month was over, Lance enrolled Zoe in a Pennsylvania kindergarten with Karen's approval.

I unfurled the fluffy beach towel I'd wrapped around Zoe, drying her with it as she giggled. Zoe giggled if she simply *thought* someone were about to tickle her. The towel sported two penguins, a girl and a boy, with leis around their necks and flip-flops on their feet. The male penguin had his flipper around the female. Between rubs, I clasped Zoe to me, hiding my moist eyes in the terrycloth on her shoulder.

She escaped from my arms, running around the room, laughing, ducking, wanting me to chase her. Trying not to cry, I said her grandmother was waiting and told her to come here and get dressed. Regretting my impatience once she obeyed, I enfolded her in my arms again, but she had had enough of hugs.

Stashing her pink Minnie Mouse swimsuit in a plastic Winn-Dixie bag, I led Zoe out by the hand. Tina, dripping wet from the pool, hugged Zoe hard. Her arms down at her sides, Zoe smiled over Tina's shoulder. Dave accompanied Zoe and Elizabeth across the recently mown lawn, and I watched the back of the little girl as she strode between her two grandparents. She walked as she always did, with a straight posture and long steps, as if she had a purpose in mind and was determined to see it through.

Tina burst into tears. "How can Karen let Zoe go off like that? And with someone she doesn't even know!" I put an arm around Tina, feeling the slickness of the exposed skin of her back and shoulder, feeling awkward hugging a wet, pregnant woman. I didn't know how to comfort her.

A year later on her first day back Zoe marched around the guestroom interrogating me. I sat on the floor, my legs stretched out, ankles crossed, watching and answering. Are these books mine? Are these DVDs mine? (No, but you may read and watch the ones for kids.) Why's this box under my bed? (That's where I store it.) Why are these coats in my closet? (Ditto.) I sensed she was testing me, and my frustration with Dave over this issue increased. I couldn't adequately explain to a five-year-old that many houses in the New Orleans area didn't have much storage space, and keeping shelves and a closet empty for eleven months out of the year to keep a child happy for one went against my grain.

My dad died that summer, and the day after his funeral Karen asked Dave to keep Zoe overnight. Tina and her family had just left for a short vacation. The majority of any time Karen spent with her daughter occurred while they slept. As soon as Zoe woke, they materialized either on Tina's doorstep or on ours. Dave never questioned Karen, who was always vague about what she was doing. Convinced that Karen was going out drinking with her new loser boyfriend on the one night she planned to have Zoe, I snapped at Dave for enabling her.

He followed me into the bedroom, and I enclosed myself inside the lightweight down comforter I bought shortly after our wedding. I was years past the fact that this handmade bed had been Dave and Nancy's, and Dave supported my converting the room's color scheme from royal blue to deep purple. Huddled into a ball, I couldn't see him but pictured him standing by the bed. I knew he wanted to help me but was bewildered as to how. I knew that later I would feel bad for making him feel bad. After a few moments he left the room, quietly shutting the door, and I erupted into tears. I heard the back door close and then the clink of the long-handled net against the high sides of the swimming pool.

The doorbell chimed, penetrating my cocoon. Noises from the backyard informed me that Karen and Zoe had left the front door and walked to the back. I heard Dave say, "Not a problem, she can stay however long you want." Desiring to drown out their voices, I flipped over and pressed the power button on the TV remote control. A baseball game appeared on the screen and I left it on, drifting in and out of sleep, crying when awake.

Dave had already lost his parents and a wife, but grief was new to me. My grandparents died when I was young and I wasn't close to them. My excessive crying all that afternoon and into the night scared me, and I didn't leave the bedroom. Dave lay on the floor of the guestroom that night, as he did whenever Zoe asked. Afterward I told myself that Dave hadn't failed me, that

I could only grieve alone, that I'd chosen the occasion.

Remembering how she felt when her mother died, Tina was appalled at her sister. But Karen knew a request concerning Zoe would always get a positive response from her dad. Dave told me he did it for Zoe, not Karen, and that I'd understand when I was a grandparent. I imagined grandparenthood to be an exclusive club that I'd have to petition for membership, one that would refuse me when they found out about my social defect.

That day was the only time Karen saw Zoe that summer. When Zoe wasn't with her aunt, uncle and cousins, she was with Dave and me. One morning Zoe woke up with an elevated temperature, vomiting once. Before going to the office for a few hours, Dave tucked her back in bed. I checked on her shortly after, trying to touch her forehead with mine, hovering while she hid her hot face from me. She smiled as I wriggled my head onto the pillow next to hers. I kissed her cheek, and she fell back asleep.

When Zoe woke up again, her fever was gone. She changed out of Barbie pajamas and into a striped sundress that Tina had bought her. She scampered outside to find Dave pulling weeds from the azalea beds. Before she closed the back door, I heard her yelling to him that she wanted to go swimming. He replied maybe tomorrow, that we needed to make sure she was well first. The door swung shut.

From the kitchen bay window, I observed Zoe standing under the grapefruit tree, her demeanor altering as she realized she wasn't going to get her way. Arms folded across her chest and her lips in a tight line, she slammed the back door with a thrust of her slight body. She stomped across the den and into the guestroom, throwing herself on the bed. She left the door open and I could see her while I prepared dinner. Zoe looked so much like Karen then that my own internal temperature flared. I felt like shaking her. She perched on the edge of the bed, a sullen look plastered on her pale face, her mouth drawn down but her eyes upward, waiting for me to notice. When she lived with Karen, Zoe existed within a habitual loop of power struggles and silent treatments.

I chopped the carrots, tossed them in a pan with the roast, and closed the oven door. Zoe lay on the bed fully stretched out, staring at the stick-on stars affixed to the ceiling. I sat next to her and she spun over, determined not to meet my eyes. I patted her back until I spotted a smile peeking between the strands of her hair. My lips located her cheek, the color returned to her face, and she giggled.

Months later I dreamed about that day. Because I hadn't seen her in so long, I kissed her cheek over and over again in the dream. She wore the same happy smile in my dream that she had on when I coaxed her out of that bad mood.

Zoe didn't visit the next summer, and Lance agreed to let her come the following Christmas. She spent every night of the holiday season at Tina's in the company of her cousins. Bringing Zoe to us beforehand, Tina and her family visited Wayne's relatives the afternoon of Christmas Day. Zoe shot me accusing looks as I explained why my mom was staying in *her* room. While Mom dawdled in the bathroom, I discovered Zoe crawling on her hands and knees, as if on a reconnaissance mission, down the polished wooden floor of the hallway toward the guestroom. Mom had left the door ajar, and Zoe crept in without needing to push it open.

I followed Zoe in as she stood up, her eyes roaming, checking to see if each thing had waited for her in its usual place and that the walls remained cotton-candy pink, though Dave had assured her over the phone that they had. Zoe gaped at Mom's cosmetics, deodorant, hairspray and curlers strewn on the floor, and at the clothing heaped on top of the bed. A pale blue nightgown spilled from the pile, the sleeves wafting to the floor, evocative of Zoe who liked to bend upside down at the edge of the bed. Giggling, she'd wait in that position, her blonde head touching the carpet, until Dave or I noticed.

"She's leaving tomorrow morning," I whispered into Zoe's ear, my hands on her shoulders, as I escorted her back to the den. Her feet dragged as she trudged in front of me.

I was being solicitous of Mom's feelings on our second Christmas without Dad and without the family home. The first Christmas after the storm the house was gutted, stripped bare of everything that made a house a home. By this Christmas the house had been sold to a young family man who was renovating it himself.

The hurricane only cost Dave and me some pecan trees, a portion of the yard fence and the aboveground pool, which had been almost as old as the twins. We entertained my brothers and their families on Christmas Eve, and Mom was spending one more night. She was residing at my aunt's until a smaller house she bought was ready, and the sisters needed a break from each other.

Mom's doctor, working from a trailer outside his gutted office and understanding her constant tears, prescribed Zoloft after we returned from our evacuation in Houston. Over a year later, I worried that Mom was drinking too much on top of the antidepressant. Role reversal came to the two of us, though my mother was neither elderly nor chronically ill as my dad had been.

I worked out of the house, my business slow with the recovery of the area ongoing. Sometimes I struggled to remember that Dave's home belonged to me too and that I wasn't living with just Greg in a rented Uptown flat or a Mid-City shotgun, a raised house that ended up with four feet of canal water inside. I drove by and saw its brown waterline. Saints and LSU theme parties were popular this past football season. Fans were ready to inject some fun into their exhausted lives, and I dreamed in black and gold and purple.

Zoe's obstinacy surfaces occasionally. I prompt her into saying "please" to soften the tone she uses when asking something of Dave. She grins in apology, her features changing from demanding to patient, as if she merely needed a little reminder. Dave doesn't ask it of his grandchildren, but Tina makes sure her kids are polite. If I pick up Karen's slack, I figure that's better than my getting angry with Dave for allowing Zoe to be rude to him.

After I finish combing her hair, Zoe hops off the bed and faces me. "How long have you lived here?" When I answer, her eyes widen in surprise. It's more years than she's been alive, and she thinks she's been alive a long time.

I send her off to brush her teeth. "Need any help?"

"No, I'm good."

While Dave tells Zoe good-night, I straighten the bathroom, rinsing the tub and removing its contents: a red boat, a damp washcloth, fish-shaped plastic bottles of orange-mango shampoo and cherry-kiwi bath gel, a yellow bucket. Replacing the hand towel in its ring on the wall, I look for the new toothbrush I left out for Zoe, expecting to see it next to the sink. The spot is bare, and I glance toward the far corner of the countertop. Zoe has stuck her toothbrush in the ceramic holder where Greg, home for summer break, keeps his. The handles of the brushes nestle into one another, the heads just barely touching.

SPIRIT OF ADOPTION

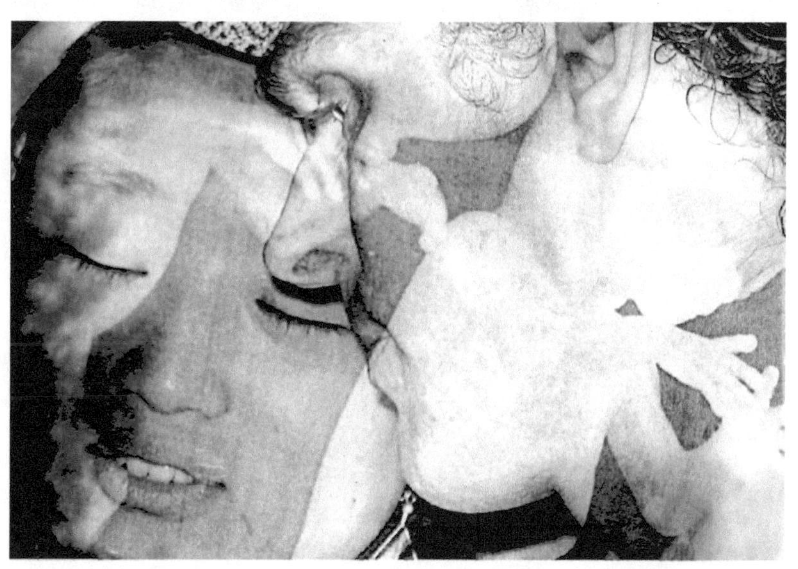

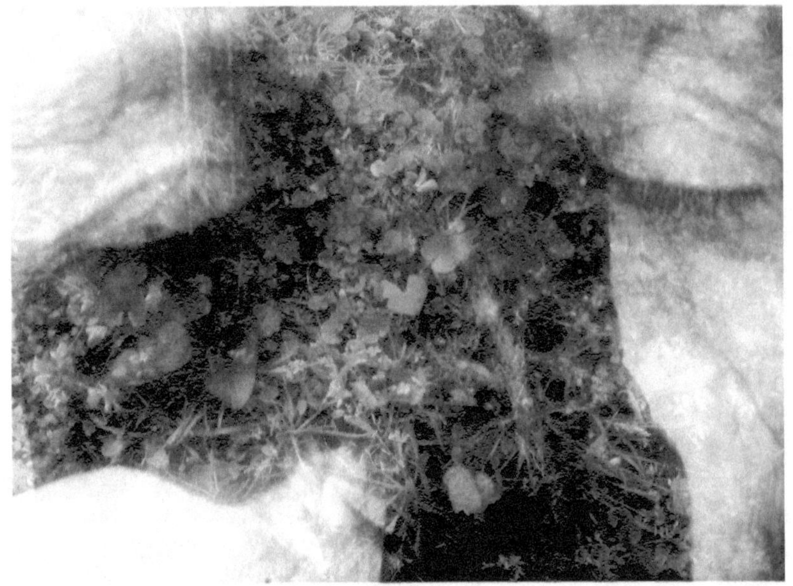

PHYLLIS LANGTON

'MOTHER' LADY

In October 1946, at age thirteen, I was discharged from the Natick, Massachusetts orphanage I had lived in for seven years. While waiting for the house mother, Mrs. Florence Kahn, whom I loved and trusted, to drive me downtown to the bus which I would take to Logan Airport to catch my airplane, I sat on the front steps of Wilber Home, looking at the flagpole for the last time. Every morning at 6:00 a.m., we stood at attention with our right hand over our heart, and said the Pledge of Allegiance as two children raised the flag. At 6:00 p.m., every evening, we sang, "Day is done, gone the sun…" while two children lowered, folded, and placed the flag in a frame, ready for the next day. These rituals brought order and security to my life. I said a mental farewell to the flag and waved. It was time to go.

I was headed for California to join my sixteen-year-old sister, Audrey, whom I hadn't seen in seven years, and our mother, whom I didn't remember ever knowing. I knew I would miss my school friends and longtime friends at the orphanage. We were a noisy bunch of girls, with great zeal for life. We were happy.

I clasped the envelope that held my airplane ticket and school records. I had little else to carry with me since we didn't own our clothes, and I had no pictures. My only treasures were a copy of Silas Marner, and a book of Mark Twain stories.

We climbed into the station wagon, chatting about my adventure. It was the first time I sat in the front seat. It felt hard, and looked like new. I noticed large circles of lights on the dashboard. As children, we sat in the back seats every Sunday on our way to the Congregational Church. Once, we rode to the movie to see Bambi, our only social outing. During the summer, we rode to the lake to swim. We used to sing camp songs and hang our heads out the window, waving to every car that passed.

Mrs. Kahn was not a fast driver, but this day she was especially deliberate as we approached downtown Natick. She slowed down on Main

Street near the common square where I had watched the Boston Marathon runners pass by several times over the years. "Phyllis, do you recognize that woman standing on the corner?"

"No, I don't remember seeing her before," I said.

We rode around the block and returned to the same spot. She asked me again.

"No. Where is my bus?" I asked.

Mrs. Kahn stopped the car at the sidewalk, where the woman opened the car door and said, "Hello, Florence. I'll take over from here."

I didn't know who she was or what she meant. The lady told me to get out of the car. Mrs. Kahn nodded her head for me to get out. She drove away so fast that I didn't have a chance to tell her goodbye.

"Who are you? Are you going to take me to my bus?" I asked.

"Yes. I am your mother," she said.

"You're not my mother. I'm on my way to California to live with my sister and my mother."

She grabbed my arm and shoved me to where a bus was waiting. "Hurry up, or we'll miss the bus. You can talk when we get on the bus."

"Is this the right one? I need to get to the airport," I said.

She continued to push me towards the bus. I got on, followed by the lady who claimed to be my mother

When we were seated, I looked her over carefully and asked, "Where did you get those stockings? When we did our concerts and choir performances at school this year, we had to put orange paste on our legs to look like stockings. The teachers told us that nobody had real stockings because of the war. There wasn't any silk to make them. Where did you get yours?"

"Oh, that is silly, I've always had stockings," she said.

I didn't like her and sat with my face pressed hard against the window, staring as miles of road passed. I was tired and scared and wondered why Mrs. Kahn had dumped me out of her car without a word. I decided to get the bus driver's help. First, I needed to get past this lady.

I pushed my face close to hers and studied it. She had the same snapping green eyes as mine, the same hook in her nose, which my school pals called my 'French crooked nose', and the same shaped teeth. The only difference was that her skin was chalk white.

"Who are you, really?" I asked.

"I am your mother. Let me see the envelope so I can help you get where you want to go."

"No, I'll ask the bus driver, and he'll help me."

I tried to leave my seat, but the lady wouldn't move. I wanted to kick her stockings, but something held me back.

"Before you bother the bus driver, let me look in the envelope to see if your ticket is in there." Her voice was slippery and smooth like the big bad wolf with Red Riding Hood.

I sat down, gave her my envelope, and hung over her lap while she opened it.

"Look. The only things in here are your school records."

"There must be some mistake. Mrs. Kahn told me I was going to California." I started to cry, something I rarely did.

"That plan has changed. You're going to Boston to live with your sister. We moved there a year ago."

"What? So why haven't I seen my sister?"

"The bus is pulling into Park Street, now. We'll get the subway to where you'll be living with your sister," she said.

"When will I see my sister?" I stifled my sobs, folded my hands on my lap and knew I would only be happy when I saw my sister.

"In about 20 minutes."

We took the subway to Massachusetts Avenue and walked down Commonwealth Avenue to a row of old gray stone buildings with several floors, opposite the Somerset Hotel, which was alight with bright fixtures at the entry way. We entered a large room on the first floor where Audrey was waiting. The room had high ceilings, two tiny beds like in the orphanage, a couch and an area with a sink and a hot plate. There was no bathroom.

I squealed at Audrey and hugged her. Her return hug was lifeless. I held onto her in case she fell over after my enthusiastic welcome. The sunshine was missing from her face, but she still had her beauty mark—a mole on her right check.

The mother lady interrupted our reunion. "The bathroom is on the second floor. Use it only when you have to. There's no food in the refrigerator. There are a few cans of spaghetti in the closet."

"Can we eat now? I couldn't eat my breakfast this morning because I was so excited, but I'm hungry, now."

"Don't interrupt. You're signed up for the ninth grade at the same place as your sister, Girls' High School, in South Boston. Take the subway we were on tonight to Tremont Street, then walk the remaining way. If Audrey feels like going to school tomorrow, she'll show you how to get there. If not, here's a map of Boston." She dropped it on the only table in the room.

"I don't know where South Boston is. Is this North Boston?"

She continued, "You're to see the guidance counselor tomorrow to get a job right away and a social security card. There is subway money in the drawer for a week, and be sure to take your school records. You'll sleep on the couch tonight."

The 'mother' lady went upstairs to use the bathroom.

"I'm tired, Phyllis. I need to sleep. I'm happy you are here." Audrey gave me a faint smile and went to bed.

I fell asleep on the couch with my clothes on. I didn't have anything else.

When I awoke the next morning, the 'mother' lady was gone. I went to school by myself.

AMY DENGLER

GLEANINGS

Treasure is often missed on first pass:
coins buried at the beach,
orchards full of fallen fruit. At Ellen's
we spy Macs and Cortlands idling on the branches
and nearly miss the profusion of drops
dappling the ground.

The windfall at my brother's house:
two adopted daughters –
knees of dark honey, cheeks like Winesaps.
Gleanings from another life
they settle into their parents' laps
the way seeds nestle at the heart of the apple.

KALIA ABIADE

UNTANGLED

I can't say that I love to do Asha's hair. I don't even like it. My fingers dread the cramps that come along with trying to grip and manipulate her short, tricky locks. My back aches at the mere thought of contorting my body to reach that last little braid at the nape of her neck. Even my head hurts in anticipation of the test of wills that is sure to come.

My neutral tone: "Asha, please try to remember to keep your head still."

With a bit of treacle: "Please try to be still, OK? It will be easier for both of us."

Getting desperate: "If you can be still for 10 minutes straight, you can watch 'High School Musical'."

Now I've lost it: "If you don't sit still right now your TV privileges for the week are gone. Do you hear me? GONE!"

It ain't pretty. This is probably not one of those bonding moments that she and I will recall fondly as some mother-daughter pairs do. Like many other aspects of our relationship, hair time is a struggle—often it is a complicated mess.

When I was a child, a lot of my black playmates wore chin-length plaits or cornrows weaved tightly against their scalps. Their heads were often adorned with colorful beads and plastic snaps. I never asked why my hair was different than theirs because I knew. My dad is African-American, which means I have dark, thick hair; my mom is Filipino, so it is also long, wavy and fairly easy to untangle. I grew up in a part of California where people were used to seeing and meeting people who were from different races or who were "mixed." But there was still an attitude toward me—sometimes spoken, sometimes not—that I was not black enough. It didn't matter that I looked like my African-American grandmother, or that I had brown skin, or that I identified myself as black. To others, I still was not black enough, and I started to believe it. That childhood feeling stuck with me and often left me trying to find ways to prove that, despite my hair, I was.

About six years ago I married an amazing man with a spunky two-year-old daughter. Asha had an adorable fuzzy 'fro that was barely long enough to twist. That first summer that she stayed with us, my job on the hair front was easy. I'd wash and comb it out, stick a cute clip on the side or place a colorful band around her head, and we were out the door.

The next summer, Asha arrived with skinny, 2-inch-long braids all over her head. "Cute," I thought. Then I panicked. Who is going to do her hair when it's time to take those down? I surely didn't know how. I spent about a week ticking off the names of all of my black friends who might know how to do hair. I thought of the girls who'd babysat her before. Then I stopped. I was her stepmom. It was my job to do her hair.

I called my mother-in-law to ask what supplies I would need. I gathered some spray conditioner, a rattail comb, a brush, and a bunch of clips. I flipped on Sesame Street, sat on the couch, and placed Asha on a small stool between my feet. I must have stared at her hair for a few minutes before I did anything. Then I flipped the comb and made the first part. I had no idea where I was going with that part, but two hours later, neat squares of braided hair covered her little head. It really wasn't that bad. As the weeks and years passed, I became more adept at braiding. It still took a solid two hours from start to finish, but it was a pleasant two hours and my parts were straight and the braids were presentable.

Just after she turned six, Asha came to live with us for the school year. It turned out to be a challenging time for us all. The summers and breaks she'd spent with us in previous years now seemed like they had been carefree vacations with flexible schedules. Now Jeremiah and I had to enforce strict bedtimes and early mornings. Asha had to adjust to being away from her mom and living full-time under a different set of rules. We found ourselves talking often with Asha's teacher about discipline problems at school. We also were experiencing a few of our own at home. On top of all of this, I was six-months pregnant.

Many of our frustrations were played out during hair time. Asha expressed herself by refusing to sit still. I responded by losing my patience. It was now taking three or four hours to finish her hair—one time it took all day. And after all of that time spent, her hair didn't look all that great. I was at a loss. I used to be able to handle this. How could it be that this task was easier when she was three and now it was nearly impossible?

I called my good friend Azizah for some advice. First she reassured me that I was doing a good job, that I was a good stepmom and that I shouldn't feel bad about being frustrated. She told me that one way I showed my love for Asha was by simply learning how to care for her hair in the first place. These were words I needed to hear. Then, she told me that when she was a girl, her mom sent her to a braider. It wasn't that her mom couldn't do her hair, but why fuss and fight over it to get mediocre results when someone with more skill can do it in half the time? Then more time was left to spend doing things they actually enjoyed.

If Asha were my biological daughter, I probably wouldn't have thought twice about sending her off to get her hair done. My love and concern for her would have been a given. But because I am her stepmother, I felt like I had to prove how much I care. I felt an enormous amount of guilt at the mere thought of not doing her hair. I was afraid that giving up on Asha's hair would be seen as giving up on Asha. On some level, I was also afraid that my inability or unwillingness to persevere would make me, once again, not black enough.

On the other hand, something had to be done. These hair conflicts were starting to take over. Instead of enjoying our time together, Asha and I could spend an entire Saturday fighting. I wanted her to look nice and feel good about the way she looked, and I wanted her to be happy. I wanted to be happy. Jeremiah, who usually looked on helplessly and rarely intervened, told me of a woman named Dee who braided men's hair at his barbershop. I was still a little unsure.

I started to think of the things Asha and I enjoy doing together. We like to bake cookies and bread from scratch. She's a great sous chef at dinnertime. We take weekly trips to the library to feed her insatiable appetite for reading. I love watching her strike poses when I take her shopping. And she's a great companion at bookstores and cafés where we like to read and sip hot drinks. I realized that hair time does not have to define or dominate our relationship. By taking that stress out of our lives, we could make room for real bonding time. I told Jeremiah to call Dee and make that appointment.

I looked up from my magazine at the barbershop just as Dee was securing the last few beads. I admired Asha's hair. Every part was perfectly straight, each little braid spaced just so, and a few dangled just above the rim of her glasses like bangs. Asha was beaming and I hadn't lifted a finger.

She skipped every few steps in the parking lot and stopped to check out her reflection in each car window we passed on the way to our car. After she strapped in, Asha touched the top of her head and gently stroked the braids that lay against her neck. She was happy.

"Wanna go to Starbucks?" I asked.

"Can I have whipped cream on my hot chocolate?"

"Of course."

"Sprinkles too?

"Sure. Why not?"

"YES!"

I wanted to shout as well. Instead I exhaled and drove ahead.

JOHN RYBICKI

SILHOUETTE

I'm folding clothes when
I notice my boy lying curled
on our street in the rain,

lying there with his hood up.
No cars, just the rain
with its soft bites.

I'm in a rush outside
when Martell begins to
rise, careful-like,

and when he's all the way up,
he stares at the dry outline
of his body on the blacktop,

his face bowed like he's
reading something.
His friend Chucky comes

trolling on his bike, skidding
his sneakers on the street.
Martell lifts his chin

and then both boys look
down again, watching
our son disintegrate.

THREE LANTERNS

There's our son at the end of my hook
riding over the Detroit River

where Tecumseh's still rowing
towards his oblivion.

This boy we're casting to the land
of the leaping frogs.

My lass lives on the floor
where the fish are frying,

her spine snapped in half
the way a Milky Way might.

She squares her thumbs and fingers together,
frames for our son

a picture window to climb through

*

Eighteen months with us,
and our dark-skinned son

still has pockets sewn over his clothes.
They're filled with stones

that keep a boy underwater,
his vowels bubbling up to us.

With our brooms and hockey sticks,
    we're swatting away

city streetlights that followed him here,
    those bulbs that bow

and peck at his back.

*

My love's trying to stop the chiming,
    her fingers so singular

since that one dark bell
    is ringing again in her neck.

I hollow this house while she sleeps,
    take my time and chisel

the proper curve so our canoe
    cuts easy through rough water.

My lass is a sweet tomahawk
    for the scalping

of moons and runaway boys.

*

We press four hands over our son's
    mouth when he sleeps

so his body blows up and floats.
    We nail our stakes in the yard

to keep him
    tethered to this world.

See how he splashes
in summer when he knocks

his mouth against moon water.
See how we paint with one finger

bright horses across his ribs,
and rivers on the outside

streaming down his arms.

*

Sometimes we sketch with smoke
a door just over

that rock in our boy's chest. You can hear it
rusty when he knocks

on our bedroom door. We take the scent
that falls from him—

baby powder, gun powder—into our skulls
because we live in an empty house,

and in each bedroom there's a bell
ringing under the covers

where a child might live.

*

We sledge the stake in our yard,
then let the line out slowly

until our son's way up there
            where the moon makes

a lovely mess of him.
            When my wife and I

are overwhelmed with this,
            we beat our skulls upon the moon,

and it empties over the earth.
            I tell you, when we kiss,

even the little bell in my love's neck
            jingles, it rhythms,

it makes a lovely sound.

TWO MOVEMENTS FOR MARTEL EPPERSON

From a Letter to Marie Howe

Dearest Marie,

There's this rope around my son's waist,
city he's towing like some glacier
across our cornfield. Forget my romance

with bricks stacked like loaves of bread.
We have little Detroit castles
crumbling all over our field.

That city of stone where blackbirds
buzz in and out of windows
blown open by rocks.

Martell is emptying his pockets.
There's a man in an orange vest tonight
wandering among those piles.

He's following a blood trail through
the scruff of prairie grass.
Just a few weeks ago Julie dreamed

our son held his BB gun
to her head
and pulled the trigger.

I was his Big Brother last summer
riding the roller coasters then dropping him off
at his own little castle.

It floats so close to our house
the front doors are kissing. Glass shatter
on his porch someone had swept

into a sparkling pile. We were chins up
to the brick-sized window on his front door
crying into an empty house for his mom:

"Annie? Annie, you in there?" My brother
Benny out of his cherry SUV and we gather ourselves
around this boy and what to do.

We're two loaves of white bread
on Martell's porch and I'm scribbling a note to his mom.
"I'm so sorry, Mr. Rybicki," Martell says,

tears in a landslide down his cheeks.
Days later, when we key into her house,
Martell crosses the hardwood floor

to the bullet holes.
The walls seem so fleshy and tall.
He slips his fingers in

the holes and leaves them there.
He's at the bottom of a climbing wall
wanting to scale his way up the sky.

And so this hawk of a boy lights in our nest.
I don't know how to hug him right.
There's something sharp like a city

in between us. So I warm his blanket
in the dryer and cover him sleeping on the sofa.
He moves in and on the third day

his lungs go bad--he's a wheezer like I am.
I pour medicine from a vial and breathe with him
when he hookahs mist into his lungs.

When he comes out of sleep, he flashes
his face at me, an oil spill made of boy light.
"Hey Scooty Puff Daddy Senior," he says.

"Hey Venison Meatball Rex," I call back.
What we say every syllable after that is for the first time.
Martell and I do Speed Racer mornings,

my coffee all rock-a-bye up our driveway
as he snatches off the dashboard a sliding plate
of toast. We're off to school

in the dark with that hawk of light in the east.
At night he races marbles along the counter
slope doing wind sprints. "They're football players,"

he says and lets them roll and bump heads.
Then he's whispering, "Go-go-go fire defense,"
playing coach to a bunch of marbles.

I'm fire in the wood stove and stir the pot,
and out of nowhere this boy who once swallowed gasoline
on a dare is dangling his Fancy Hamster Ginger

so her back paws light on his little skateboard.
I'm talking rubber band wars where cowboys
dive for cover, bullets whizzing past

our book shelves, or taking off an ear.
So many miracles our roof's no more
than the lid to a baby grand tilted up

so the singing can ring and rafter up.
"You're living two lives now," I tell him rolling out
of Detroit in my truck with glass tabletops,

sofas, plastic fruit (his mom is being evicted).
"You slip your arms out of a fur coat made of bricks.
And when we get home, trade it

for a fur coat made of cornfields."
He smiles one deep breath and says,
"I like the fur coat made of corn the best."

*

Dearest Marie,

Your letter brought music to our branches
after so hard a day here. Today Martell smacked
in the head a little boy named Hunter.

Tonight we gathered in the field with his teachers,
principal, basketball coach and lay hands on
his old house, that whale thrown up on our land.

And when the good boy gets tired
and drains out of him, we haul our son to Lake Michigan.
He's such a beautiful kite

smacking up and down the dunes.
The light on the water and sand he loots
into his pockets and shoes.

At home he paints on his bedroom wall
freighters and beach fires and waves
that spray out at you.

In the foreground, there's a black dot
of a boy with a white mom and dad.
The boy's flying up the wall holding our hands.

The sand Martell brought back,
he piles on his bed sheets shaping it into castles
and hills.

I have seen him bow to his snare drum
and place his mouth inside it
like he's drinking from a birdbath

or shimmering pool--the drum skin vibrating
so its molecules flow in and out.
He hawks his wings over the drumhead,

but Julie and I are gone. We're out in the field
tearing bread from the cornerstone of some old house,
gathering warm bits for under his pillow.

ELIZABETH DI GRAZIA

COMMUNITY

Sitting in the park with the other playgroup mothers, I watch as they place Veggie Booty—green speckled yellow puffed food—in front of their children whose tentacles reach for it eagerly. Immediately following comes the soy yogurt, the blueberries, the applesauce, and wheat crackers. There I am handing my son a circus shaped cone of Kentucky Fried popcorn chicken. In the recess of my mind . . . way back there . . . hours ago when it was still morning, I recall the newspaper article about employees at a chicken factory swinging chickens against a wall, stomping on their heads. Shrugging my shoulders, as a reminder that I don't care what they think, I look at my chipmunk son, cheeks bulging, hoping that he swallows the animal flesh instead of spitting up the spoils. He's gotten in the habit lately of masticating forever then expelling in one giant blagh the dregs.

"Oh, I've never tried Kentucky Fried Chicken," says the mother with the Veggie Booty. She also has two children so I can't say that she doesn't have the dirty diapers, the tired toddlers turned whiny. People say expressive is a better term to use then whiny. I know that they don't have a whiny child then, cause I know whiny: the incessant chord of a bee, not in search of sweetener but working my edge, wanting, wanting, wanting what! . . .I don't know . . .and . . .they don't either. When I say, "Stop!" silence reigns . . .until . . . their engine jumpstarts, the constant off-key thrum lodging in my inner ear, unbalancing me . . .again.

"No, you can't have another cracker until you eat a spoon of applesauce," a mother says.

I say to my son, "No, that's milk. You won't like it." Not wanting to be wasteful, I open the carton and drink the warm chalky liquid. As the liquid dribbles down the back of my throat I think, maybe . . . maybe I should have my children try milk again. Their tastes are always changing, so much so that I can't keep up with them.

I'm new to this Guatemalan playgroup. It used to be my partner Jody's thing when she stayed home part-time. It's my thing now since Jody is working fulltime and I'm the full-time stay at home mom. I placate myself by saying, "It's for the children." Five mothers, eight children—one to three years of age, make up the group: three boys, five girls, four lesbian and one non-lesbian mother. After a conversation with one of the moms, we came to realize that in our past life—before partners—before children—we had dated the same woman (not at the same time). This shouldn't have surprised me, that being the way in the lesbian community.

The playgroup rotates to each other's home or park for three hours, once a week. Usually it takes Antonio and Crystel an hour to become accustomed to the other children and their surroundings. Sitting on the floor, I point to what their friends are doing, encouraging them to say hello. It's my job to show them how to be social, I think. What I told the other mothers when I became the playgroup mom was that I don't like community. As soon as I said that, I realized it wasn't a good icebreaker. I've had life-long problems joining, getting along in groups. Ultimately struggling with the coach or leader (formal or informal) because I had a difference of opinion. Maybe Antonio and Crystel will help me learn to get along. I stay at their side until they walk away, engaging with their playmates.

When the playgroup is inside, sometimes, Antonio becomes agitated. "Too loud," he says. "Too loud." We take a break outdoors with Crystel joining us. In the shaded back yard, with the scrambling squirrels and busy, busy birds, I'll question what I'm teaching the children. Is it to be unlike others, independent, distinctive? After a lapsed period, I urge Antonio and Crystel to rejoin the group. Soon, Antonio will say, "Eat, eat." I'll open our lunch bag, hand him crackers. I don't insist that they wait until the other mothers gather their children, setting them down. My parents didn't see to my needs, tend to me, or keep me safe. I'm determined to do different by my children even if this means being contrary.

Is community not essential to me because I'm not any good at it? One could say that I have an attitude about the whole playgroup community thing. But I'm a parent. It's my job to show my children how to join, get along, and be a part-of. I also want to teach them to have a self, a voice, and a willingness to stand apart when the situation doesn't feel right.

A week ago in playgroup, two-year-old Marie was whaling on one-year-old Alex, violence, meanness and determination showed in each swat of her hand before her mother could grab her arm, stopping the pummeling. Giddy, I rolled on the floor laughing, happy it wasn't my child. Antonio was playing Buddha-like with the other children, while Crystel sat next to me fiddling with a toy bank. A moment later, little Marie asked me for a doll that I was holding. "Marie you can have anything you want of mine," I said. "You better give it to her," responded her mother. The mother understood my laughter as I understood her jesting. Maybe I am learning how to get along.

Who is Antonio and Crystel's community? Where do they belong? Is it this Guatemalan playgroup composed mainly of lesbian moms? Do Jody and I have a responsibility as parents to facilitate our children in discovering who and what community will be to them? Will Antonio and Crystel choose the same community? Or will they find belonging in different places?

Driving me to ask about community for my children is anticipating Antonio and Crystel as teenagers saying to Jody and me that we should have known something, done something, or made an effort to place them in situations where they could find belonging. I want to be able to show them that their parents made every effort to see them as individuals, Guatemalan, and distinct from their white, Minnesotan lesbian mothers.

Will the gay community be a safe haven for Antonio and Crystel, a place where they won't need to explain their family, their life, and their moms?

Rainbow Families provides services to 2000 families in the upper Midwest, and is one of the strongest LGBT family organizations. Families are created in many different ways; children come from marriages, partnerships, and single parenting; some come through adoption, foster care, and guardianship, and others by birth.

Though Jody and I have attended functions held by Rainbow Families, I'm cautious about belonging to a select group. The family I grew up in was a select group, and this has left me with a fear of joining any community. In contrast, Jody enjoys community. She takes steps to not be the same as her mother—inept in social situations. She'll approach people and visit though her tendency is to be quiet. Jody wants to be a role model for the kids, showing them how to belong and be a part of a group.

This summer we camped with Rainbow Families. Thirty children were present under the age of five—four children from Latin America (including ours) and two African-American children. If there were any children adopted from European locales—Russian and former Balkans, they would have blended in with the other white children.

A group of women in their twenties sat on the withered grass, chatting, and playing with their babies. When a child escaped out of the circle, one of the mothers would fetch the baby, bring him or her back to the safety of sprawled legs. Leaning against a picnic table, I alternately watched the women and Jody who was pushing Antonio and Crystel on the swings.

Slapping at a mosquito, I asked myself, why am I shocked and uncomfortable with the white women and their white babies? Is it because Jody and I had both failed to conceive through artificial insemination? I listened to my children's familiar timbre, "Higher, higher," and observed Jody's lean form, one hand reaching out to push Antonio, then Crystel. "Underdog, Mama Joey, Underdog." Jody swooped under Antonio's swing, then ducked beneath Crystel's on her return.

Why didn't I approach the women to visit? After contemplating this question, I decided that I would have if the babies were adopted from a Latin American country. Does this mean I only stick to my kind?

Parenting the two African-American children were two men (the only men at camp). As is the case, Antonio and Crystel gravitate towards darker skinned children, therefore Jody and I were in proximity of the men and had an opportunity to talk with them. When dinnertime was announced, I took the initiative to sit with the men and their children. Did I make this decision to isolate myself from the other women or was I concerned about the men sitting alone? Driving me to look at my behavior are my issues with community and how they will affect our children. Later at our campsite, Jody spoke of her disappointment with our seating arrangement. Though she said she had no expectations about developing new women friends, she at least wanted us to be approachable and by sitting with the men we were not accessible for conversation.

Our neighborhood community of ten houses is a potluck of Republican and Democrat, straight and gay, young and old, married, widowed, divorced and single. We're white, African-American, and Guatemalan. We have children, grandchildren, dogs, indoor and outdoor cats or we borrow from the neighbor the same as we borrow a cup of brown sugar.

Mornings at six our phone rings. Our bichon/cocker salivates, her tail quivers, she whines at the door. The children yell, "MAGGIE'S FRIENDS ARE CALLING!" I unlatch the front door and the dog pushes through the opening. She jumps off our steps, shoots left across the neighbor's driveway to the front door held open by one of the two elderly women who live there. After having her belly scratched, a dish of chicken and a nap, they'll walk her home. Or if it's real cold, they'll call, and I'll hold the door open, and whistle for Maggie.

The first time our toddlers wandered off for a walk before I realized it, Grandma Jo, a widow, stepped out into the rain flagging which way they went. Down the street, across the intersection, I caught sight of the beacon that their yellow slickers made.

Standing at the bay window in the afternoon, the children wait for their friends, the divorcee and her teenage son, who live across from us. After seeing her car pull in the drive, they run to her house to have Oreo cookies and milk.

Another neighbor's son has babysat the children since they arrived on this block at seven and eight months old. He is now sixteen. They are four.

Before the children came, Jody and I didn't know our neighbors beyond waving hello. It was only after Antonio and Crystel were a part of our family, that we started hosting the block party in our back yard twice a year. The children changed our relationship with the neighbors by being—kids. Walking down the street on a sunny summer day, we'd stop and say hi, visit, and inspect front and back yards and people sitting on their stoop.

Our block could be an evangelical community. One family has a cross embedded in the brick structure of their home; another family are musicians for their church; and yet another family owns a business making and selling religious plaques. Barriers broke down over a serving of baked beans and a commitment for the common good came forth over warm brownies with ice cream. After one block party, our neighbor had two gift plaques made, (Antonio "PRICELESS ONE" and Crystel "FOLLOWER OF CHRIST") to hang in the children's bedroom.

Because we got to know our neighbors, our views about Christians have changed: a nice bunch and not so scary. Perhaps the Christians say the same about us. I attribute feeling more at home in our neighborhood to Antonio and Crystel.

This holiday season when Crystel was four and she would see a nativity scene she'd yell, "It's the little people!" It soon became a contest to be the first to sight a manger. On the way to their swim lessons, I noticed a stable on the roof of a church. "The little people are up there!" I shouted and pointed. This brought as much hurried talking as seeing Santa Claus stuck in a chimney. All season long we looked for the little people.

Jody and I don't belong to a spiritual community, though we believe that it's important that the children have a spiritual foundation to draw on. We've begun researching congregations, looking for a fit. A strong children and youth program is a priority and the community that we have penciled on our calendar to visit states that their congregation draws strength from people of all racial, ethnic and national backgrounds, of all sexual orientations, and of a wide range of abilities. Over 400 children and youth are formally enrolled in classes.

One day the children will learn the truth about Santa. This is sure to make them sad. Will they also lose the joy, excitement and thrill at spotting the little people?

Jody and I have created an extended family for Antonio and Crystel with eight chosen aunts and uncles. These men and women, heterosexual and homosexual, single and married, are tied to us by choice.

Sprouting this family community for Antonio and Crystel began before the children came home from Guatemala. These aunts and uncles agreed to be significant in the children's lives. It's this family that celebrates their birthdays, holidays, and visit on a regular basis.

At the infants' christening their aunts and uncles prepared wishes for the children. Aunt Amie said:

"My wish for you Antonio. . .Is that you know how much you are cherished, that you have a life filled with love and laughter, that you have a spirit filled with courage and strength, and that you always feel a sense of peace, joy and pride in the person that you are and in the person that you will become."

"My wish for you Crystel. . .is that you know how much you are loved, that you have a heart filled with warmth and close friendships, that you have a mind filled with curiosity and confidence, and that you know that the power of your inner strength and beauty will make your dreams a reality."

Tears cloud my eyes when I watch Crystel cup her uncle's nose, laughing as she tries to get her hand around the honker, than scampers with Antonio through their aunt and uncle's house to the toy cupboard. After visiting their relatives they return home stuffed with love, showing it in different ways: Antonio struts, Crystel wiggles with joy. Their first decipherable word wasn't Mom; it was Scott, their uncle.

Antonio and Crystel's relatives have multiplied many times over. This was an unseen outcome. Aunts and uncles have introduced them to friends, nieces and nephews, cousins, siblings, parents and grandparents. Their inner circle is a village.

"Me, me, me," Crystel said jabbing at a picture of Latin American children on the Spanish Immersion preschool welcome pamphlet. Through tears, I peered at what she was seeing, and realized how much it meant to her to be among children that were of the same color.

Will the children find acceptance in the Latin American community?

More than 90% of the Spanish-speaking world is Roman Catholic. The church influences family life and community affairs, giving spiritual meaning to the Hispanic culture. Since the Roman Catholic Church is negative about homosexuality, would Hispanic parents discourage their children from being friends with ours, not allow them to swim in our pool, not permit them to have a sleepover at our house? Or will Antonio and Crystel break down barriers as they did with our neighbors?

Like many other communities of color, Latinos have an established history of informal adoption: grandparents, aunts and uncles, and godparents have long raised children. When Antonio and Crystel say, "I'm adopted," will they be questioned as to why their blood family didn't keep them?

The children's tightest community is with each other.

One afternoon I came upon Antonio and Crystel in the bathroom. She was sitting on the stool and Antonio was carefully taking the snarls out of her hair with a doll comb. After straightening her hair, he bundled it into a ponytail. That same day Antonio asked his sister to scratch his back. Antonio holds a place for his sister at the top of slides on the playground, causing a jam-up of children. Once she's sitting next to him, or right behind him, he slides to the bottom. They hold hands crossing streets, and he asks, "Have your feelings on me, Cissy?" when she's crying. Driving home from their Spanish Immersion preschool, I asked them if they had danced that day, painted, played in the gym, sung songs, or read books. I was met with silence. Trying to spark up a conversation, I took a different tack. "What did you like best today?" I asked.

"I like Toe best," Crystel said.

I looked in the mirror. A grin worked its way across Antonio's face. "I like Cissy best," he said.

DIANE RAPTOSH

ON NEED AND SATIETY: SOME MEDITATIONS ON BEING A MOTHER TWICE

I am the single mother of two daughters, one biological—but what child is not "biological"?—and the other adopted. Said another way, one child came about as a result of a swapping of body fluids on a bed of leaf litter and fern in the mountains of Stanley, Idaho; the other, as the consequence of sheaves of written words exchanged with nameless Chinese officials. In short, I have been pregnant once and expecting twice. These two ways of having a child seem, in retrospect, more or less equally difficult, both awkward and elegant, each unequivocally right.

The pregnancy with my first child, Keats, was filled with the usual ups and downs: the quirky high of being kicked in the gut from the inside for the first time, the low moments exacerbated by the very fact that I was what I was: a single woman living on my own, soon to be marked, doomed to become highly conspicuous. I was suddenly no longer alone—was in fact unexpectedly housing someone, or more accurately, a potential someone—I could not yet know. I became instantly lonely. Dour. I sensed I could be in peril.

I teach at a small, relatively conservative, private liberal arts college in Idaho. During my pregnancy, which coincided precisely with the academic year, I lived in daily abject fear of losing my job. The college president at the time, I imagined, would have had no difficulty expelling such a wanton young (I was 29) female faculty member in only her second year of full-time teaching. To avoid being fired, therefore, I told my department chair that over the summer I had gotten married and that oh, by the way, I was expecting a baby sometime that spring, perhaps early June. He congratulated me with a planter of yellow mums. I strategically told one other member of my department, who I knew would be sure to spread the above news posthaste campus-wide. I revealed the real truth to the few colleagues I think of as close friends and considered my duties of professional disclosure fulfilled.

On the personal front, Keats's father—I will call him Michael—and I alternately huddled together and hid from each other, trying to figure out how to proceed. We had only known each other a number of months. We are similarly independent and solitary, yet we both thought that having a child could enhance our lives. We had both reckoned, correctly, that rushing into a marriage when neither of us was ready for such a commitment would be the wrong move. So we left things open-ended, remained in separate homes, and I made it through the pregnancy and the academic year in quiet terror. I went into labor late on the last day of classes, spring term, 1992. Forty-eight hours later, face-down and drowsy with pain killers I'd taken hours before, Keats was coaxed into the world with forceps, dented head like an over-ripe peach, furred in vernix, the hands of a pianist. My brother Eric cut the cord. Michael wept and mumbled something joyous about family, which I couldn't quite catch.

While our mutual devotion to Keats has remained unwavering over the past nine years, our own relationship, Michael's and mine, has remained more or less undefined. We like each other and live apart. We both date others. We love each other and are not lovers. Sometimes we nap together from two sides of a room, Keats at the kitchen table doing her math homework. Michael and I talk daily, either live or over the phone, about the usual parental issues: Did I remember that her Tae Kwon Do lessons were canceled for this week? Don't I agree she should be learning Idaho history in the fourth grade? Would he mind stopping at ZamZows to pick up some pinhead crickets for the lizard before he brings Keats here this evening? Last night we all four, including Colette, the baby, ate cous-cous, potato salad, and red grapes for dinner at my house.

The urge to have a second child, which caught me entirely by surprise, began dogging me when Keats was three. "Give it another year," my friend Elizabeth admonished. "The desire will melt away." I told Laura, a good friend and (married) mother of two girls that I was thinking up ways of having a second daughter. "You haven't figured the math," she said. "Two kids add up to more than twice the work of one. Consider yourself lucky with just Keats." I waited. Years. I analyzed layers of this yearning as though it were an intricate fossil: Am I trying to patch up some void I am unwilling to face by having a second child? Is this about the terror of having only one body? Am

I afraid of the possibility of my own increased freedom? Am I afraid I would fail as a writer if I allowed myself more time to devote to that? Or is this desire a supreme example of what James Baldwin calls "writer's greed?":

The writer's greed is appalling, Baldwin insists. *He [sic] wants, or seems to want, everything and practically everybody, in another sense, and at the same time, he needs no one at all; and families, friends, and lovers find this extremely hard to take.*

I went back through several sketchy journals I kept when Keats was an infant, looking to scare myself out of my own craving:

Monday? 10/19/92: I am so tired I can taste it. . . I have so few moments to myself—even less a sense of what a self is meant to be . . . Monday, 12/7/92: My sleep is fragmented, my house is in pieces; by day I am frayed, but here is a fragment from Heraclitus: 'The most beautiful order in the universe is a heap of sweepings, piled up at random.' Thursday, 12/10/92: excerpt from Louise Erdrich's <u>A Woman's Work:</u> 'One reason there is not a great deal written about what it is like to be the mother of a new infant is that there is rarely a moment to think of anything else besides the infant's needs. Endless time with a small baby is spent asking ***What do you want? What do you want?*** *The sounds of her unhappiness range from mild yodeling to extended bawls.* ***What do you want?****" . . . Sunday, 12/13/92: A reminder from the play <u>Saturday in the Park with George</u>—The only things worth leaving the world are children and art . . . children and art . . . .*

I continued to discuss my obsession with friends. Michael was supportive, if a bit nervous about how I would be able to handle the increased responsibility a second child necessarily entails. Gary, the patient and kind man I have been dating for seven years, did not say much on the subject but vowed he would try to be helpful however possible. "I thought you wanted to be a writer," my child-free writer friend Vicki in Wyoming razzed into the phone, listening like a crystal for a virus. *It's irrational,* Terry, the philosopher, explained, and I agreed. "Maybe you just want a bigger family," suggested the school nurse.

So how does a more or less willfully single working mother of one go about having a second? And how do so without mucking up the relationship with the first? I did not dare ask Michael if he'd like a go at having another:

I knew that being the father of Keats—intelligent, compassionate, radiant child that she is—provided him utter satiety, a sense of abundance beyond what he had probably imagined possible for himself. What is more, we were not a "couple" in the truest sense of the word. Likewise, having a child with Gary did not seem a reasonable option. His two kids were already teenagers. Besides, he had had a vasectomy: What were the chances of a successful reversal? And if it did work, we would all have to share the same house—become, in the vernacular, a blended family. A family with four children! While Keats liked Gary's children well enough, she would not necessarily have wanted to live with them. Likewise, why should they have wanted to live with us? As for me, how would I ever find solitude? When would I write? And where would Michael fit in? Surely, he would no longer feel free to drop by to oversee the completion of Keats's homework or share a quick meal. I searched—to no avail—for a gay man with a drive to procreate. I considered artificial insemination for a while and realized I did not necessarily feel compelled to pass my genes on to the next generation a second time; and certainly, the planet is sufficiently crammed with people already here. Nor did I think I could endure another pregnancy more or less alone. Having investigated what I thought were the best possible options, I began to settle into the idea of adoption.

I began the rather massive paperwork necessary to adopt a baby from China in July, 1999, beginning with the first letter that would go to China. Addressed simply to "Honorable Chinese Officials," this missive featured a series of adoption agency-recommended promises: I vowed never to abandon or abuse my Chinese daughter, never to place her in servitude. I pledged to steep my new daughter—and the old one, for that matter—in the traditions of Asian literature. I affirmed that I would provide my Chinese daughter with the best education possible, that she would be heir to my property as well as beneficiary to my life insurance. I described the somewhat irregular contours of my family and the overall tenor of my home, pausing over such particulars as the trio of raccoons that make off with half the dry cat food on our back deck, the sense of good will that characterizes my relationship with Michael, that family of foxes living in the drainpipe up the street to whom Keats and Michael and I bring baked chicken legs every spring: We imitate the squeals of a mouse by kissing the backs of our hands.

On a cool Friday in September, 2000, I stopped by the office of Meg Simonton, the new department chair, just for a chat, something I often do.

We talked about what the new school year was likely to bring: preparation for assessment, accreditation. A slew of curricular change. On my way out, I mentioned that I was expecting another child some time in the next couple of months. That I had no idea who the father was. That I might need to miss a day or two of class. She shot me a bemused look and laughed.

On October 22, 2000, at age 39, I was to find out which of the roughly one hundred million orphans (almost four times the entire population of Canada) would become my second daughter: I received from the China Center of Adoption Affairs what is somewhat awkwardly called a "referral": a photo of the adoptive child accompanied by a very brief general status report on the child (all in Mandarin) from the orphanage and a letter seeking confirmation from the potential adopter. The English translation of the Mandarin script of the letter reads as follows:

Ms. Diane Josephine Raptosh:

Based on your application, the following child has been assigned to you. You are kindly requested to give your decision as soon as possible . . . through your adoption agency.

Decision of Adopter

____ I (We) accept the child mentioned above.

____ I (We) can not accept the child mentioned above. The reason is:

Signature of Adoptive Father

Signature of Adoptive Mother **Date**

I studied the 3" x 4" color photo of "Gao Ji Hui," the nine-month-old girl in a red onesie with a shaved head (to keep down the incidence of lice), a pair of chins, and a grave look in her eye. I drew a black *X* by *accept.* Only after that did I ask one of my students to translate the general status report into English:

This baby was found at the back door of People's Hospital in No. 116 Fuquian Street, Gaoyou City, on March 19, 2000, covered in dark brown cotton.

She was approximately three days old and yellowish in color. Her weight was three kg. The hospital staff took good care of her, and now the baby is quite healthy and cute. She is now, at five months of age, 65 cm. long and weighs seven kg. She does not have many bad habits. She has two to three bowel movements per day and urinates approximately eight times per day. She drinks milk and liquid fruit and noodles. She kicks all her blankets off while she sleeps and sometimes tries to tear off her shirt.

Told to prepare for an early to mid-December trip to China, I reviewed the agency's document checklist on November 30th:

____ Form I-864 & I-864A Both completed & notarized
____ Form I-600 Completed & notarized
____ Form OF 230
____ Form I-604
____ Travel Letter from China
____ Explanation of why one spouse did not travel Notarized *If applicable*
____ All other blank forms in the packet received from Guangzhou
____ 3 years of most recent income tax returns
____ 3 years of supporting W-2 forms
____ Original I-171H form
____ $325 in American Currency for Visas
____ Current Pay Stub or notarized letter from employer for both spouses
____ Letters confirming assets *If needed to meet 125% of poverty level*
____ Power of Attorneys (2 authenticated, 1 notarized) if applicable
____ Birth Certificate(s)
____ Marriage License *If applicable*
____ Divorce Decree(s) *If applicable*
____ Copy of Home Study Dossier
____ Child Referral Information
____ Passport
____ 2 Visa pictures

On December 10, 2000, I left Boise for Nanjing. On December 11th, wearing six layers of clothing, nine-month-old Gao JiHui was handed to me by a tearful orphanage caretaker in my room on the seventh floor of the Grand Central Hotel in Nanjing. She stared into me an inscrutable look, black eyes pearl-lit. She could not sit up on her own or roll to either side.

In roughly 78 hours, Colette and Keats and I will celebrate our one-year anniversary of being a family of three. During this time, Colette has learned to walk, climb small foothills, trot on a broomstick, jump on a trampoline, and turn forward somersaults. Her yogic mountain pose rivals the angular perfection of the Owyhees; so too, she is able fold herself into a damned fine downward-facing dog. And she does a terrific breath of fire—which clears the lungs and vibrates the *ng* at the root of the nose—both on command and simply when she feels like it. Colette's determination to do whatever Keats does is keen (and Keats's patience with Colette astonishing), her legs strong as the titanium teeth of police dogs. She has sufficient manual dexterity at 21 months to maneuver a Phillips screwdriver into the tiniest of screws on the rocking horse Michael and I set up in the living room last week. At the supper table, faced with virtually any food, ranging from a bowl of lightly oiled broccoli to a platter of moussaka, she is happy as a toad with a fat waxed worm—so long as she can feed herself. She is wildly independent and peaceful as snow, the large cowlick on the left side of her forehead—curlicue straight from Van Gogh, a symbol of her fierce intelligence, according to the Korean/American woman in the navy lapels, who, greeting us in customs in San Francisco, proceeded to give me a detailed translation of the marks and contours of Colette's face and head: the lack of a clear bridge on her nose, helping to offset what would otherwise be an unbearable stubbornness, those little pouches of fat packed at each of her temples, bringing to mind a very large heart.

Over the course of this year, I have taken to middle-of-the-night meditations—usually the only free time I have—on the new state of my life. I awake and walk into Colette's bedroom, marveling at the nighttime quiet, at the fact that Colette is not mewling or making a fuss but rather snoozing soundly, most frequently in the position of Jesus on the cross.

Sleep, apparently, is something she excelled at in the orphanage, having spent roughly 23 of every 24 hours in a crib during her first nine months of life. I have to wonder at my good fortune: to have been handed a child whose temperament and health and habits are so excellent. I have to wonder too how I will get everything done. I have to wonder how Keats will continue to fare, how I will successfully serve as both Colette's father and mom. How I will continue to keep my own body and mind sound. Though I do sleep my fair share, I feel as if I have been exhausted for an entire year. I think of William Blake's reminder that you don't know what is enough until you know what is too much.

A couple of months ago, we moved into a larger townhouse across the street, which, from every south-facing window allows a view of the entire city of Boise and its environs. At two A.M. on a clear December night, it looks like some raw galaxy's stretched out across earth: to the east, the downtown lit in gold and white pulsations; just southeast of that wink the pink lights of Edwards Stadium 21 Theatres; to the west, the Owyhees heave in their white nightgowns. The living room is littered with student papers still to be graded and kid paraphernalia: Keats's favorite CDs; the rocking horse; the red and yellow Rescue Rider; the talking alphabet desk; plastic Oreo cookie halves with shapes in the middle—ovals, moons, plus signs, stars—strewn across the carpet. Drop cloths bunch up in the main hall, waiting for the second coat of paint Michael will be applying any day. I haven't seen Gary in more than three weeks, though he doesn't complain. I haven't written a poem in two months. I haven't gotten any exercise in over a week. It occurs to me I prefer a life that will never quite cohere. I am back to reading Heraclitus, as fragments are all I have time for:

Fragment 8? [Heraclitus said that] what opposes unites, and that the finest attunement stems from things bearing in opposite directions....Fragment 55: Whatsoever things are objects of sight, hearing, [and] experience—these are things I hold in higher esteem....Fragment 65: [And he calls fire] 'need and satiety.'

Keats has been sick much of the night, wafting in and out of sleep with some stomach ailment; Madonna's "What It Feels Like For a Girl" wafts softly from her room: I told her she could play her boom box as late as she wanted, if doing so helped her get through to morning. In the company of a wriggling candle flame, I, at the same time, am trying to listen to the Cuban folk vocalist and acoustic guitar player Silvio Rodriguez sing "Casiopea" on the living room stereo. It is a somewhat disjunctive listening experience—really too much to take in—layers somehow plain and complex; city and country; water and word; paean, flirtation; boyish, girlish, and I rather like it.

JESS WELLS

THE SEE-SAW FAMILY

"Tuxedo Shirts"

I was standing on a street-corner when I felt the tilting and, though it might have been someone's brakes or the door to the diner behind me, it sounded like the screech of old metal pressed into service. Two dapper young lesbians walked by in perfectly pressed tuxedo shirts and short hair, dressed for night though it was early morning, striding in that way that my sisters walk, but even in San Francisco discreetly not holding hands. For 23 years of my lesbianism, dapper butches had been my favorite. A woman in slacks. Cognac, the New York Times, erudition.

But today, as a single lesbian mother, I clutched my son's hand tighter and felt chilled by how remote they seemed.

I had left yet another relationship but this break up was more devastating, more profound. Three years of cautious weekends and separate arrangements only to hear "gosh, I don't really want to be in a family."

I had been an idiot, I see that now: I thought we could win her over, that time would draw her to this marvelous life spent raising kids, and to my incredible child.

After she left I started dating, but was told by my beautiful, witty artist that "she didn't want kids." And not knowing any better, telling her that I didn't want her to discipline my child or cover my finances, that I could keep my family life separate. How deluded was that? She knew better, and disappeared.

No, separate wasn't going to work. It was family or celibacy and my friends point out that I'm really not built for celibacy.

Searching the internet, this time for lesbians who clearly stated a desire to be in a family, I found only femmes. Any woman who checked the box "would consider it" was ruled out. "Yeah, I like kids," they'd say, and it sounded like "sure, I like…dogs." I wasn't going through that again, have some woman exercise her right to change her mind, or become involved only to reject us.

It was a slow, cautious business. You can't move too quickly when kids are involved, you can't have flings, or give it a try. They take it personally. They believe in happily-ever-after. They want and need things settled, and they're incredibly traditional about parents. Serve them a sippy cup you're a parent in their eyes.

But I'm not a woman to be alone. I didn't know what to do.

Taking one last look at the lesbian night owls, I saw a man coming up the walk, pushing a stroller with another kid in a shoulder pack. He was in his early thirties though sleep-deprivation made him look older. He schlumpped down the street, his socks mismatched and his bed-head hair ignored. The stroller rider had a bottle and was well tucked into blankets and the back-pack rider was bouncing up and down on the lumbar rung in that giddy callisthenic that makes a parent seem to be trudging through sand. You could tell he was tired, that his needs came second, that someone was at home reaping the rewards of his generosity. And that he was happy about that. He had the strength and self-confidence to live in the wrinkled world of parenting. Believe me, it takes a lot of confidence and exhaustion (or is it good values and clear priorities?) to make you not care if your clothes match.

And that, it turns out, was the crux of my becoming bisexual, to jumping the fence, or deserting the flock, or throwing in the towel: The sexual allure of nurturance drew me in. There's nothing sexier to me than evidence of generosity.

There is a sensuality to parenting. It sure isn't dapper, but it's very sexy.

People will grant you that parenting is a different world, but I've never heard that it's got a really hot streak to it. That care of children is a parent's foreplay. And I hadn't expected that a rumpled dad with happy kids would be way more attractive to me than a dapper someone focused on themselves.

I knew that family life was a different world, but I didn't know that the world of good parenting is so all-consuming, so entirely defining, that it can transcend the confines of gender, orientation, and social definition. It's not just that you spend all your time with parents, it's that the ability to focus on someone else is an indicator of a heart that's open and giving. And that's about as hot as it gets.

It was a surprise to me that it would be easier to find a man willing to put someone else first, to devote himself to nurturing, than a woman. It was a surprise to me that it was damn hard to find a lesbian who didn't lean back and proclaim to be "too selfish for kids." And so began the journey of discovering that some of our lesbian mainstays just weren't true for me anymore.

"A Movement Lesbian"

Twenty-three years with women is a long time. A lot of sex can be had in 23 years. I had done the committed relationship thing. I had done the SM thing, the non-monogamy thing, the orgy in the country thing. What was left?

I guess when you've been a lesbian long enough, sex with men is the only thing left that's taboo.

And I hadn't been one of those lesbians who knew at age 6 that she was gay. In fact, I had no desire to have sex with women but 25 years ago men were a piggish lot, especially in Europe where I was living. I was between the boat and pier. So when a German woman told me, "You're called a movement lesbian," (women who go for the politics and stay for the sex), and then pressed me into the wall like a good top should, I stayed.

Twenty five years ago, orientation wasn't a fluid thing. You were in or you were out. Going 'back to men' was like a nun who gave up the frock, it was giving in to The Man. It was aiding and abetting the oppressor.

But I seem to re-invent myself every decade or so. I became a lesbian and 10 years into it became a mother. Ten years into motherhood I became bi-sexual. If my mother were still alive she would be afraid of the future.

"The Swinging Closet Door"

It's odd to tell people about this. "I've gone bi," I practice but it sounds like I've gone by the store, or gone by the river, by the wayside. There are people who see a picture of my boyfriend Simon (ok, not his real name but he deserves a little privacy) on my desk at work who have no clue that I 'used to be' a lesbian. I come out to gay people on the job and it's an awkward conversation that makes them suspicious, the new millennium version of 'some of my best friends are gay' but now it's 'some of my best years were gay.' I have new friends who have never known me as a lesbian and old friends who are just getting used to the idea of my not being a lesbian. Twice as many awkward conversations, twice as many closets.

Like having dinner with a straight man in the Castro. Clearly a bi-type move. Or maybe it was the move of a lesbian who didn't know what she was doing on an internet het-date site. Well, it was late at night. Sitting at Orphan Andy's counter eating, my 'date' mentions that the gay people around us seem nervous. As if they haven't seen straight folk in a while, he whispers. But it's me, sitting there at total odds with myself, eating a salad with identity crisis dressing. Who is this guy? And who are men, really? What do I know about them? I've only got one male friend and he's a radical fairie. Of course there are all the dads I hang around with, they're pretty cool. But what about this guy?

I've never been on the outside of the outside before. A bi-sexual in the Castro is on the outside of the fringe. Assumed to be the inside. I had whip-lash.

And having dinner, again, with my boyfriend Simon, in the Castro, where the waiter treated us like breeders, camping it up as if we'd never seen a queer before and making all kinds of references to how 'we gays' do things. I wanted to raise my hand like Hermine Granger, 'ooh, ooh, I'm a sexual outlaw too!!'

But there are advantages, I admit. Even here in San Francisco gay people on the street stiffen up and drop hands when they walk past people who appear to be heterosexual, and I don't have to do that anymore. My guy's not really the hand-holding kind (he tolerates my hand looped through his arm) but hey, I don't have to stiffen any more. The world's definitely safer, I'll attest to that.

"Future Tense"

Simon leans back against the kitchen sink and wants to know why I don't call myself heterosexual now.

I proclaim, almost with hostility, that it would be to suggest that the last 23 years of lesbianism was a mistake.

He presses on. "If this relationship didn't work would you consider going back to women?"

I want to remind him of how much I love him, how devoted I am and how good we are together, but that's not the question in front of us. (Nor the focus of this piece. No one asks 'why do you love Simon the man'; they ask 'why are you with men the gender.')

His question makes me see my former selves spin out of my shoulders like a vapor trail. Women full of piss and vinegar. Full of righteous confidence that I just hadn't found The One. The just-shout-'Next'-and-you're-on belief that love was out there. But I'm nearly 50 years old now, and not only am I looking at my own middle age (exactly middle, since I want to live to be 100+) but I'm filled to the brim with the knowledge that I can't put my kid through another breakup, desertion, another set of readjustments. It's this or nothing.

If he leaves, I give up on love altogether. I mean that. I've tried every configuration and gender. I sincerely think I would shave my head and become a Buddhist nun. Not so far-fetched, really: I'm a Buddhist who has taken refuge. My Buddhism is central to my belief system and is at the core of my coping skills. I'd be a nun with saltpeter in her begging bowl, though.

What does that say about my sexuality? I won't base my sexual identity on my current heterosexuality so I can honor my past. Simon will give me my bisexuality if there's a chance of having sex with women in the future. If I intend to be celibate in the future, then am I pre-celibate? Is that a category?

Whatever it is, though, I'm definitely queer. I'm the B in the LGBT so I still get to march in the parade. I may not be gay but I'm definitely in the "woman with unusual sexuality" category. You can't have double-closets and not be considered queer.

"Coy on a Barstool"

Lesbianism is the land of the outward women. The self-made women. If there's one cultural trait that you can attribute to lesbians it's that they say what they mean and mean what they say. They don't do coy. They don't do phony demure. You don't sit coy on a barstool waiting to be selected and laid. It's a self-selection process among lesbians, you make your world right down to the sheets. So when I 'decided' to have sex with women it was a darn difficult process, since I thought I could just switch bars, perch myself among women and they'd pick me up. Maybe it was because they were Dutch (coldest people on the planet, statistically proven) and I didn't speak the language. Or maybe it was because I was already known in the bar as a straight girl. It just seemed to take forever.

"A Different Kind of Straight Girl"

All that lesbianism has made me a very different sort of woman and I'm not sure Simon appreciates it (but that's ok.) There are a number of things that drive me crazy about straight women (and always have). For example, I'm appalled that they use sex as a manipulative behave-or-you-don't-get-any tool. No lesbian would tolerate that. Sex tapers off and falls away, but no lesbian would use it to get the lawn mowed.

And who the hell taught straight women that they could have a house where there wasn't any sign of a man living there? I went to a (straight) colleague's house and every inch was covered with chintz and Laura Ashley prints. No sign of the husband's hobbies, past, pictures, shoes. Nothing. She toured me through the whole thing, out into the back yard.

"Here's John's special place," she said, opening the back end of the garage. No Rosanne set with beer fridge and old Laz-Y-Boy, this room was perfectly finished with white carpet and pale taupe walls, a minimalist modern sofa. He was in there. The room was so small that the three of us couldn't be in it at the same time. And there was no dust or socks or personal objects, even here. Turning, though, she saw a flat screen TV.

"What's this?" she said incredulously.

"I…bought a TV."

"When were you going to tell me?" my friend said.

"Ahh. . .today," he said quickly.

Busted, I thought.

There are times, however, when I do ask 'what would a straight woman do?' to double-check the extent of my rights in this new world I live in. Looking at the filth and the disheveled mess men seem perfectly happy to live in, I think maybe it's reasonable that straight women exercise control of the interior decorating. Can I do that without becoming my colleague the Chintz Diva? Can't I say no you can't put that dirty old milk crate full of albums in the living room?

While I was single, really single as in not dating at all, I started a list called Butch Things I Can Do Myself Now, which included things like getting up onto the roof (treacherous activity), changing fuses. A few things like that. I was very proud. And Simon, being devoted to equality, wants to know every time I can't open a jar or ask him to investigate a plumbing problem, what I would have done prior to his arrival. The truth is I would have paid someone, or waited for a friend to come to open the jars. My son and I used to line them up on the counter until my butch friends would come over. Why don't I do it, he wants to know. Because he's more capable than I at things like that, right? Hell, he's an electrician but so was one of my ex's and she opened the jars and spackled the walls. On the other hand, the truth is that while we were hiking in Desolation Wilderness and had to make our way from cairn to cairn over steep rocks, I wouldn't have had the confidence to forge on if I had been alone with my son. I just wouldn't. Despite my lesbianism and my confidence, I wouldn't have done it alone.

"A Cross-Cultural Experience"

"Is that a guy thing?" I ask.

Or, "don't straight women get to do that?" Not apologize for caring about table linens at Thanksgiving. Set the dress code for the night out. I hear that some of them even get veto power over articles of male clothing. No lesbian would stand for that.

Simon's completely baffled by the phrase "will you butch it out and get the drinks?" Or "straight women are the laziest lovers."

Or here's a great one. Simon says "I don't understand. What is a 'control issue'?" And I think "Toto, what land are we in now because this is *so* not the Lesbian Nation."

And the time I was trying to explain feeling fragile that day, a bit afraid or as if something would push me over the edge into being blue, or I was describing some sort of oatmeal of shame, fear, and powerlessness. And he's craning his neck and knitting his eyebrows while he's shaking his head no.

"You know, fragile."

"No, baby, I don't know."

I thought I knew that men were confident enough to do all kinds of things that women second-guess themselves about but I didn't understand that confidence could be that pervasive.

He doesn't understand why I have two locks and a chain on my door, why I keep the house locked at all times, why I lock the car doors the second I sit down, even before my seat belt. Early on I railed at him that it was very nice for him that he didn't have any experience with rape or sexual assault, and I trotted out my theory that men do extreme sports because they're not in danger on the municipal bus. But it *is* nice for him that he feels safe in the world: I wouldn't wish fear on anyone. And I send him to the door when the homeless guy comes to harass me to clip the bushes because the guy scares me.

Sometimes he says "Is that some kind of lesbian philosophy or something?" (I've developed the habit of saying 'go forward' in the car rather than 'go straight'. It's a hold-over from the early 80s chest-pounding days. "Go straight? Never!!" Seems a bit ridiculous in this day and age. And try explaining it to a car full of teenage boys.)

My favorite cross-cultural experience, though, was the discovery of the pedicure. I've never had a pedicure and I had always thought that straight women painted their toe-nails because they were utterly powerless and relegated to decorating every surface inch in their lives. Especially when I heard that men don't really care about women's shoes or women's feet. Well one night it hit me that it's so the chick has something to look at over his shoulders. It's het sex self-entertainment!

Who knew?

But then I started wondering if that meant that the women with the toe rings and the ankle bracelets and the pedicure were openly displaying their boredom with sex or, at the very least, that they are narcissistic at the one moment they should be focused on someone else. Is that it? Is that some unwritten code that straight girls have with each other?

"Six to 23"

You can imagine that I must have been pretty disillusioned after my last lesbian relationship to have taken such a drastic turn. Some friends tried to keep me on the path and called to invite me to a Butch-Femme dance. Maybe with an Uzi, I told them. Bitter. Sick of the processing, and the self-righteousness, and the judgementalism. Scouting on Match.com (divorced dads with higher educations and liberal politics—that was my database search), I came across a profile where the guy said "it takes about 23 conditions to keep a woman happy, and about six to keep a man." Well that was it. I wanted a life where it only took six factors.

My lesbian friends claim that men are emotionally shallow. Aside from the statement being glib and rude (and oh so righteously lesbian), I just don't think it's true. It might have something to do with men's pervasive confidence that I mentioned before. Men don't have any reason to be as suspicious, worried, frightened, or conflicted as women. Maybe it's because men only need six factors in a relationship and they seek fulfillment in 17 other areas of life. Maybe it's because they don't need to re-open every conversation and re-visit every fucking discussion, they don't need to have it proven over and over that they are loved. Things are what they are: holidays are holidays not tests of love. Presents are objects not yardsticks of emotion. It may be that men are not shallow, they're content. They are willing to let something that is true remain true until big movement proves that it isn't. What's true for a man, is true. Until it's proven to not be true.

My friends call it shallow. I call it stable.

"Systemic Shock"

And all of this is new on all kinds of fronts: when I met Simon it had been 7 months of no lover; it had been 4 years since my last full-time relationship; 7 years since I lived with anyone; 23 years since my last man; and I had never had other children in the family at all. Talk about old metal pressed into service!

Of course this would all be much more shocking if I didn't already have a son, if I had a daughter and wasn't used to boys wiping their noses on their knees and bashing into things because their elbows have grown overnight. Or with the mantra that I learned early on that my son was like a puppy: meat before 10 and run hard before noon or there would be no socially acceptable behavior out of him. None of this light breakfast, read quietly then sit like an angel for brunch. Good god, no.

I went to Santa Barbara on a train with my 6 year old son and there was a jet fuel spill on the tracks so the train was stopped for hours and my guy started to go bananas. The only thing I could think of to do with him was to have him run down the entire length of the train car, give a mighty kick to the panel on the door that opened it, get into the next car and run its length. Kick, run, kick run, turn around and do it over again endlessly. At one point a mother was sitting there quietly and smiled at me. "You have children," I asked, seeking absolution. "A daughter," she said with a knowing smile, "and she would be just standing here turning pirouettes in front of me." Sons. And a wired up son at that —oh so like his mother, who can't sit for more than 10 minutes to save herself even at 50.

"A Sudden Din"

It's odd to have other children around. When you have one kid and you're a single parent, you talk to them and they talk to you. But get a car full of kids and they talk bullshit to each other. A din of it. A head-pounding dose of bullshit while you're relegated to the role of chauffeur.

And when they're somebody else's kids, you're not really a parent, but you are. I want to notice when they don't brush their teeth, or to inspect their hands before dinner but that's the last thing his kids want me to do. Especially the youngest who was 2 when his parents divorced. He's never had to share his father. He is the one least pleased with this new arrangement.

It was odd to read that the best thing to do in a 'blended family' is to let the biological parent do the parenting. My philosophy had always been that everyone does the very best they can for every single child. The whole 'it takes a village' concept means that everyone in the village gets to be involved.

"See-Saw"

We had been arguing about the kids' comings and goings, about schedules and being notified of things because I'm a planner and Simon's plan-phobic.

Simon hates to plan. He doesn't know what he's going to do at the end of the day, even after morning coffee. He never makes a reservation for anything and he thinks even the smallest calendar or note pad with dates on it is giving in to The Man. Weekends that I thought were scheduled with the kids, weren't. I assumed it was because his wife (count-down to the divorce) was running the show, but it isn't. He just admits to having a serious deficit in the time-management skills department.

But life takes planning, I argued. It doesn't, I know, but I'm a professional project manager. Grant charts, spreadsheets, rolling deliverables and all. I can only 'be here now' if I have a plan of action for immediately after 'now' and a backup plan for that plan, just in case.

Simon went seven years after the separation without dating at all and I think that after he dropped his kids off at their mother's house he would just fall into a stupor, as if life was on hold until they returned. He never wanted to go anywhere until his kids came back: things didn't matter unless they could be shared with the kids. Life on pause. The see-saw tips, he's stuck at the bottom.

When an opportunity came up to be with them, even if it was a spur-of-the-moment change of the family constellation, he would jump at it. He'd go off to Marin to drop off the kids and come back with one. Or walk through the door (when I had dinner for 3 in the oven) with two extra mouths to feed.

Finally I put my foot down, pointing out that putting everything on hold until his kids returned made me feel like my son and I didn't count. And if he's not going to plan ahead or let me know when they're going to be around, I can't schedule things only for the weekends that they're there.

It was my 'life goes on' speech. Which was a bit ridiculous of me because I am incapable of being without my son. That's why I'm a single parent by choice: better do it all alone than have to have him just half-time.

That's when the 'oh my gawd' moment came and I could see things more clearly. Simon was talking about how difficult it is for him to be without his kids, how painful it is for him to only see his kids half-time. And I could see it in his face: more than the demise of his marriage, the central pain in his life is his separation from his kids. Relationships come and go but you want pain, take a parent away from their kids. That pain over-rides all schedules or menus, that's for sure. Simon now tries harder to let me know what's going on, and he's getting used to doing things with just the three of us. In return, I cook for five, almost always.

"Single Parent by Choice"

I am a single parent by choice—rare, I know. Not a 'broken family' or a it-didn't-work dream. Single parent by choice because I figured that if there's a 50% probability of divorce among heterosexuals then there has to be a 75% chance of divorce among lesbians. And I just wasn't going to have my son living out of a suitcase, shuttled back and forth. I've seen too many disorders generated by that uncertainty. My son would come home to the same house and sleep in the same bed every night, regardless of whether I had to incur the huge karmic debt and my ex- bear the huge emotional scar of my refusal to co-parent with her. Besides, I am mom who wants to be up to her elbows in motherhood, so there just wasn't enough kid to share. Fifty percent parenting wasn't enough parenting for me. I suggested she have one as well (so handy, this lesbian parenting) but she declined.

So I walked into this relationship with a divorced father with a deeply held dislike of the see-saw lifestyle. I need order and stability.

The fluctuating cast of characters was difficult for me because the see-saw was tipping. It caused a couple of hours of the oldest mouthing off at his dad (read transition behavior) or the young one talking incessantly (read transition behavior). I faced rising panic every time I knew they were about to arrive (read transition behavior) and would need to retreat to my room and close the door to have some control. Everything changed. My son never spoke at the dinner table when Simon's kids were there, as if we were watching someone else's dinner theater. If he did speak, it was to make outlandish claims as if he had to open with a zinger of a punch-line (transition behavior). And for the first year there was nothing I could do to keep my son at his homework or on his usual regimen because Simon's youngest was there and there were video games and the Simpsons. I lost my son to the pack whenever Simon's kids arrived. And Simon, so hungry for their company, would walk down the street shoulder to shoulder with his oldest, the rest of us trailing behind. Waiting our turn.

Then Simon would fall into a funk when they left and put life on pause while my son would get wacky and out of control to fill up the space they had vacated.

Up and down. Up and down.

"Cave of the Clan Bear"

The joy, of course, is that all things balance out in time. I am blessed to be in a situation in which the care of children takes primacy. Simon and I recite the litany of sporting events and play dates that will keep us jetting around town all day Saturday and there's no resentment or inequality. There's no issue if I work all evening with my son on his homework and it's assumed that Simon will play guitar with his oldest, go to dinner alone with his kids after aikido, and go to the swim meets of his youngest. At 10 p.m. every night it all shuts down and it's time for the two of us (gosh, a whole 30 minutes). We try to get away every couple of months for a weekend, and once a week we grab a few hours when there are no children in the house at all. I think it's pretty healthy. No one is left behind. Neither of us is lonely or neglected. And we get along even better when the kids aren't around, which we recognize as a darn good thing because in a short seven years the house will be empty. We're in a clan now, and it doesn't make any sense to pretend we're alone in a couple, or that the configuration is any different than it is. Some of the clan members move more than others, but we're a clan anyway and trying to be careful and kind.

AUTHORS

Kalia Abiade sat many childhood mornings between her own mother's feet as she figured out what to do with her "mixed" hair. Kalia is stepmom to 8-year-old Asha and mom to 2-year-old Adam. She and her husband, Jeremiah, are planting the family's roots in Southwestern Virginia—for now. When she is not working her full-time job as a mom and wife, she is a newspaper copy editor and freelance writer.

Karen Aschenbrenner, a graduate fellow at University of Wisconsin-Milwaukee, studies literary representations of disability and narrative healing. Karen's most recent short stories appear in *A Fly in Amber* and *Halfway Down the Stairs*. She is currently writing her first novel, a farcical fantasy.

Annabelle Baptista is a poet and short story writer born in Indianapolis, Indiana. She is a spoken word poet from Boston, Massachusetts and currently lives in Heidelberg, Germany with her husband. She has been published in the anthology *Coloring Book: An Eclectic Collection of Fiction* and *Andwerve* magazine.

Elinor Benedict has published five chapbooks and a collection, *All That Divides Us*, which won the May Swenson Poetry Award from Utah State University Press in 2000. She also publishes short stories and creative nonfictions. Her work has appeared in *Poetry, Shenandoah, Indiana Review, North American Review, Image, Green Mountains Review* and other magazines and anthologies. With degrees from Duke University, Wright State University and the Vermont College MFA Program, she has worked in journalism, teaching and editing.

Teresa Tumminello Brader was born in New Orleans and lives in the area still. She holds a B.A. in English from Marquette University. As a single, working mother, she raised two children, now grown. Remarried to a man who now has nine grandchildren, she joined him in raising her youngest stepson. Her stories have appeared online at *Rumble, Brink, Hobart, 971 Menu*, and elsewhere; links can be found at http://teres-nola.blogspot.com/.

Yu-Han (Eugenia) Chao was born and grew up in Taipei, Taiwan. She received her M.F.A. from Penn State University. Her books include a short story collection, *Passport Baby*, forthcoming with Rockway Press in 2008, and a poetry book, *We Grow Old: 53 Chinese Love Poems*, forthcoming with Backwaters Press in 2008. Sample her writing and artwork at www.yuhanchao.com

Amy Dengler lives and writes in Gloucester MA. Her work has been published in *Atlanta Review, IDEALS Magazine, Thema* and the *Christian Science Monitor* and many other anthologies, journals and newspapers. She is the recipient of a Robert Penn Warren Award and her collection, *Between Leap and Landing*, was published in 1999 by Folly Cove Books.

Elizabeth di Grazia has published work in a number of journals, including *The Phoenix, Rockhurst Review, Beginnings, Penniless Press, Hackwriters, Minnesota Parent, Adagio Verse Quarterly, The Mom Writer's Literary Magazine, SLAB*, and four essays with *Edge Life*. Her work has been anthologized in *Illness and Grace/Terror and Transformation.* She was the winner of the Minnesota Literature sixth annual Essay Contest. Elizabeth can be reached at edigrazia@msn.com

Benjamin Arda Doty is an MFA student at the University of Minnesota. His fiction has appeared in *Paradigm, Whistling Shade* and *r.kv.r.y.* and is forthcoming in *Verdad.*

Catherine R. Fiorello is a psychotherapist, musician, and the mother of five grown children. She has lectured extensively on family issues and has conducted workshops for parents, youth workers and teachers. In 1998, she coauthored and music-directed *Voices,* a multi-media production featuring the artwork and poetry of sexual assault survivors. She has been published at *utmostchristianwriters.com* and her work is forthcoming in *Haruah: Breath of Heaven.*

Debra Gingerich received an MFA in Writing from Vermont College. Her poems and essays have appeared in *Mochila Review*, *MARGIE: The American Journal of Poetry*, *Whiskey Island Magazine*, *The Writer's Chronicle* and others. Her first collection of poems *Where We Start* was published by Cascadia Publishing House in 2007. She lives in Sarasota, FL where she works as a Web communications and publications manager.

John Grey's latest book is *What Else Is There* from Main Street Rag. He has been published recently in *Agni, Worcester Review, South Carolina Review* and *The Pedestal.*

Andrei Guruianu, Romanian-born, is the author of *Days When I Saw the Horizon Bleed* (FootHills Publishing, 2006). Individual work has appeared or is forthcoming in *Paterson Literary Review*, *Ted Kooser's American Life in Poetry* project, *River Oak Review*, *Saranac Review*, and *White Pelican Review*. He is pursuing a Ph.D. in creative writing at Binghamton University and teaches writing at Ithaca College. In 2007 he founded the literary journal *The Broome Review.*

Cheryl Hicks has had creative nonfiction included in *Crate, Halfway Down the Stairs, Southern Hum*, and *The Best of the First Line*. Her poems appeared most recently in *Literal Translations, Toward the Light, Sigurd Journal, Ginosko, Eskimo Pie, Heliotrope, HerCircle, Orphan Leaf Review, the delinquent, Silent Actor, Word Riot, Clockwise Cat*, and *Monkey Kettle*. Hicks is also a mixed media artist whose work has been shown across Texas and in New York.

Daniel M. Jaffe is author of the novel, *The Limits of Pleasure*; editor-compiler of the anthology, *With Signs and Wonders: An International Anthology of Jewish Fabulist Fiction*; and translator of *Here Comes the Messiah!*, a Russian novel by Dina Rubina. He teaches creative writing in the UCLA Extension Writers' Program. http://danieljaffe.tripod.com

Bonnie Wai-Lee Kwong was born in Wisconsin and raised in Hong Kong. She began writing poetry as an undergraduate in Comparative Literature at the University of Michigan. She currently lives in California and works as a piano teacher and mother. Her poetry has appeared or is forthcoming in the following publications: *Bamboo Ridge, Blue Collar Review, Crab Orchard Review, Earth's Daughters, Runes* and the anthology *Yellow As Turmeric, Fragrant as Cloves.*

Kerry Langan's short fiction has been published in more than three dozen print and online literary journals during the last fifteen years. Her stories have been published in the United States, Canada and Hong Kong. Her non-fiction has appeared in *Working Mother*. "Eternal Youth" was originally published in *Thema*. Regarding this story, Kerry says, "I wrote this work years before my husband and I had any idea we'd be adopting two beautiful daughters on the other side of the world. Family is more, much more, than DNA."

Phyllis Langton, PhD, RN, is Professor Emerita and Professor of Management, George Washington University, Washington, DC. Her specialty fields include: Health and Illness, Health Policy, and Management of Large Organizations. Widow, and grandmother to Claire and Lorna Ramage, her essay, 'Mother' Lady", is an excerpt from her memoir in progress, Sweet Abandon. She lives in McLean, Virginia. Langton72@cox.net

Janice Levy is an award winning author of thirteen children's books about bullying, parenting, multiculturalism, foster care, Hispanic holidays, intergenerational relationships, family values, and just plain fun! Three-time winner of Writer's Digest Competition/Literary Short Story. Credits include: *Glimmer Train, StoryQuarterly, Greensboro Review, Iowa Review, Alaska Quarterly, Quarterly West, The Sun, Mid-American Review, North Dakota Review, Hawaii Review, Confrontation, Chattahoochee Review* and numerous anthologies. Website www.janicelevy.com

Jessamyn Luong is an undergraduate student at Bradley University in Peoria, IL, where she is majoring in Philosophy and Religious Studies. She is also a part-time music instructor and tutor, and she enjoys writing songs, essays, and poetry. Jessamyn is married to a Chinese-Vietnamese-American, whose family is the subject of the poem included in this anthology.

Michele Markarian is a writer whose plays have been produced across the United States and the UK. Her ten-minute play "Old Friends" was a finalist for the 2006 Heideman Award from the Actors' Theatre of Louisville. Her play "Phoning It In" can be read in the anthology *35 in 10* by Dramatic Publishing. Michele's essay "Miles in the Morning" was published in the Spring 2008 edition of *Mom's Literary Magazine.* She is a member of the Dramatists Guild.

Daniel Martinez, a poet and writing instructor, lives with his wife and family in New Mexico. He teaches at a small, four-year liberal arts college. You can reach him at http://www.geocities.com/danielrmtz/ and danielrmtz@yahoo.com

Precious McKenzie holds a Ph.D. in English from the University of South Florida. She teaches writing and literature at the college level. Her writing and research interests currently focus on issues of gender, class and power. She has published poetry, short stories and academic articles and is currently working on a picture book for children. In her spare time she enjoys walking with her dogs, horseback riding, and music.

Wendy Jones Nakanishi is an American by birth, but she has spent seven years in Britain, one in France, and the past twenty-four in Japan, where she is employed as an English professor in a small, private Japanese university. She has published widely in her academic field of eighteenth-century English literature but also writes in recent years of her experiences as the wife of a Japanese farmer and the mother of three sons.

Sheryl L. Nelms is from Marysville, Kansas. She graduated from South Dakota State University. She has had over 4,500 articles, stories and poems published, including twelve individual collections of her work. She is currently the Essay Editor of *THE PEN WOMAN MAGAZINE,* the NLAPW publication.

Carl Palmer, 2008 nominee for the Pushcart Prize, is the author of *Telling Stories, Memory Moments* and *Family Matters*, books of flash fiction and poetry performed at open mikes in the Puget Sound region of the Pacific Northwest. www.myspace.com/carl_papa_palmer

Diane Raptosh has published two collections of poems and has a third collection, *Parents from a Different Alphabet*, due to be published later this year through Guernica Editions. The winner of three Idaho-Commission-on-the-Arts-sponsored fellowships in creative writing, she teaches literature and writing at The College of Idaho. She lives with her family in Boise.

Donna Lee Richardson was born November 16th, 1954 in in the city of Syracuse, New York. She has three girls ages 27-25-22, Yai'sa, Denova and Katherine. The two older ones are in college. Each child lives in a different state. The youngest, Katherine, lives in Virginia with her only grandchild Rachel Elizabeth. Donna longed to write from sixth grade on, but wrote her first five poems at the age of 18.

John Rybicki's latest collection of poems is *We Bed Down Into Water*, Northwestern University Press. His poems have also appeared in *Poetry, Ploughshares, Field, TriQuarterly, the North American Review*, as well as in numerous anthologies. "Three Lanterns" also appears in *The Best American Poetry 2008*. Associate Professor of English and Writer-in Residence at Alma College, he also teaches creative writing (Wings of Hope Hospice) to children who have gone through a trauma or loss.

Patti See teaches developmental education and women's studies courses at the University of Wisconsin-Eau Claire. Her work has appeared in *Salon Magazine*, *Women's Studies Quarterly*, *Journal of Developmental Education*, *The Wisconsin Academy Review*, *The Southwest Review*, *HipMama*, as well as other magazines and anthologies. She is the author of *Higher Learning: Reading and Writing About College*, 2nd edition (Prentice Hall, 2005) and a poetry collection, *Love's Bluff* (Plainview Press, 2006).

Lorena Smith was born and raised in Sri Lanka where her Swedish mother and Sinhalese father ran an orphanage and various social empowerment programs. She has been published in several anthologies and magazines including *Redbook Magazine, Rambler Magazine, Ascent, Sketching Stone, The Smoking Poet, Door Knobs* and *Body Paint*. She writes on life and family, special needs kids, social involvement and women's issues. She lives with her family in Dallas, TX.

Anna Steegmann, a native of Germany, is a bilingual writer and translator. She lives in New York City and teaches writing at City College. Her work has been published in *The New York Times, sic, Promethean, Epiphany, 138 journal,* and several German newspapers. Her translations from German to English, *Absinthe* and *Dimension,* have been published by W.W. Norton.

Bruce Taylor, Professor Emeritus at the University of Wisconsin, Eau Claire is the author of seven collections of poetry including *Pity the World: Poems Selected and New* and editor of eight anthologies including, with Patti See: *Higher Learning: Reading and Writing about College.* His poetry, translations and fiction have appeared in *Carve Magazine, The Chicago Review, The Columbia Review, The Nation, The New York Quarterly,* and *Poetry.*

Jess Wells is the author of the historical novel, *The Mandrake Broom,* and of 12 other volumes of work including two novels and five books of short stories. A winner of a San Francisco Art Commission Grant for Literature and a four-time Lambda Literary Award finalist, she is included in more than two dozen literary anthologies and journals, university curricula, and European publications. Her books, stories, podcasts, and essays can be found at www.jesswells.com

Cherise Wyneken is a freelance writer, whose stories, poems, and articles —adult and juvenile—have appeared in a variety of journals, periodicals, anthologies, two books of poetry, a memoir, a novel, and a poetry chapbook. She studied creative writing at Florida Atlantic University, Florida International University, and various writers conferences and workshops. She is an active member of the Bay Area Poets Coalition in Berkeley, CA.
http://www.authorsden.com/cherisewyneken

ACKNOWLEDGMENTS

Elinor Benedict's "Glimpses" (as "Nearly,") "Immolation of a Stranger," and "Paper Flowers" were originally published in *All That Divides Us* (© 2000 by Elinor Benedict). Reprinted with permission of Utah State University Press.

Amy Dengler's "Gleanings" first appeared in *The Christian Science Monitor*, Nov. 6, 2003.

Yu-Han Chao's "Mail Order Bride" first appeared in *The Externalist: A Journal of Perspectives*, June 2008.

Debra Gingerich's "Thoughts After Hearing a Lecture on Translation", "To My Yugoslavian In-Laws", "Two Mothers and a Baby", "My husband Becoming a Naturalized Citizen", and "Video from Boston" are all reprinted from her book *Where We Start* (Telford, PA.: DreamSeeker Books, an imprint of Cascadia Publishing House, 2007) used by permission of Cascadia Publishing House.

Daniel M. Jaffe's "Marla and Billy, A Triptych" previously appreared in its entirety in *Triptych* and in segments in *The Forward.*

Kerry Langan's "Eternal Youth" previously appeared in *Thema.*

Janice Levy's "Bagels and Bialys, They Got Rules" previously appeared in *Cicada.*

John Rybicki's "Three Lanterns" also appeared in *The Best American Poetry 2008.*

Patti See's "Family Story" previously appeared in *VerbSap*, May 2005. http://www.verbasap.com/2005may/see.html

Cherise Wyneken's "It's Time" first appeared in *A Time of Singing and Seeded Puffs* and is reprinted with the permission of the publisher, Dry Bones Press, Inc.

Photographs by Heather Tosteson.

EDITORS/PUBLISHERS

HEATHER TOSTESON is the author of *Visible Signs* and *Hearts as Big as Fists.* She has published poems, short stories and essays in numerous literary magazines, received a Nation/Discovery prize for poetry and fellowships for poetry, fiction, and photography from MacDowell, Yaddo, VCCA, and Hambidge. She holds a B.A. (Sarah Lawrence College), M.F.A. in Creative Writing (University of North Carolina at Greensboro), and Ph.D. in English and Creative Writing (Ohio University). She is founder and co-director of Universal Table and Wising Up Press.

CHARLES BROCKETT, having worked from an early age in a small book bindery co-owned by his father, is delighted decades later to be developing a second career as a book publisher—and co-director of Universal Table. He has written two well received books, *Political Movements and Violence in Central America* and *Land, Power, and Poverty: Agrarian Transformation and Political Conflict in Central America*, and many journal articles. A professor of political science at Sewanee: The University of the South, he is a recipient of several Fulbright and National Endowment for the Humanities awards. His Ph.D. is from UNC-Chapel Hill. He lives in Atlanta.

See our booklist and calls for submissions for new anthologies
www.universaltable.org
wisingup@universaltable.org

www.ingramcontent.com/pod-product-compliance
Lightning Source LLC
LaVergne TN
LVHW091038080826
845145LV00002B/546

* 9 7 8 0 9 7 9 6 5 5 2 3 4 *